love
blooms
-a bluestar novel, book 1

_____

by Jennifer Faye

Copyright 2021 © Jennifer F. Stroka

Published by Lazy Dazy Press
ISBN-13 (digital): 978-1-942680-12-3
ISBN-13 (paperback): 978-1-942680-13-0
Thanks & much appreciation to:
Content Editor: Trenda London
Copy Editor: Lia Fairchild

Bluestar Island series:

Book 1: Love Blooms
Book 2: Harvest Dance

Table of Contents

Dedication
To my readers, who are the sweetest, kindest and most
supportive group.
Thank you for all of your support!

ABOUT THIS BOOK

He's an injured firefighter. She bakes the most delightful treats. When their worlds collide will the baker help heal the firefighter with a mix of blueberry muffins and her caring way?

The elegant baker, Hannah Bell, has always lived on Bluestar Island with her family. While still grieving for her father, who died in a fire, she focuses all of her energy on making her dream come true—opening her very own bakery. But when a broken water pipe washes away her carefully laid plans, she's on the verge of losing everything.

New York firefighter Ethan Walker's life is in a tailspin after he's injured on-the-job. When an urgent call detours him to Bluestar Island, he agrees to help his lovable but meddlesome great-aunt. But organizing the island's Spring Fling proves a lot harder than he originally imagined. He needs help...and fast.

Under the magic of Bluestar Island's sea breeze and warm sunshine, Hannah and Ethan must not only face their immediate obstacles but also their own turning points in life. Will they have to do that alone? With a leap of faith and a dash of romance, they might just find the perfect mix to make their dreams come true.

Includes a delicious recipe for The Elegant Baker's Blueberry Crumble Muffin!

"With the bloom of springtime flowers...
comes the opportunity for new beginnings."

CHAPTER ONE

Brooklyn, New York

"Hello..." *Static.* "Call..." *Static. Static.* "Hospital."

Ethan Walker's heart stuttered at the mention of the word *hospital.* "Mom?" *Static.* "Mom, I can't hear you. Who's in the hospital? Are you all right?"

As Ethan stood in the Engine 256 Firehouse where he worked, the world came to an abrupt halt. He clutched the phone tighter to his ear. Maybe he'd misunderstood her. Maybe she hadn't said *hospital.*

"Mom." He raised his voice. "I'm going to call you back." He disconnected the call.

His parents were on the trip of a lifetime, spending a month touring Europe. This was their first week away and if he recalled correctly, they had just arrived in Paris. He was thankful his mother had set her phone up with an international calling plan. He liked hearing about their travels and experiences. But he'd never appreciated the ease of calling her more so than now.

He rushed to pull up her number. The phone rang once.

"Ethan?" His mother's voice was clear, as though she was standing next to him.

"Mom, what's going on?" He willed her to say everything was all right—that he'd misheard her.

"It's Aunt Birdie. There's been an accident. She's at the hospital."

Aunt Birdie was technically his great-aunt, which meant she was getting on in age and a fall could be serious. Aunt Birdie was his mother's aunt and the only living relative on her side of the family. Aunt Birdie had grown up in Brooklyn, just like him, but when she married, she moved to Bluestar Island just off the Massachusetts coastline. It was a

9

lesser-known island than Nantucket or Martha's Vineyard, but it still had its own charms and distinct folklore.

His great-aunt was more than just a fun aunt; she was more like a loving grandmother to him. He remembered as a child visiting Bluestar Island for Christmas and especially for the Fourth of July celebration. He'd even spent part of his summer vacations with Aunt Birdie. They were some of his favorite memories.

With great trepidation, he asked, "How bad is it?"

"I...I don't know. Must have just happened. I missed the call. Someone left a generic voicemail saying she fell, but they gave no other details about the extent of her injuries. I tried calling but with all of the rules and regulations, I couldn't get any details. I'm trying to get a flight home but everything is booked."

The thought of his parents abandoning their once-in-a-lifetime trip, when they didn't know the seriousness of the situation, didn't sit well with him. "Mom, hold off on the reservations—"

"But I have to be there for her. Aunt Birdie doesn't have anyone else." Her voice was filled with worry.

"She has me."

"But you have to get back to work." She momentarily paused, as though shifting her thoughts. "You're all right now, aren't you?"

She was referring to his on-the-job accident that had sidelined him for weeks, but he was feeling much better now. In fact, he'd just gotten his medical release. He knew his mother worried about him. She always had. He supposed she always would. It's what mothers do. And it was all he could do to get her to quit fretting about him and leave on this long-planned trip.

"I'm all better, but I have a lot of vacation time saved up—"

"Ethan," called out his captain. "Just the man I want to see."

Ethan turned to the large man standing in his office doorway. "Mom, hold on a second." He held the phone to his chest. "Cap, I'll be right with you."

The man, who was always way too serious, glanced at the phone in Ethan's hand before their gazes met once more. "Make it fast."

"Yes, sir."

After Captain Morales turned and walked back into his office, Ethan said, "Listen, Mom, I've got this. Don't worry." He did have a lot of vacation time. He was always working; just ask his ex-girlfriend, Mary. "I'll drive up to Bluestar and find out what's going on."

"I don't know."

"Listen, it's going to be a lot faster for me to get there than you. I'll call you when I find out anything. How many hours are there between us?"

"It doesn't matter about the time difference. I don't care what time it is. When you find out something—anything— call me."

He nodded. "I'll do that. I have to go." Before they disconnected, he said, "Mom, try not to worry. Everything is going to be all right."

"I hope you're right. Call me when you get there. And be careful." She always worried about his safety, no matter his age. "I love you."

"I will. And I love you too."

Ethan slipped his phone into his pocket and then turned to head into the captain's office. Ethan paused at the doorway. Captain Morales, or Cap as the crew liked to call him, was ten or so years older than Ethan. The man was good at his job—at following the protocols. Perhaps if Ethan was more of a rule follower, he wouldn't have been sidelined with his injuries.

Cap sat behind his large desk with its neatly stacked papers and files. The captain's dark hair was lightly peppered

11

with gray. Ethan had been told more than once that he was responsible for a few of those gray hairs.

Cap glanced up and signaled for Ethan to join him. Ethan stepped inside, closing the door behind him. The room suddenly felt as though it had shrunk considerably.

He'd been in this room many times, some of the visits good and others were, *um*, stern warnings about him taking too many chances out in the field. Those chances had finally caught up with him this last time. But he didn't want to think about that now. He shoved the troubling thoughts to the back of his mind.

"Have a seat." Once Ethan was seated, the captain continued. "Thank you for keeping me updated on your recovery progress. You've done well in such a short amount of time." The captain's serious gaze met his. "But don't forget, it could have been a lot worse."

"Yes, sir."

Cap's chair groaned as he leaned back in it. He steepled his fingers together. "I just received your work release forms."

Ethan rubbed his palms on his jeans. "About that, sir, I was wondering if I could take some vacation time?"

The captain's brows scrunched together as his brown eyes probed him. "Are you still having issues?"

"No, sir. It's not that. I'm ready to get back to work." He wished he felt as confident as he sounded.

He glanced down at his hands, with their red burn scars that trailed up under his jacket sleeves. They served as a vivid reminder of his near miss with a blaze that quickly flamed out of control. He tugged down his jacket sleeves.

The worry lines on Cap's face smoothed. "That's good to hear."

Ethan shifted in the cushioned chair, not able to find a comfortable position. He was beginning to think his discomfort came from being in this office, and it had absolutely nothing to do with the chair itself.

Ding.

A text message. Ethan's gut told him it was a message from his mother.

Ethan cleared his throat. "Excuse me, sir. It's important."

Cap didn't say anything, so Ethan took that as a sign to go ahead. He retrieved the phone from his pocket.

Talked to the doctor. Possible pelvic fracture. Maybe surgery.

His pulse picked up its pace. Surgery at Aunt Birdie's age would be risky. His jaw tightened. He texted his mother back.

I'll be there soon.

He slipped the phone back into his pocket. He lifted his gaze to meet the captain's inquiring look. "Sorry. My great-aunt was just rushed to the hospital. I'm her only family in the States, as my parents are in Europe. I need to go to Bluestar Island."

Cap's dark brows rose high on his forehead. "I'm sorry to hear that. I hope it isn't too serious."

"Me too." Ethan refused to think of what life would be like without Aunt Birdie in it. "I'm sorry to put you in this bind after everything."

"We've got everything covered. The sub is fitting right in with the crew." Cap frowned as he rubbed his clean-shaven jaw. "I was just looking at your file. You have rollover vacation time from last year that you didn't use. If you don't use it by the end of this year, you'll lose it."

"I know, sir." His ex had often reminded him that he never spent enough time with her. He was always too busy working. "We've had a busy year at the firehouse and were shorthanded at times."

Cap pulled something up on his computer. "You have five weeks available. Go see to your aunt. I hope everything is all right."

That was easy. Perhaps too easy. Was it possible he was no longer needed? In the next breath, he realized he was

13

reading too much into the man's words. He'd been a firefighter all of his adult life. Experience counted for a lot.

"Thank you, sir. But I shouldn't need that much time." Ethan hoped. He stepped toward the door and then paused before turning back. "Are you sure about this?"

Cap nodded. "With what you went through, I wasn't sure when you'd be back. So no worries. Do what you need to do."

"Thanks." Ethan rushed down the stairs and then stepped into the busy bay. When he first arrived, he'd slipped in undetected through the side entrance. He hadn't wanted to speak to anyone until he'd met with the captain.

The floor was abuzz with activity. Some of the crew were checking hoses. Others were spiffing up the engine. It took them a moment to notice him standing there, but when they spotted him, he was greeted with smiling faces.

"Ethan!" his buddies called out in unison as they stood and moved toward him.

The first to shake his hand was Tom, the driver on his truck. His friend went to pull Ethan close, in order to pat him on the back, but then hesitated, as though recalling Ethan's injuries. Instead he gave him a smile and firm handshake.

Ethan wondered if that was how it was going to be from now on. Were the people on his crew always going to treat him differently? Treat him like he wasn't the same man he used to be? Was he the same man? Ethan pushed the troubling thoughts to the back of his mind.

"I've got to go," Ethan reluctantly said. He hadn't realized until now how much he'd missed these guys. "Some family stuff came up."

"Hope to see you back in action soon," Fred, a longtime co-worker and friend, said.

The other guys chimed in their agreement.

"Thanks. I'll be back as soon as I can." Ethan headed for the door. As he stepped outside, he squinted in the bright morning sunshine. A mid-March breeze rushed past him as he headed for his pickup. He ducked his head against the cold air. Any day now the springtime weather would warm up. He couldn't wait.

He climbed into his new pickup and started it. The soft purr of the engine filled the cab. He adjusted the heat and then glanced out the window. The red brick building of Engine 256 Firehouse stood proudly. The American flag hung between the two big white bay doors. The red, white, and blue material fluttered in the breeze.

It was within those four walls where he'd spent so much of his life. As a child he would come to this fire station with his father. He'd been in awe of the big, shiny trucks and the brave men and women who rode in them.

As an adult, he'd stepped into his father's boots, becoming a firefighter himself. It was what was expected. It was a Walker tradition.

Since the accident, Ethan had struggled with returning to work. He knew if he didn't push himself—if he didn't get back to the business of putting out fires—that he might never ride in a fire engine again. And where would that leave him?

But family always came first. He put the truck in gear and headed home. He'd grab a few things and hit the road. He hoped there had been some sort of mix-up and he found his aunt ready to go home.

CHAPTER TWO

Three days later...
Bluestar Island, Massachusetts

She was one of the lucky ones.

She got to do what she loved every single day—bake.

And best of all, she was able to put smiles on people's faces.

Hannah Bell remembered how excited she'd been as a little girl receiving a play-oven for Christmas. She'd baked up countless imaginary cakes with it. Eventually, pretend cakes gave way to real ones.

And now her life's dream was coming true. She'd just bought the sole bakery on the island—the Bluestar Bakery. The ink wasn't even dry on the loan papers. And yet it was all hers...at last. Or at least it would be when the renovations were completed.

In the meantime, she was baking special orders in her apartment. It wasn't ideal, not by a long shot, but it brought in enough money for her to put food on her table and pay the bills. Thankfully, the arrangement was only temporary.

This particular Saturday morning, Hannah found herself sitting in her friend's kitchen. She rested her elbows on the table and leaned forward. "I'm so happy for you both. I know we talked about the cake a while back, and you hadn't decided on all of the details yet. But with the wedding a few weeks away, I need to know exactly what you want."

Amelia Johnson's face lit up as her cheeks grew rosy. "I can't believe Jake and I are finally getting married. It seems so long ago when we met online. I don't think I told you but we texted for a long time before we met in person. And then when we started to date, I lived in Boston and he was here on the island. Well, that is when he wasn't out at sea on a fishing boat. After a year of that, Jake said he'd had enough of the separation and asked me to move here. Anyway, here I am planning a wedding."

"You better believe it." Hannah smiled. How could she not? Amelia's joy was infectious. "You and Jake make a perfect couple. And I'm so glad you moved to the island. I can already tell that we're going to be great friends."

Amelia's lightly freckled cheeks filled with color. "I'd like that."

"And it's going to be a beautiful wedding." Hannah reached into her backpack purse and pulled out a pen and notebook. She didn't want to forget any details. She had so much on her mind these days that it was best to write it all down. "When we talked before, we'd discussed a three-tier cake. Does that still work for you?"

"Yes. Jake and I were talking and we don't want anything too fancy."

Hannah nodded as she took notes. "Are you thinking fresh-cut flowers?"

When Amelia agreed, Hannah went on to ask her more detailed questions about the colors and details. She would order the flowers locally at Bea's Posie Patch.

"That just leaves us with the flavor." Hannah had baked a lot of cakes for the citizens of Bluestar over the years—some at the bakery and others on her own time. Her former boss at the Bluestar Bakery believed in the basics such as vanilla or chocolate cake with the standard butter cream. Any time Hannah had tried to introduce a different style of decorating or different fillings, Mr. Hamil said it took too much time. He was a nice man, but he was set in his ways.

"We decided on red devil's food with the cream cheese filling."

"Oh, that will be nice." Hannah continued jotting down the details. "What about the people that don't like chocolate?"

17

"Do people like that exist?" Amelia wore an expression of mock horror.

Hannah smiled and nodded.

"Oh, well, in that case our second choice was yellow cake with a lemon curd filling."

"Sounds perfect. Will you need anything else...say for your wedding shower?"

Amelia kept smiling though the light in her eyes dimmed. "I'm not having one."

Hannah was confused. Everyone she knew had a shower. "Don't you want one?"

"It's not that. It's just that I'm new to the island and I don't know many people. It's okay. I don't need one."

Hannah hadn't known Amelia for very long, but according to Agnes Dewey, gossip extraordinaire, Amelia didn't have any family and grew up in the foster system. Whereas Hannah had grown up right here on the island where it was like she was part of a huge wonderful family. And when her father tragically died, all of the island's residents had been there for her.

She could still recall how the whole island turned out for the funeral. Business that day had practically ground to a halt. And the casseroles had kept coming for weeks. When tragedy struck, the island pulled together. She couldn't imagine how rough it would be to go through life alone.

"You leave the shower to me." Hannah already had her hands full with renovating the old bakery to reopen next month, but help was what the people of Bluestar did for each other.

Amelia once more blushed. "I couldn't ask you to do more. You're already making the cake."

"You aren't asking. I'm offering. Do you have a list of wedding guests?"

"Yes, it's..." Amelia sifted through the stack of papers on the table. "It was right here." Halfway through the second stack, she smiled. "Here it is."

Hannah glanced down over the list. Almost a hundred guests. All of them were residents of Bluestar. "Do you have a preference as to who is invited to the wedding shower?"

They went over the list and whittled it down to a reasonable number.

"Good," Hannah said. "I'll get back to you with the details."

Hannah had a feeling this was just the beginning of a close friendship. Amelia was going to fit right in on Bluestar Island. She tucked the final notes for the cake and the guest list in her backpack and said goodbye.

She rushed out the door and moved toward her bicycle. It had come from her grandmother's estate. With a rusty frame, two flat tires, and a torn seat, it'd been designated for the junk heap. But Hannah remembered her grandmother's smile when she rode it around the island and knew she couldn't part with it.

A little sanding followed by a coat of hot pink paint, new tires, and a replacement seat gave the bike new life. The woven basket on the front just needed to be cleaned and it looked like new. And just like her grandmother, Hannah couldn't stop smiling when riding it.

She slung her backpack purse over her shoulders and then set off. It was finally time to check on the progress of the bakery. She hadn't been able to make it there yesterday, as she'd had a large baking order and she'd been exhausted when she finished.

Each day the crew was making marked progress. A smile tugged at her lips. It was going to look amazing when it was finished.

As Hannah rode through town, she waved at everyone she passed. She couldn't imagine there was any nicer place to live. Spring had blossomed in vibrant shades of red, purple, yellow, and so many other lovely colors. The tulips were in full bloom. They were such a welcome sight as the colorful flowers encircled the tree trunks lining the street.

This was going to be the best year ever. These days she felt as though she were walking on clouds—big, white, puffy ones. Yes, life was that good. And dreams did come true.

"Good morning." Agnes Dewey's weathered face lifted with a smile as she paused from sweeping the sidewalk in front of her house.

Agnes knew everyone who lived on the island year-round, as well as everything that happened within the town limits—and probably even what was going on in the outlying areas. The woman was a fount of information. And what she didn't know, she surmised—usually in a dark foreboding manner.

"It's going to be a beautiful day." Hannah paused pedaling.

"That it is. Too bad it's not going to stay that way. Today's horoscope was troubling—"

"So sorry to hear that but I don't have time to chat." Hannah resumed pedaling. She knew stopping to talk would deflate her good mood. Some days Agnes predicted good things. And then there were days like today where doom and gloom lurked in her words. "Hope you have a good day."

Agnes's brows drew together. And with her gray hair pulled back tightly in her customary bun, she looked a bit intimidating. "You don't want to hear about the prediction?"

"Maybe another time. I'm late." She kept pedaling right past Agnes. Nothing was going to ruin her good mood.

A couple of blocks later, Hannah paused to speak with Lisa West, an old schoolmate of hers, and peek in the stroller at her sleeping little girl, who was already nine months old. How had that much time passed already? It seemed like she was just born.

As Hannah continued on her way, she realized she was the same age as Lisa, but their circumstances were quite different. Lisa was happily married to the manager of the hardware store. And she'd just quit her job at the fish market in order to stay home with the baby. Hannah couldn't help but wonder if she'd been so focused on having her own bakery that she'd missed out on having a family of her own. Was it true that you couldn't have everything in life? And if so, had she made the right choices?

Being the middle child of three kids, Hannah sometimes felt invisible. Her big brother, Sam, had been the best at everything he touched from sports to taking over the family farm. And then there was her younger sister, Emma, who had won one of those nationally televised singing competitions. And she was now off in Nashville, cutting a record. At least Hannah thought that was the right terminology. On the rare times that Emma called, she was always so excited that her words all ran together.

And that left Hannah to make her own mark on life. Thirty was still young, right? She still had time to have it all. She shoved the thoughts of her ticking biological clock to the back of her mind. Right now, she had a business to build. She'd risked every single penny she'd saved since she was a teenager, plus the money her father had left her, on this dream.

She braked in front of the bakery and got off her bike. She glanced up at the front of the bakery with a great big smile on her face. Her worries about her choices in life completely disappeared. This was her destiny.

Sure, there was paper over all the windows, but that was just because she wanted to keep the makeover a surprise for the townspeople. The siding had been freshly painted white, and she had plans to buy decals for the large storefront window and the black door with the large window. She was thinking of a large cupcake decal smack dab in the middle.

With it being the weekend, no one was working on the bakery. Knowing the workmen had left some supplies by the front door, Hannah made her way to the side door that led to the kitchen. Excitement bubbled up in her when she placed *her* brand-new key in *her* new deadbolt of *her* back door of *her* very own bakery. Who said dreams don't come true?

She turned the key. The deadbolt easily gave way. She grasped the door handle as her smile broadened. She pushed the door open—

Water whooshed over the doorstep.

Hannah gasped. Cold water soaked her shoes. She stumbled back. Her arms waved about as she struggled to regain her balance. A scream tore from her lungs.

CHAPTER THREE

One day had turned into two.

Two days had morphed into three.

Ethan was still on the island, looking after his aunt's beloved dog, Peaches. He had no idea when he'd be returning to New York. Aunt Birdie had cracked her pelvis, but thankfully it would heal without surgery. However, her recovery required her to spend a bit of time in physical rehab. Sunny Days Rehabilitation Center—the cheapest of the expensive alternatives—was located just outside of Boston.

The bad news was that Ethan had been sleeping on the lumpiest couch on earth. He shrugged one shoulder and then the other before rolling his head, trying to work out the kinks. He'd already tried his aunt's bed, which was too soft and too short with a footboard that prevented him from dangling his feet over the end.

Too bad his aunt's house was a small one-bedroom bungalow. He knew why she never sold the house. It was situated on the edge of town along Surfside Drive. The sweeping covered porch had an unobstructed view of the ocean. Talk about your million-dollar view. And in the summer, Aunt Birdie would open all of the windows to let in the sea breeze.

He closed his eyes again, not quite ready to face the day. The clip-clip of footsteps over the hardwood floors let him know that Peaches was growing impatient for him to get up.

Last night, after giving his parents an update on Aunt Birdie's progress, he might have stayed up until well past midnight watching an action movie, but it wasn't like he had any place to be until later in the day. His aunt had therapy in the mornings, so he tried to be at the physical rehab facility at lunchtime.

Though the last time he was there, she had insisted he not make the lengthy journey from Bluestar Island to Boston each day to visit her. She was making friends at the center and promised she'd be fine. She said it was more important that he spend time with Peaches. That was his aunt, always thinking of others before herself.

A whiff of dog breath preceded a swipe of a wet tongue over his cheek. Yep, it was time to get up. Ethan ran the back of his hand over his face. And yet the rest of him didn't move. It was just too much effort.

"Just a little longer," Ethan pleaded with the dog. With his eyes still closed, he reached out and ran his hand over Peaches's furry back.

Arf. Arf.

With a groan, he got up. After letting Peaches out in the small fenced-in yard, Ethan grabbed a quick shower, hoping the pulsating hot water would ease his stiff muscles. It didn't. At least not much.

Once Peaches ate, they headed out for their morning walk to Beachcomber Drive and a stroll to the far end of the park. Peaches wagged her tail and greeted a few familiar faces. At that hour, most people were working or getting on with their day.

Ethan loved listening to the roar of the surf as the salty sea breeze rushed past him. It was as though it swept away all of his troubles—at least temporarily.

He paused at the intersection, checking for traffic before crossing. It took him a moment to remember there wouldn't be any cars or trucks zipping up the street. With this being a small island, vehicles were prohibited unless issued a special day permit. He'd left his truck at one of the many parking lots on the mainland and taken the ferry to the island. Once on Bluestar, people got around via golf carts, bikes, or walking. It had always been that way. And he supposed it would remain that way. Bluestar was steeped in traditions that went back generations—

A scream pierced the peaceful morning air.

Peaches ears immediately perked up.

"Come on, girl."

His feet pounded the sidewalk. Peaches kept pace with him. The firefighter part of him instantly took over. Adrenaline flooded his system. He listened for another scream to make sure he was headed in the right direction, but it was quiet now.

He slowed down and glanced between each building. And then he spotted a young woman with auburn hair pulled back in a ponytail. She had a hand pressed to her mouth. She was staring straight ahead at the side of a building.

He gave her curvy figure a quick once-over. She appeared to be physically all right. Could the scream have come from her?

His gaze moved to the building. It didn't appear to have any smoke coming from it. After all of these years on the job, it was one of the first things he checked.

He approached the young woman. "Excuse me. Do you need some help?"

When her wide-eyed gaze met his, he felt a distinct jolt. It felt like the Earth had spontaneously sped up for just a moment, leaving him unsteady on his feet. And yet he knew nothing like that had happened. Logic dictated that the Earth continued to spin at its same steady rate—even if Ethan's world felt a bit off center.

Whatever the reason for the strange sensation, he didn't have time to evaluate it. She was in trouble and he was there to help—just like he'd been doing for strangers year after year.

The closer he got to her, the wetter the ground became. What in the world? He didn't recall it raining while he'd been on the island.

"My bakery." She never moved her gaze from the building. "It's ruined."

He stepped up next to her as water continued to gush out the door. To have this much water, it had to be a burst water pipe. *What a mess!*

"I have to stop it." She took a step toward the door.

Ethan immediately reached out, grabbing her arm.

She turned to glare at him. "What are you doing? Let go!"

He wouldn't release his hold. Not yet. "You can't go in there."

"Of course, I can."

"You'll get electrocuted."

"What?"

He pointed to the wires hanging from the partially collapsed ceiling that were arching, hissing, and snapping. "Until the electricity is off, you could get electrocuted."

"But the circuit breakers are on the other side of the kitchen. I have to go in." She yanked on her arm, but he tightened his hold.

She wasn't the first person he'd had to restrain from doing something dangerous. When people were panicked or in shock, as this woman appeared to be, they didn't make the safest choices. Experience told him to keep his tone steady and level. Getting frustrated would only make matters worse.

"Let go of me now!" Her jade green eyes shot daggers at him.

"If I do, will you promise not to rush inside?" He had to be sure she wouldn't risk her safety.

She hesitated. "Fine. Yes."

He continued to hold her for just a moment longer. "Did you call for help?"

"No. I didn't have a chance." She yanked on her arm again.

This time he let go. However, he didn't take his gaze off her. He didn't care how mad she got at him; he wasn't going to let her get hurt. Not on his watch.

She gave him another distinct frown as she reached in her purse and pulled out her cell phone. She punched in the numbers. A brief conversation ensued. After she disconnected the call, the distinct wail of the old fire whistle, mounted atop the fire station, peeled through the air.

26

"Stay here. I'll be back," he said.

"Where are you going?" The anger that reflected in her eyes had been replaced with worry.

"I'm going to see if I can shut off the water at the road. There should be a shut off valve there." On second thought, he didn't feel good about leaving her alone. He still didn't trust her. "Come with me."

"Why?"

His brain raced for a plausible reason. "So you can hold onto Peaches's leash while you flag down the fire truck."

She gave him a strange look. "They know where the bakery is. It's the only one on the island."

He inwardly groaned. "Would you rather stand here and argue, or you could come with me and I'll see if I can get the water turned off?"

"Fine. Let's go."

He handed over the red leash. While the woman moved to the curb and looked down the street for impending help, he searched the bushes in the front of the building. And then on the other side, he found a metal cap. He pried it off and found the water shut off. But it was down deep.

He took off his jacket and then lowered himself to the grass. With his chest flat on the cold, hard ground, he reached his arm down the narrow pipe. He grasped the valve. He attempted to turn it. It didn't budge. He gripped it tighter. Gritting his teeth, he gave it every bit of strength he possessed.

He wasn't sure it was going to budge. And then it gave way, turning with a screech.

He got to his feet and dusted off his shirt and then his hands. He walked over to where the young woman was standing next to the curb. "The water's off."

"It is?" she asked as though needing reassurance that this nightmare wasn't going to get any worse. When he nodded, she said, "Thank you."

It wasn't the first time he'd been thanked for his efforts, but the look of relief reflected in her eyes and the sincerity in her voice stirred a warm spot in his chest.

As though recalling that she was still holding Peaches's leash, she held it out to him. When he reached for it, their fingers brushed. A tingling sensation started in his fingertips and then worked its way up his arm before settling in his chest.

She jerked her hand away as though she too had been affected by their brief connection. Her gaze met his briefly before she glanced back at the quiet roadway. "You...you don't have to wait."

"I don't mind." He didn't want to leave her alone when she was clearly upset.

"It takes them a little bit since it's a volunteer service. They don't stay at the station. They all have other jobs and stuff."

"I understand." He didn't know what to say next. His mind drew a blank. And so he stood by quietly while the young woman knelt down to love on Peaches, who happily ate up the attention.

A few quiet moments passed and then the truck siren could be heard in the distance. As the fire engine grew closer, Ethan glanced over at the young woman, there were tears in her eyes.

"It's okay," he said softly. "Help is here."

She swiped at her cheeks. "I...I know. Don't mind me."

He should say more—something comforting. But before he could speak, she moved to the street to greet the firefighters. He had this gut feeling that something more was troubling her, but being a stranger, it wasn't his place to pry.

A short, stout man with his turnouts on and *Chief* emblazoned in gold on the front of his black helmet moved from the engine to the sidewalk. "Hannah, what's going on?"

So that's her name. A pretty name for a pretty lady.

At that moment, she looked as though she was having problems keeping her emotions in check. Ethan felt sorry for her. He spoke up and filled the chief in on everything that had happened so far.

"Thanks," the chief said. "We've got it from here."

The chief started yelling orders to his men before speaking into his mic to dispatch, requesting the power company cut the electricity to the building. Ethan took a step back and watched as the firefighters rushed past him. He wasn't used to being relegated to the position of mere observer. It felt wrong to do nothing.

The firefighters had a pump, a generator, and some fans prepared to take in the building once the power was cut. For a volunteer company, they moved with practiced ease. Their chief obviously kept a tight house.

Ethan's attention turned back to Hannah. A frown pulled at her pink lips. Her fine brows were drawn together, creating worry lines. It was only then that he noticed her pale complexion.

With the men rushing back and forth in the narrow space, they were in the way. "Come with me," Ethan said to her. When she resisted, he said, "We won't go far. Let's just move out of the way so they can do their work."

She hesitated. But when a firefighter bumped into her, she turned to Ethan and nodded her agreement. He led the way to the sidewalk across the street. He moved to a quiet spot and sat down. She looked at him and then at the sidewalk.

"What? You never sat on the curb as a kid?" Growing up, he'd spent a lot of time sitting or standing on a curb in Brooklyn near his buddy's house.

She didn't say a word as she left a respectable distance between them. Peaches sat between them. Hannah stared straight ahead, looking as though she'd just lost her best friend. The longer the silence wore on, the more he worried about her. She was taking this hard. It wasn't like it was the end of the world.

"Do you work at the bakery?" he asked, trying to make conversation.

She shook her head. "Worse."

He found the response rather odd. "I don't understand."

"I own it."

Oh. He opened his mouth. Then he promptly closed it. He'd forgotten her saying "*my bakery.*" Now all of her prior actions were starting to take on a new meaning. No wonder she'd been so desperate to save the building.

The sadness reflected in her eyes prompted him to speak. "I'm sorry this happened."

"Me too." Her voice was soft, but the raw pain was still evident.

"If there's anything I can do to help."

She shook her head. "Thanks."

Somehow he knew that was what she was going to say. But he wasn't going to give up that easily. There had to be something to say—something to do—that would ease some of her distress.

"Hannah!" A blond young woman that he recalled seeing around town came rushing up to her.

Hannah jumped to her feet. Immediately the women hugged. He felt bad for not being able to comfort her, but he was glad someone was now there for her.

When the women parted, he realized where he'd seen the other woman—at the café. If he spent enough time there, he was pretty certain he'd bump into everyone in town. The Lighthouse Café was popular when he was a kid, and it appeared things hadn't changed over the years.

He got to his feet. He considered saying goodbye, but Hannah was already engrossed in conversation about the incident. He was no longer needed here.

Ethan turned his attention back to the bakery. He knew from experience that there was going to be a lot of damage from the water, starting with the caved-in ceiling. But he had no doubt it was all fixable. And now that the fire department had a pump and line running, the water was quickly being drawn out.

Just then the fire chief started across the street. He came to a stop in front of Ethan. "You did good work shutting off the water."

Ethan shrugged off the compliment. "I just did what needed done."

The man eyed him up. "Most people wouldn't have known what to do."

"I'm a firefighter."

The chief's gray brows rose. "It's nice to meet you." He stuck out a hand. "Chief Campbell."

He shook the man's hand. "Ethan Walker."

"What house are you with?"

"Engine two fifty-six in Brooklyn, New York."

The chief nodded. "A ways from home."

"My aunt, well, my great-aunt got hurt and I'm sticking around to help her out."

"You wouldn't be Birdie's nephew, would you?"

Ethan smiled at how small Bluestar was that the chief would be able to deduce who his aunt was. "Yes, sir."

"How's Birdie doing?"

"Much better than originally thought. The doctors thought she'd need surgery, but luckily it was a hairline break and a lot of bruising. It should heal on its own."

"That's good to hear."

"I won't keep you."

"Hey, you should stop by the firehouse. Visitors are always welcome. And we could use a new volunteer. That is if you're sticking around for a bit."

The invitation appealed to him. He did miss his buddies back in Brooklyn. "Thanks for the invite. I'll stop by, but just for a visit. I still have a job waiting for me back in the city."

31

The chief nodded in understanding just as someone called out his name. "I'll see you soon."

As the chief made his way along the side of the bakery, Ethan knew it was time for him to get a move on. He needed to catch the ferry to the mainland in order to visit his aunt.

When he turned to leave, he caught a glimpse of Hannah. Her face was still pale and drawn. Then again, maybe he'd stick around for a few more minutes just to be sure the pretty lady with the stroke of bad luck didn't need any other assistance.

Ethan turned and made his way back toward Hannah. He wasn't sure what else to say to her, but that didn't slow him down.

CHAPTER FOUR

This can't be happening.

It was a horrible nightmare.

Hannah wished she would wake up and all would be right with the world. Oh, how she wished that were the case.

And to make matters worse, she'd let her emotions get the best of her when the fire truck had pulled up. She inwardly groaned over what the good-looking stranger must think of her—weak and helpless. Frustration knotted her stomach.

The truth of the matter was that it had been the first time she'd seen the fire truck with its lights on rolling up the street since her father's funeral—since he died in a fire. In her mind, she could clearly see his casket draped with a flag and placed atop the fire truck. He had been driven to their family's private cemetery on the edge of her brother's farm.

Her heart ached for him. Her father should be there now. He would have known how to fix this mess. He'd always been great with offering advice.

She blinked, bringing herself back to the present. Her gaze moved to the big red truck now parked in front of her. If her father hadn't been a firefighter—if he hadn't been so willing to put his life on the line for others—he would still be there with his family. She knew it was selfish. She knew the world needed more people like her father. But did her father have to lose his life for doing a good deed? Life wasn't fair.

Inside she was weeping for her father—for her damaged business—but on the outside, she maintained a stiff upper lip as she stood quietly next to one of her best friends, Josie Turner. They'd been friends, well, since forever. Their mothers had been best friends all of their lives. Hannah supposed she met Josie when they were both still in diapers. There just wasn't a time she hadn't known Josie as a dear friend—through the good and bad. And now was definitely one of those bad times.

It felt as though all of Hannah's hopes and dreams had been washed away with the flood water. She didn't know how extensive the damage was to the building, but from what she'd witnessed from the doorway, it was bad.

Her heart sank down to her purple tennis shoes. How was she going to get all of this repair work done, as well as the rest of the restoration, and still open on time? With the bakery's large loan payment looming in her future, everything had to stay on track.

Right now, it all felt so overwhelming. But she was a Bell and Bells didn't give up. It was what her father used to tell her before her math tests—her toughest class in school.

If her father were here now, he'd tell her to hang in there. He'd insist there was a way to fix this mess. And he would be right. She'd invested everything in this dream. She couldn't give up now.

Hannah's gaze settled on a familiar green golf cart headed their way. "Oh no."

A worried look came over Josie's face. "What's wrong?"

Hannah nodded to the road. Her brother's green golf cart pulled up to the curb. Next to him was their mother, who was wearing a worried expression. In the back seat sat her six-year-old niece, Nikki. This wasn't good. She didn't want to worry her family.

"It was bound to happen," Josie said. "You know how fast news travels on the island."

It was only then that she turned around, noticing nearly half the town checking out the commotion. She should have known it was too much to hope that word wouldn't get back to her family. But still she'd hoped to downplay it so her mother wouldn't worry.

"Josie, you should go back to work," Hannah said. "This might take a while."

"I don't know." Josie looked hesitant. "Are you sure?"

"Positive. I've got it."

"I do need to get back to the inn. We're expecting some guests on the next ferry." Josie gave her another hug. "Let me know if there's anything I can do, including buying a couple pints of rocky road ice cream. For me, it's the best medicine."

"Thanks. I just might take you up on the offer."

Josie glanced over her shoulder at Hannah's family rushing toward them. She turned back to Hannah. "And if you need a place to hide away from all of the well-meaning fussing, my place is available."

And with that Josie walked away, leaving Hannah alone to face her concerned mother. And her frowning big brother, Sam. And her anxious little niece who held Sam's hand as they approached Hannah.

Nikki paused to stare at the fire engine with its red lights still flashing. "Isn't that the truck Grandpa used to ride?"

"Yes, it is," Sam responded as he too stared at the truck, most likely thinking of the father they'd lost too soon.

Hannah was astonished that Nikki could remember back to when she was four-years-old—back when her grandpa was around to give her ice cream treats and make her laugh. As her gaze returned to the big red engine, Hannah could remember how proud her father had been when the island had purchased the truck. It seemed like it was yesterday.

"Oh, my goodness." Her mother pressed her hands to her cheeks as she watched the firefighters rush around, adjusting equipment to drain the water from the building. "What happened?"

Nikki let go of her father's hand and ran up to Hannah. She wrapped her arms around Hannah's legs. "I was worried 'bout you."

Hannah ran a hand over her niece's straight brown hair. "There's nothing to worry about." Hannah painted a smile on her face for Nikki's benefit. "It's just a little water. Everything will be fine."

"A little water?" Sam was normally the most laid-back man she knew, but even he looked concerned.

The last thing he needed was to worry about her. He had enough of his own problems. He'd lost his young wife only a few years after they'd married. It had all been so heartbreaking. But he'd made a go of tending to the farm he'd taken over from their grandparents.

And he was doing a mighty fine job raising his daughter as a single parent. If only he'd find love again, maybe those worry lines around his eyes would smooth, and he wouldn't look so tired all the time.

But who was she to try to fix his problems when she had no idea how to fix her own? Still, she had to act like she was in control of the situation. "Everybody, stop worrying. It's not as bad as it looks."

"Who's he?" Her mother's voice interrupted Hannah's thoughts.

When Hannah's gaze followed the direction her mother was pointing in, it landed on the handsome stranger. It was only then she noticed how tall he was—six feet or more.

He wasn't looking her way, and it gave her a chance to take in his chiseled jaw with some scruff on it. Not bad-looking. Not that she was interested.

Just then he turned his head. His brown gaze connected with hers. Her heart skipped a beat or two. Heat swirled in her chest and rushed to her cheeks. She glanced away.

Her mother was still looking at her, expecting an answer. What was his name? Had he told her? Try as she might, she couldn't recall. Her thoughts were a jumbled mess.

When her mother's question garnered the man's attention and he stepped forward, Hannah felt pressured to say something. "Mom, this is the man who helped me by shutting off the water before the fire department showed up. Without him this all would be so much worse."

The man extended his hand. "The name's Ethan Walker. It's nice to meet you."

Her mother studied his face as she shook his hand. And then her gaze lowered to Peaches. Her face lit up. "You're Birdie's nephew, aren't you?"

He smiled, showing off the dimples in his cheeks. "Yes, ma'am. That's me."

"How's she doing?"

"Really good considering."

"Give her my best and if there's anything I can do, let me know."

And then Hannah watched as he introduced himself to her brother. The men chatted for a couple of minutes about the bakery. It was like she was introducing her boyfriend to her family for the first time. As soon as the thought came to her, she quickly dismissed it. She didn't even know this man, nor did she have time to get to know him. She had more than she could handle at the moment.

"Honey, I'll be right back," her mother said. "I just need to speak to someone." Without waiting for Hannah to say anything, her mother moved away.

Curiosity had Hannah watching as her mother crossed the street and approached Chief Campbell. Not thinking much of two old friends greeting each other, Hannah turned her attention back to the firefighters working to pump out the water.

She recalled her grandmother telling her that baking was in her blood. Her grandmother spent a large portion of her life creating amazing desserts for her family and friends. Hannah had been taught from a young age how to make a flaky pie crust and a fluffy angel food cake. When she was too short to see over the table, her grandmother would pull out a chair and let her kneel on it. Her grandmother used to say there was a certain elegance to Hannah's cakes.

And then Hannah had gone on to be an employee at this very bakery for close to fourteen years now—ever since she was in high school. When the bakery reopened, she would no longer be an employee—she'd be the owner. Correction, she was the owner.

Agnes Dewey rushed over to her. "You poor girl." She gave her a hug. "It's just awful. I knew this was going to happen. You should have listened to the horoscope this morning."

Hannah was so caught off guard by the woman's hug that she didn't know how to react. It was all so uncharacteristic of Agnes. And then the woman pulled away as fast as she'd hugged her.

"I...uh..." Hannah struggled for the right words.

Agnes clucked her tongue. "It's just a shame that everything is ruined."

Hannah wanted to disagree. The bakery wasn't ruined. She opened her mouth but then wordlessly pressed her lips together. Was the woman right? Had Agnes overheard something about the building's condition on the inside? Was the bakery beyond repair? Hannah's heart once more sank down to her still-wet sneakers.

"It was going to be so amazing." Agnes continued to talk as though she hadn't even noticed that Hannah wasn't taking part in the conversation. "I just feel so horrible that all of your dreams are ruined. But you gave it your best shot. If only you'd caught the leak sooner." Agnes's gaze latched onto someone else. "There's Betty Simon. I have to speak to her about Spring Fling." Agnes's pitying gaze moved back to Hannah. "You take care of yourself." And then she was gone.

Agnes was right. As the owner, she should have foreseen something like this. She'd worked so hard planning the renovations to bring the bakery into the modern era. She'd even made sure to budget in rewiring the entire building. But she never thought the place would need to be replumbed too.

Honestly, she wasn't aware, until now, that pipes could wear out. *Maybe I should have asked more questions. Maybe I should have had a different contractor. Maybe I should have—*

38

"Stop blaming yourself."

Hannah blinked as she glanced at Ethan. "What?"

"Don't let that woman get in your head. There's no way you knew this was going to happen."

"But I should have known. I should have been prepared."

"This is not your fault."

"If it's not my fault, whose is it?" She didn't wait for a response. "I should have known that everything in the building would need replaced. After all, the bakery is practically as old as the town."

"It's a broken pipe. Those things happen. The building is still standing. Still sturdy."

At least she hoped so. But what was going on behind the walls? Was there another disaster lurking someplace she hadn't thought to look?

Lily Adams, her other bestie, came running up to her. Her short dark hair was styled in a pixie cut. And her golden-brown complexion was done up with just a bit of makeup. The only thing missing that day was her cheerful smile.

They'd been friends since elementary school when they'd both reached for the pink modeling clay in art class. They'd both withdrawn their hands. And then they'd both reached for the purple clay. They'd both started to laugh. In the end, they decided to share all of the colors and they'd been friends ever since.

Before Lily said anything, her friend hugged her. "I'm so sorry." When she pulled back, their gazes met. "What happened?"

"A pipe broke. It must have been leaking for hours. There's so much water and...and the ceiling has partially caved in."

Lily didn't say anything at first; she didn't have to. The sympathy reflected in her warm brown eyes said it all. "I'm so sorry. What can I do to help?"

Lily ran a small crafts shop called The Lily Pad. Some of the items were hers—mostly the jewelry—the rest were items on consignment. It was a great place to find a unique gift.

Hannah shook her head. "There's nothing to do now. Everything is soaked and they had to cut the power."

Lily draped an arm around her and rested her head on her shoulder. "Thank goodness you found it when you did."

"I know, but it was Ethan who stopped the water before the fire department could get here."

"Ethan? Who's that?"

Hannah glanced around but found he was gone. "He was literally just standing here a moment ago. Where did he go?" She visually searched the crowd of people but didn't see him. His long legs must have allowed him a quick escape. She turned back to Lily. "Anyway, it's Birdie's nephew."

"Oh... Is he cute?"

She gently elbowed Lily. "I can't believe you asked me that right now."

Lily ducked her chin. "I know. Bad timing."

"Yes, it is." But Hannah felt bad about snapping, so she admitted, "And yes, he is."

Lily's gaze met hers and she smiled. "Not exactly a meet cute but a memorable one."

"Stop. It wasn't any sort of meet. I don't need a boyfriend. Been there, done that. What I need right now is someone to fix my bakery."

She hadn't dated anyone since she'd broken off her engagement with Brad seven months ago. She had no interest in investing herself in a relationship. Now was the time for her to focus on her career.

Brad had never understood that. In fact, when she'd told him about her dream to buy the bakery, he'd told her that it was a waste of her money. He'd said she would be better off investing the money her father left her in a beach house for them. A beach house was never anything she'd longed for, but it was something Brad had desperately wanted.

40

For a time, she'd told herself it would be nice to live by the beach—to be able to walk out her door each morning and step onto the sand. It took her a bit of time to come to her senses and realize that she'd miss living in the middle of town. She loved being a regular part of the Bluestar community. Brad never understood that—he'd never understood her.

"You're right." Lily's voice drew her from her thoughts. "First, the bakery and then we'll find you someone."

Hannah shook her head. "Why am I the one who needs a guy when both you and Josie are still single?"

"One of us has to take the plunge first."

"If you're talking about what I think you're talking about, it's not going to be me." Marriage flashed through Hannah's mind, right before the tick-tock of her biological clock echoed in her ears. "I've got too much to do. And why are we talking about guys when my business is in ruins?"

"Because it distracted you for just a bit."

And then there was a gentle tug on her hand. She glanced to her side, noticing her niece. How long had Nikki been standing there?

Nikki's worried gaze met hers. "Auntie Hannah, are you sad?"

Her niece's concern tugged at Hannah's heartstrings. She knelt down so she was on eye level with her niece, who acted so much older than her tender age.

"Everything is going to be all right." Even as she said the words, she didn't believe them.

Nikki leaned forward and wrapped her arms around her neck. "I love you."

Hannah blinked back tears. "I love you too, sweetie."

Just then Sam approached them. He adjusted his green ball cap. "The electricity is off and most of the water has been pumped out. What can I do for you?"

Hannah straightened. "Thanks. I've got it."

41

She loved her big brother but knew as a single parent he didn't have any spare time. Even with their mother helping out with Nikki, there was still too much work for one person between running the farm and taking care of the laundry and cleaning the house.

He arched a brow. "Are you sure?"

She nodded.

His eyes said he didn't believe her. "In that case, I need to get back to the farm. One of the goats is about to go into labor."

"That's so exciting. I wish I could be there." Hannah meant it. "I love those goats."

Sam shook his head. "Sometimes I think you're in the wrong line of work."

"But if I wasn't a baker, who would make you a double chocolate, peanut-butter-filled cake with peanut butter candies on top for your birthday?"

His eyes lit up at the mention of his favorite cake. "You have a good point." He gave her a hug. "Sorry this happened to you. Call me if you need anything at all."

"I will." She glanced over to where her mother was now chatting with Betty Simon. "Want me to get Mom?"

Sam shook his head. "She's staying in town. She has an appointment later."

"Oh. Okay." And then she gave Nikki a big hug and kiss. "Be good for your daddy. And let me know as soon as the goat is born. Send me pictures."

Nikki smiled. "We will. Love you."

"Love you more."

As her brother and niece drove away, Hannah's fingers moved rapidly over the screen of her phone. She retrieved the number for the insurance company. The conversation was brief. They were sending out an adjuster today. She was certain they'd have more questions for her.

Next she did a little research and found a disaster restoration company located in Boston. She read their description and yes, they worked with water damage. And then she read the reviews. All except one review said they had done an exceptional job. And the one bad review was so bad she couldn't help but wonder if it had been placed there by their competition. Then she checked out their Better Business rating. It was a stellar A+ rating.

These were the people she needed. Because even though her family and friends were offering to help, they didn't know anything about water damage or replacing water pipes. And her insurance would cover the professional help. She made the call. After a brief moment on hold, she was able to speak to a human. They'd be there as soon as the insurance company approved payment.

So now she had a plan. It was a small comfort. But it was something.

"Hannah!" Newly-elected Mayor Tony Banks strode up to her. "I just heard what happened. I'm so sorry. I can't imagine how devastated you must be."

Though he was only a couple of years older than her, Tony always acted so mature for his age. He was always so serious with his collection of bow ties and suits. He kept his brown hair cut short. He was always so put together. And now that he was in office, he had plans for the island—plans to mix things up a bit.

"Thanks." She wasn't sure what else to say. She was still grappling with the devastation to the business and the threat to her dream.

"The whole town is going to be so disappointed about this setback. I know everyone was looking forward to the grand opening. Do you know how long it'll take to fix everything?"

Her mouth opened but she promptly closed it. It was best not to speak. He might expect spontaneous answers at town hall meetings, but things were different out here in the street. Instead she shook her head.

His gaze moved to the bakery. "At least the outside looks fine. Hopefully the inside isn't so bad. Tourist season will be kicking into high gear early this year thanks to the early spring, so if there's anything I can do to speed things along, just let me know."

"Thanks. I will." She knew how popular the bakery was with the tourists. It was what she was counting on.

He glanced at his watch. "I have a meeting in ten to go over this year's tourism guide. I hope we'll still be able to list the bakery."

Her chest tightened as the consequences of the flood continued to grow. "I'll do my best."

The mayor nodded in understanding. "I better go. But I wanted to stop by and let you know that the town is totally behind you."

"I appreciate it."

And then the mayor was off in a rush. She liked Tony, but she'd never met anyone on the island that was in such a rush like him. No wonder he wasn't married with a family of his own. He never slowed down long enough for a lasting relationship.

At last the firefighters packed up their equipment, drew up their hoses, and stowed away their pumps. She knew them all and had gone to school with a handful of them. The chief told her they'd done as much as they could. She was warned to be careful of the damage and not to have the power restored until the building was inspected. And then not just the fire chief but each firefighter either offered encouraging words or gave her a hug.

The kind gesture launched her heart into her throat. The last time they'd hugged her had been at her father's funeral. Each member of the department had been in their dress uniforms with badge covers. Hug after hug, she struggled to maintain her composure. They had no idea how much their presence reminded her of her loss.

And then the fire department left and it was time to go inside. Her stomach twisted into a knot. Would the interior look as bad as she'd initially thought? Or would it be worse? Though her mother encouraged her to wait to go inside, nothing was going to stop her.

On wobbly knees, she made her way to the front door. It was hanging wide open. She stepped inside, not sure what to expect. But this section didn't look bad. She moved to the stacked boxes of flooring. Most of the upper boxes were still dry. She wanted to breathe a sigh of relief, but she knew the worst of the damage was in the back—in the big kitchen.

Her mother and Lily were following her, but they remained quiet. She was grateful for their silence because right about now, she didn't trust her voice. Until this point, she didn't know how much she'd fallen in love with this bakery—how her dream for its future had taken on a life of its own.

Hannah eased open the door separating the kitchen from the storefront. The breath hitched in her throat. The long light fixture with fluorescent tubes dangled by one end from the ceiling. There was a giant gaping hole in the ceiling where she surmised the pipe must have burst.

Tears stung the back of her eyes. She blinked repeatedly to keep her emotions in check. She lowered her gaze, finding crumbled plaster and other building supplies scattered across the stainless-steel countertops.

Her heart lodged in her throat, choking off a cry of despair. This was so much worse than she'd ever imagined possible. She just couldn't see how it'd be possible to fix all of the damage in time for the grand opening in three weeks. Definitely not possible.

As her gaze lowered, she saw the muck and debris on the kitchen floor. She blinked away the unshed tears. There weren't available funds to replace everything, so she'd opted to keep the kitchen floor. No one would see this area but her and her employees. She'd worked so hard to clean and patch the floor after the contractor had finished priming and sanding the walls. She'd been all prepared to make it shine once the renovations were over. And now...now who knew if it was salvageable.

She'd wanted everything to gleam before her inspection. Inspection! She made a mental note to call and have that delayed.

Her mother moved to her side and placed an arm around her back. "I'm sorry about this. But it can be fixed. I can stay and help you clean some of this up." Her mother's voice was soft and full of love. "Whatever you want, just tell me."

"I can stay too," Lily said.

Hannah shook her head. This was her problem. "Thanks, but you both had things to do. I've got this." She wondered how many more times she'd have to say that today. "And I don't want to clean anything until the claims adjuster gets here and takes some photos."

"When will that be?" her mother asked.

"They didn't say." As she spoke, her gaze was still inventorying all of the damage.

Her mother and friend finally left, but not before she repeatedly promised them she was all right—that she wasn't going to fall apart. It was a lie.

She was crumbling on the inside, but no one needed to know that. After all, she was strong. She'd get through this. It was like Ethan had said; it was an old building. These things happened.

And she already had repair plans in motion, but would they happen quickly enough to save her business?

CHAPTER FIVE

"How's Peaches?"

Not a "hi" or "how are you?" Ethan smiled as he gave a slight shake of his head. It was just like his aunt to get straight to the point.

Ethan stepped farther into Aunt Birdie's private room at the Sunny Days Rehabilitation Center. The light-blue walls were cheerful, and the morning's sunshine lit up the room. It was certainly far nicer than the hospital room he'd stayed in for days after his on-the-job incident. His fingers ran over the uneven skin on the back of his hand. As fast as the disturbing memory came to him, he shoved it away.

He stopped next to a tan high-back armchair. "Hello."

His aunt's alert blue eyes met his. Her ivory face drawn with worry. "Don't keep me waiting. Is she okay?"

Every time he walked into the room, his aunt's first question was about her beloved dog. He nodded. "Peaches is good, but she misses you."

"She's not used to being away from me." Aunt Birdie visibly breathed a sigh of relief and then smiled. "Tell her I miss her too."

"I will."

Aunt Birdie was wearing a bright pink-and-yellow-flowered robe while being propped up in bed. Her white hair was swept back in a neat bun. Circumstances hadn't dimmed her smile as her aged hands resumed moving the wooden knitting needles along the deep-plum yarn. If not for their surroundings, it'd be hard to tell anything was wrong with her.

Taking a seat next to the bed, Ethan couldn't help but admire her strength. She'd lived through a lot, from not being able to have kids of her own to the premature loss of her beloved husband. She was the only grandmother-figure Ethan had ever known. And he was so grateful she was going to be all right. He couldn't imagine life without her gentle prodding for him to be happy or her insightful comments about life in general.

"Is she eating?" His aunt continued to quiz him on her cockapoo's routine. He sat down and proceeded to answer all of her questions, knowing if he didn't, she'd worry.

"Don't forget to walk her. At least twice a day. We don't want her gaining weight. The vet was adamant that she gain no more weight."

"I'm walking her." He suddenly felt as though he were twelve as his aunt instructed him on how to puppysit. "I promise."

"Thank you. You don't know what a relief it is to know you're caring for Peaches. I couldn't stay here and rest without knowing you're taking care of her."

"Where else would I be?" Ethan asked, not expecting a response.

"Well, for one, your job. I feel terrible for dragging you away from it."

"You can stop worrying. I have a lot of saved-up vacation time. So I'm here as long as you need me."

Aunt Birdie's gray brows drew together. "And they just let you take all of that time off at once?"

He shifted uncomfortably in the chair. This was a question he'd been dreading. Until now, Aunt Birdie had been thoroughly distracted with urging the doctors to release her.

Aunt Birdie's hands ceased movement. He knew from past experience that very little kept her from knitting. She could knit without even looking at what she was doing. But now her entire attention was focused on him. He glanced away, not wanting her to read too much in his eyes.

"Ethan James Walker, what aren't you telling me?"

He didn't want to tell her. She had her own problems to worry about. However, a lifetime of experience told him when she used his full name, she wouldn't give up until she got the whole truth.

He drew in a steadying breath. His hospital-assigned therapist had told him he should talk about it, but that was easier said than done. "I just haven't returned to work yet."

"Look at me." He raised his gaze, meeting his aunt's straight on. She studied him. "Are you having complications from your injuries?"

He shook his head. "Physically I'm fine."

"What else aren't you telling me?"

He shrugged. "It's no big deal."

That wasn't quite the truth. There was a lot he was leaving out, but he wasn't ready to talk about it with her or anyone else. Not yet. The therapist had also said that until he was willing to talk about it, the nightmares would persist.

"You can't hide from life."

"I'm not." His voice was firm.

Her insightful gaze continued to study him. "You're strong. Perhaps stronger than you think. Sometimes the best intentions can lead us down the wrong path in life. It's not a weakness to turn and follow a new path."

He glanced down at the white tiled floor. He didn't know what to say. What was she trying to tell him? That she didn't want him there? Or was she talking about him taking time off from the fire department?

He cleared his throat. "I'd much rather talk about you—"

"What about your girlfriend? She must miss you."

He kept his gaze lowered. "You don't have to worry about that. We broke up."

"Ethan, I'm so sorry."

He raised his gaze to meet hers. "Don't be. It wasn't meant to be."

"I see." She grew quiet, as though considering all of this information. "So tell me what is happening in Bluestar."

With the change of subject, he breathed easier. "Now that you mention it, something happened in town." He leaned back in the chair. "It's why I was late today."

Her eyes widened as she sat up a bit straighter. "Tell me no one got hurt."

"Everyone is fine. The bakery, on the other hand, isn't doing so well." He couldn't help wondering how Hannah was making out now that the shock had passed.

Aunt Birdie set aside her knitting, giving him her full attention. "How horrible. What happened?"

And so he regaled the tale of his morning walk with Peaches and the ensuing saga of the burst pipe. His aunt hung on his every word. He took his time, going into more detail than he normally would do.

Aunt Birdie's face creased with worry lines. "Poor Hannah. She hasn't had an easy time of it. How's she doing?"

Hannah's beautiful image filled his mind. He wondered what his aunt had alluded to about troubles in Hannah's life, but he resisted the urge to inquire. "She was pretty upset."

"I can imagine. Thank goodness you were able to stop the water. It could have been so much worse." Her gaze met his. "I should have been there."

"There's nothing you could have done."

She shook her head in disagreement. "There's always something to do, even if it's just being there for moral support."

The way she looked at him, he started to wonder if she was still talking about herself, or if she was giving him some sort of subtle hint. In the next breath, he dismissed the notion.

Hannah had her own family and friends to help her. He was certain she wouldn't want or need his help. Still, the memory of the devastated look on her pretty face dug at him.

"When you see her, please let her know how sorry I am."

He opened his mouth to say he didn't expect to see her again, but wordlessly he pressed his lips together. After all, Bluestar was a small island. The odds of running into her were high.

"I'll do that," he said, liking the idea of bumping into Hannah.

"Oh, before I forget." Aunt Birdie's face lit up. "I have something for you."

"For me?" He was confused. How could his aunt go shopping when she'd been in the hospital and now in this physical rehab facility?

She smiled and nodded. She reached over to her bedside stand, but when her yarn rolled off her lap, she rushed to grab it. Ethan sprang into action, grabbing it before it fell to the floor. He handed it back to her.

"Thank you." Aunt Birdie rolled up the yarn and placed the ball securely on her lap.

"Tell me what you want," he said, "and I'll get it for you."

"It's in the drawer."

He opened the top drawer in the bedside table. Inside he found a package of cheddar cheese crackers stuffed with peanut butter. A smile pulled at the corners of his lips.

He picked up the cellophane package. "Is this what you wanted?"

She nodded once more. "Yes. I saw them and remembered how much you used to enjoy them when you were a little boy."

A smile tugged at his lips. "I haven't had them in years. But how did you get them?"

"There's a vending machine at the end of the hall. When I was taking my mandatory walk last evening, I saw them. I went back to my room, got some change, and went back."

"You walked the hall twice?" He knew how painful walking was for her, so this gift—this memory from the past—meant so much more to him.

She nodded. "Don't tell anyone but I wanted to do it. The more I move, the sooner I can go home."

He knew how anxious she was to be discharged, but he also recalled the doctor saying that her recovery would take

time. "Well, thank you. They bring back good memories."
He placed the package of crackers in his pocket. "Now what
can I do for you? Maybe I can bring you something from
home to make you more comfortable here?"

"Now that you mention it, I could use some more yarn. I
have this plum shade in a red bag next to my desk in the
living room. Would you be a dear and bring it with you when
you come back?"

"Do you need it today?" He was willing to take the ferry
back to the island and return if it'd make her happy. It wasn't
like he had anything else planned for the day.

She shook her head. "I have plenty of yarn for now. But
I'm making a blanket for one of the nurses, and it needs to be
bigger than what I can manage with this." She held up a
couple of skeins.

That was his aunt, adopting the people around her and
treating them like family. "Are you sure you won't be
overdoing it?"

She waved away his concern. "It's my hip that's injured.
The rest of me is fine. I can't just lay here and watch
television. I need something to do—"

"I've got something for you to do." The male voice came
from the doorway. "It's time for your physical therapy."

Ethan turned to find a man who looked to be around his
own age and of average height and build. He had a pleasant
enough smile on his face, but his eyes said that he meant
business.

"Not again. Didn't I walk enough this morning?" Aunt
Birdie protested. "I made it to the end of the hallway."

"And now it's time to do it again. Too much sitting
around isn't good for you."

It was at this point that Ethan got to his feet. Something
told him this physical therapist was used to dealing with
stubborn people, and he would deal with his aunt just fine on
his own.

52

"Wait," Aunt Birdie said to Ethan. Then she turned to the PT guy. "Can you give us a couple of minutes?"

The man's lips pursed as though considering the ramifications of telling Aunt Birdie no. In that moment, Ethan liked the guy. PT guy recognized that his aunt wasn't one to be bossed around.

"Okay. I could use a coffee. But five minutes only. No more." His serious expression said he too meant business. And then PT guy turned and walked away.

"What's so important?" Ethan asked. His curiosity piqued.

"I have a problem."

Ethan sat back down. "Tell me what it is, and I'm sure we can work out a solution."

"I need to go home." When he opened his mouth to speak, she said, "I'm serious. I have responsibilities. The town is counting on me."

"We talked about this," he said calmly. "You know you aren't ready to be at home. Not yet. I'm sure people will understand."

She shook her head. "This is too important. I have to leave and you have to help me get out of here."

He couldn't imagine what had her so worked up. "Just tell me what it is and I'll take care of it for you."

She paused as though considering his words. "You'd do that?"

He nodded, still not knowing what he was agreeing to. "If it'll keep you here. So what is it?"

"Well, if you're sure about this?" When he nodded once more, she continued. "I'm in charge of Spring Fling. I need to make sure everything is organized. You can find my notes in my desk. They are in a purple binder."

He struggled not to frown as he realized what he'd volunteered to do. Still, Bluestar was a small island. How hard could organizing it be? And it would give him something to do besides walk the dog and watch movies on television.

"Don't worry. I've got this."

Aunt Birdie beamed. "Have I told you lately that you're my favorite great-nephew?"

"I'm your only great-nephew."

They both laughed. It was a real laugh—one that came from deep inside. It felt good. Maybe this time off work wasn't so bad after all.

Just then PT guy stepped back into the room. "Everything taken care of?"

Aunt Birdie smiled and nodded. "Everything is just fine." She turned back to Ethan. "And don't forget my yarn."

"I won't." If he didn't know better, he'd swear his aunt just pulled a fast one on him.

"Okay," the PT guy said. "Let's get you out of that bed."

Ethan turned to his aunt. "That's my cue to go. I can stop back this evening."

Aunt Birdie shook her head. "That's okay. Once he gets done with me"—she gestured to the therapist—"I'll be exhausted. So you and Peaches can hang out together." She held out her arms to him. He leaned over and gave her a hug. She placed a butterfly kiss to his cheek.

"Love you," she said.

"Love you too." He straightened. "Don't give your physical therapist a hard time."

"And make this torture easy for him? I don't think so."

Ethan smiled and shook his head once more as he walked away. He wondered what exactly he'd gotten himself into. As he searched his memory, he vaguely recalled attending an Easter egg hunt on the island many years ago. How hard could that be?

Her PT session was finally over.

Beatrice "Birdie" Neill leaned back against her pillow and sighed. She'd given her all. The older she got, the slower she moved. It wasn't fair that her body was failing her, because mentally she still felt as though she were a spry and energetic thirty.

In all of her eighty-one years, she'd never been sidelined before. If only she'd paid a little more attention when she was walking Peaches. Instead she'd been focused on chatting to Agnes Dewey. She hadn't realized how close to the edge of the sidewalk she'd been and her foot had slipped off the side. She cringed as she recalled landing in the street with a painful thud.

Still, something good had come of it. Ethan was back on the island. Her frown lifted into a smile because she was thrilled to have him back in her life. Sometimes she regretted not picking up and moving after her husband, Gilbert, had suddenly died. She could have been close to her family once more.

But the people of Bluestar Island were also her family. Maybe they weren't blood kin, but she loved them and them her. Plus, all of her happy memories with Gil were there on the island. She couldn't leave. And she didn't want Ethan to leave either. Not yet.

There was something bothering him—something he wasn't ready to talk about. But she knew something about this island that he didn't. It was good at helping people heal. The walks on the beach were good for clearing your mind and straightening out matters of the heart.

However, she knew her nephew and suspected he'd soon grow bored. Organizing Spring Fling would draw him into the community. It would keep him busy, and hopefully it'd help him through whatever troubles were plaguing him. And then she recalled how he'd lit up when he spoke of Hannah.

Birdie reached for the phone and dialed a familiar number. "Hello, Betty."

"Birdie, how are you? We've been so worried."

Birdie smiled. It felt good to know people cared.

Betty Simon had become her first friend when she moved to the island. They'd shared late night talks and weekends at the beach. And when she lost Gil, Betty had been by her side, making sure she ate and dressed as well as helping her through the difficult transition from loving wife to widow.

"I'm good," Birdie said, "but it's my nephew I'm worried about."

"You mean Ethan? He seemed fine when I passed him in town earlier."

"Physically he's fine, but I'm worried he's growing bored with island life. I don't think he's putting himself out there and getting to know the islanders."

"I have the feeling you already have a plan on how to fix this problem."

Birdie smiled to herself. "You know me so well. I've put Ethan in charge of Spring Fling."

"You did what?" The horrified tone of Betty's voice said she didn't approve of this idea at all.

"Hear me out. With me being stuck here on the mainland, I need someone on the island to step up. And I know you would have done it, but I also know you have a lot going on in your life, whereas Ethan doesn't at the moment. Walking Peaches just isn't enough for him. He needs this."

"You don't think it'll be too much for him? He's never done it before."

"Ethan's resourceful. I'm sure he'll ask for help."

"Sounds like you're hoping he does. But who do you have in mind to help him?"

Immediately Hannah came to mind. "How are things with the bakery?"

"Oh, you heard about the flood already?"

"Ethan filled me in."

"He did, huh?"

Birdie's smile broadened. "He's concerned about our dear Hannah."

"Birdie, if you're thinking about playing matchmaker, you shouldn't do it."

"I'm not." Not exactly. But she had a feeling Ethan and Hannah's paths were destined to cross once more. Maybe they just needed a little push in the right direction.

CHAPTER SIX

The sunshine flickered through the leaves.

Monday morning Hannah yawned as she pedaled her perky pink bike along the road. Sleep had evaded her for much of the night as she'd come to terms with this setback with the bakery. The images of destruction had flashed repeatedly through her mind, but she refused to give up on her dream.

She yawned again. It was definitely time for a jolt of caffeine. After mailing the wedding shower invitations for Amelia, Hannah stopped at The Lighthouse Café. If she could afford it, she'd stop there every day. But ever since she could remember, she'd been saving her money. She was so strict with her budget her family teased her that she squeaked when she walked, but they wouldn't joke anymore. Everything was changing.

She passed beneath the black wooden sign with the painted image of a red and white lighthouse and the name, Lighthouse Café, scrolled out in white paint. She'd been coming to this restaurant all of her life. Her family celebrated birthdays there, and she'd even gone there on her first date. She smiled at the memories. It all seemed so long ago now.

Hannah stepped up to the door and pulled it open. With it being mid-morning, the place didn't have many customers. She headed straight for the end of the counter where the server, Darla Evans, was refilling the salt and pepper shakers. Her short blond ponytail swished to the side when she glanced up and smiled.

"Morning." Hannah dispensed with the good part. So far nothing had gone the way she'd hoped.

Darla's smile faded. She'd been a few years behind Hannah in school. "I'm so sorry about the bakery."

"Thanks." Hannah forced a slight smile to her lips.

Hannah had experienced a lot of those awkward moments in the last couple of days. No one knew exactly what to say to her. Even her sister, the rising Nashville star, had dropped what she was doing when she'd heard about the flood. She'd called and offered to come home and help out. Hannah wouldn't hear of it. She knew her sister was busy following her dreams, and Hannah hadn't wanted to interfere with her sister's amazing career.

But the magnitude of Emma's offer didn't go unnoticed. Until this point, her sister always had one reason or another that she couldn't make it home for birthdays or holidays. Hannah wondered if perhaps she'd made a mistake by turning Emma down. But it was done now, so she had to move on.

"What can I get you?" Darla poised her pen over a notepad.

"A large coffee to-go with milk."

Darla slipped the pen and paper back into her black apron, which coordinated perfectly with her black pants and white knit top. "You got it."

The jingle of the front door caught Hannah's attention. She turned in time to see Lily stroll in. "Hey, what are you doing here?"

"I needed some fresh air and some caffeine." Lily smoothed her windswept curls. "The better question is, what are you doing here?"

Just then Darla returned with Hannah's coffee. "Here you go."

Hannah paid for her drink as well as an identical one for Lily. Then she stepped aside to speak to Lily. "I needed a pick-me-up. I've been on the phone all morning. The bakery is supposed to open in three weeks, but I just don't see that happening."

"I'm so sorry." Lily's brown eyes reflected her sympathy. "What can I do?"

Hannah shook her head. "Nothing. But thanks for offering. I've got things under control." At least it's what she liked to tell herself. "On Saturday the claims examiner showed up and took pictures. He approved the emergency restoration. And Sunday the restoration company sent out an inspector, who made an assessment of the situation. They didn't waste any time. They didn't want to give the mold a chance to set in."

"That's a relief."

Hannah nodded. "This morning they've set up commercial dehumidifiers. The inspector said the big units would dry the place out in a day—two days tops. The faster, the better."

"You'll have everything back on track in no time."

"I don't know about that." All of Hannah's insecurities came rushing to the surface. "Maybe trying to start my own business was a mistake."

Lily studied her beneath her long, dark lashes. "Why did you buy the bakery?"

Was she serious? Everyone knew why she bought the bakery. "You know why."

"Humor me. Why did you buy the bakery?"

After Lily received her coffee, they moved to a table. Hannah didn't have time to sit around, but without some caffeine, she didn't have the energy to keep going. And it'd been so long since she'd slowed down and spent time with her friends. Work was important but so was spending time with those you cared about.

Hannah pursed her lips, not sure she wanted to answer Lily's question. But when her friend arched her brows expectantly, Hannah sighed. "Fine. I bought the bakery for the same reason you bought the Lily Pad."

Lily shook her head. "Totally different reasons."

"How do you get that?"

"Because..." Lily paused as she stared down at her coffee. "When I bought the Lily Pad, my life was at a crossroads. I had to choose between venturing out on my own or stepping up in the family's business. Our reasons"—Lily waved between them—"for going into business are different. But

60

this isn't about me. It's about you. And it's about your lifelong passion for baking. The flood is a minor hiccup in the grand scheme of things."

"Minor?" Her voice rose with emotion. When a couple at the next table glanced over in their direction, Hannah made a point to speak softly. "It's more than minor. After I pay the insurance deductible, I don't have enough cash left to finish the renovations or buy the fixtures."

"But I thought the insurance was fixing everything."

Hannah shook her head. "They'll only make it look like it did before the disaster. So I will still have unfinished walls and ceiling. The new flooring got ruined by the water. And I have no fixtures to give the place some personality."

"Personality? I thought that's what you were for?" Lily sent her a teasing smile.

"Ha-ha. I just wanted to spruce it up. When I bought it, it had all of the basics, but they're beyond worn out. I knew the place needed work and some updates, but I had no idea just how much."

"But you're almost there. Three more weeks and it's opening day."

"I'll have to delay the opening if I can't afford to get the inside finished."

Lily pursed her lips together as though giving the problem some thought. "I don't know anything about renovations, but I'm sure there are videos online that we can watch and learn from. They have videos for everything these days. We'll figure it out."

Hannah shook her head. "Thanks. But this is my problem."

Lily shook her head. "Friends help friends."

"Speaking of friends, you could help me out by coming to Amelia's wedding shower."

Lily's dark brows scrunched together. "I hadn't heard about a shower."

"That's because I just learned that no one was throwing her one. I felt so bad for her. I told her I'd do it. I just mailed a bunch of invitations this morning."

"You're such a good person."

Heat rushed to Hannah's cheeks. "I didn't do anything you or Josie wouldn't have done."

"But you don't have time to plan a party on top of opening the bakery."

"I'll make it work." Hannah wasn't sure how but she'd figure it out. "There isn't much time to plan it, so it can't be anything fancy."

Lily nodded in agreement as she sipped her coffee. "Usually these things are planned well in advance, but we'll do our best."

"We?"

"Yes, I'm volunteering Josie to help plan the party. She just doesn't know it yet."

"But I can't ask you to do it—"

"You didn't ask. I'm offering since you won't let me help with the bakery. Besides, you'd do the same for me. Wait. As I recall you did when I opened the Lily Pad. You and Josie are always there when I need you, so let me help you now."

"Thank you." Her voice wobbled. "I don't know what I'd do without you and Josie."

"And you'll never have to find out. The only thing you have to worry about is finding a date to take to the wedding."

"I'm not going with anyone." Hannah said it firmly.

"You can't go alone."

"Why? You don't have a date...do you?"

Lily shook her head. "But you haven't dated one single person since Brad. Everyone is talking. They all think you regret breaking up with him."

This was news to her. "They do?"

Lily nodded. "They all feel sorry for you. They're talking about setting you up."

"With who?" The thought of being set up with anyone horrified her. What could be worse than being expected to hit it off with someone you're not the least bit attracted to?

"One candidate I heard mentioned was Agnes Dewey's nephew, Ralph."

Hannah resisted rolling her eyes. "Her nephew? Isn't he in his forties or fifties?" Her nose curled up. "He's way too old for me."

"Well, there were some other younger candidates—"

"Never mind. I get the idea." Suddenly finding a friend to go with her to the wedding had moved up on her to-do-list. "I'll find someone to go with."

Lily sent her a pleased smile before glancing past Hannah toward the group of tourists that had just entered the café. "Looks like the early spring weather is bringing out the tourists. Hopefully they'll make it to my shop next. And if I'm lucky they'll bring some friends."

Hannah knew how the island businesses struggled through the winter months. An early spring was a true blessing. "You should go."

Lily shook her head. "I don't want to just leave you here."

"I'm fine." Hannah smiled to prove it. "Besides I have more phone calls to make."

Lily looked hesitant. "Are you sure?"

Hannah nodded. She'd feel better when the restoration work was complete and the renovations resumed—if only she could make the finances work. She needed to open as soon as possible in order to get listed in the island's visitor brochure and most importantly to make her loan payment.

Lily stood. "We've got your back. Just concentrate on the repairs and finishing the renovations so the islanders can all enjoy your cupcakes."

"Those always were your favorites."

"Always will be. Talk to you later." Lily walked away.

Hannah took another sip of coffee, and then she too headed for the door. How did she get so lucky to have such good friends? A smile pulled at her lips as she stepped outside. She had a renewed drive to solve this problem.

CHAPTER SEVEN

Another restless night...

Monday morning, Ethan awoke tired and out of sorts. He wanted to blame it on the lumpy couch, but he could only lie to himself for so long. It was the recurring nightmare of the fire he'd narrowly escaped that had him waking up in the middle of the night in a cold sweat.

Not even the television playing in the background had kept the nightmares at bay. He knew with time they'd pass. It was what the old-timers had told him. The question was: how long would it take?

Not wanting to dwell on the subject, he turned his thoughts to the promise he'd made his aunt. He'd decided he'd put it off as long as he could. Now it was time to find out what was involved in planning Spring Fling. He was certain when he saw his aunt next that she'd have questions for him. He didn't want her thinking he wasn't taking this task seriously. The last thing either of them needed was for her to get upset, thinking he was going to let her down.

He moved to his aunt's wooden desk and started opening the drawers, searching for the purple binder. He honestly didn't think Spring Fling would be that big of a deal. He'd make a few phone calls. Maybe he'd organize a few events. And then he would be done and when his aunt returned home, she could take over.

In the bottom drawer, he found the purple binder. But surely this couldn't be the right one. It had a three- or four-inch spine. It was huge. When he lifted the binder, it was rather hefty.

As he started to wonder what he'd gotten himself into, his blood pressure inched upward. He took the thick binder to the living room couch. Peaches got up off her dog bed in the corner of the room and snuggled next to him, resting her head on his thigh.

65

He drew in a deep breath and blew it out. Then he opened the binder. The first page was dated back more than fifty years. The date had been crossed out and replaced with a new year. That was repeated all the way down the left margin.

He noticed there were more than a dozen colored tabs with labels. The first he noticed was *Bloomin' Tulips*. And if it had just stopped there, he would have been okay. But there was the jelly bean relay, the Easter egg hunt, and the tabs went on.

Was he expected to organize all of this?

"I think I'm in big trouble," he told Peaches.

She lifted her head, let out a big whiny yawn before settling her chin back on her paws and once more closing her eyes. He focused on the pages. The more he read, the more he felt out of his depth.

Five pages into it, he closed the binder and set it aside. "I'll deal with it later."

Buzz. Buzz.

He glanced at his phone. It was his mother. Why was she calling so early? His body tensed.

He pressed the phone to his ear. "Mom, what's wrong?"

"Nothing. I just feel guilty that you're missing work to take care of things for Aunt Birdie."

"I told you I'm happy to help out." His thoughts turned to Spring Fling—maybe he wasn't happy to help out that much.

"But?"

His mother knew him so well. "There is no but."

"Are you sure because we could catch the next flight home—"

"No." This was exactly why he hadn't mentioned his reservations about planning a festival. "Don't you dare come home early."

She sighed. "If you change your mind—"

"I won't."

"You're so stubborn, just like your father."

"Isn't that something like the pot calling the kettle black?"

His mother laughed. "I'm pleading the fifth."

They went on to discuss Aunt Birdie's improving condition and his parents' plans for the rest of the day. By the time he got off the phone, he was hungry.

With Peaches fed and walked, he decided to head to The Lighthouse Café. It might not be the fanciest place on Bluestar Island, but it by far had the best food—certainly better than anything he could cook. He shrugged on his jacket and then headed for the door. His mouth salivated at the thought of over-easy eggs, hash browns, and sausage links.

His long legs made rapid strides along the walk. He noticed how different Bluestar Island was from the city where people pretty much kept to themselves. But here the islanders said hello and smiled or asked him how he was or inquired about his aunt's health. It slowed his pace but he didn't mind. He enjoyed getting to know Bluestar's residents.

The café wasn't much farther. He made a left on Main Street. The delicious aromas wafted through the air and down the street. He found himself smiling as he stepped inside the restaurant. Happy memories flooded his mind. He recalled how his uncle used to bring him there for breakfast before they would catch the ferry for the mainland.

Uncle Gil had been an appliance repairman and it wasn't beyond him to make early morning trips to the mainland to pick up parts. On those days, his uncle had let Aunt Birdie sleep in while they grabbed breakfast there. Those good-old days seemed so far away now.

When Ethan's gaze settled on the community bulletin board, curiosity had him stepping forward for a closer look. His gaze lingered over the for-sale ads for cars, trucks, and motorcycles. He kept scanning, finding invitations to the quilting group, a card club, and some other organizations. He didn't stop to read those. He was surprised at the number of accommodations for rent. He knew in another month they'd all be taken as the tourists flocked to the island.

And then he stumbled across a flyer for Spring Fling. He stepped up closer. He noticed the dates and nearly choked. His aunt failed to mention it took place in a few weeks' time. He thought he'd just be helping out until Aunt Birdie could take over. But this made it seem as though he'd be doing a lot more than lending a hand. He swallowed hard.

As he considered how this information changed things, he entered the dining room. The walls were painted a beachy blue with ocean murals. The spacious room was filled with small wooden tables made of whitewash wood. And there was a long counter at the back that faced the kitchen. He headed for one of the blue stools.

The café was modestly busy, but it was also the end of March and the middle of the morning. He was certain as it grew closer to lunch, the crowd would pick up. He sat down at the white Formica counter, where he used to sit as a boy and order a chocolate milkshake. He hadn't had one of those in years. His gaze moved down the counter area until he spotted a milkshake machine. A smile pulled at his lips. He wondered if they served them this early in the day.

He didn't need to view the menu. He knew what he wanted. A server, dressed in black pants and a white top, with a bouncy blond ponytail and a nametag that read *Darla*, took his order.

He barely had time to read the headline news on his phone when there was a ding of a bell as the cook shouted, "Order's up." And then his eggs and fixings were served up piping hot as was a large mug of coffee, not one of those puny coffee cups that were more like thimbles.

The delicious food made him feel more human. And the hot coffee pumped some energy into his sluggish body. Things were starting to look up—if only they'd stay that way.

With his stomach appeased, he ordered a chocolate shake to go. Ethan headed out the door with a quick errand to run. He wanted to check in on Hannah. After all, he had promised Aunt Birdie to pass along her regards. And the bakery was just a couple of blocks away.

The more he thought of Hannah with those big green eyes that drew him in, the faster his feet moved. And soon he found himself standing in front of the bakery.

For some reason, he thought it'd be abuzz with activity. However, only one pickup was parked in front. There was a yellow day-pass displayed in the windshield. A man stood next to the bed of the truck and closed a cargo box. He turned with an orange extension cord in his hand.

Ethan approached the man. "Excuse me, do you know where Hannah is?"

The man paused and gave him a puzzled look before he shook his head. "I don't know any Hannah."

Ethan decided to try again. "How about the woman who owns the bakery?"

"Oh her." A big smile lit up his face. Apparently he wasn't the only one Hannah had made an impression upon. "Sorry. I didn't catch her first name. She was here first thing this morning to let me in. I haven't seen her since."

"Thanks." Ethan's anticipation waned.

He told himself he was disappointed not to be able to deliver his aunt's message. It had absolutely nothing to do with not seeing Hannah. After all, he hardly knew her, and he certainly wasn't interested in her romantically. Not that she wasn't pretty enough—in fact he found her quite beautiful. However, he wasn't about to start another relationship. Once bitten, twice shy and all of that stuff.

He continued walking with no particular destination in mind. He wasn't ready to dive into the festival planning. The longer he could put it off, the better. It wasn't like he was going to avoid it forever.

When Ethan stopped walking and glanced around, he found himself standing in front of the Bluestar firehouse. He didn't know what had drawn him there. And yet he approached the front door.

After all, Chief Campbell had invited him to stop by any time. Ethan was certain he would just stand quietly off to the side, observing all of the activity. Still, it was either that or go back to his aunt's bungalow and figure out where to start with Spring Fling plans.

He pulled open the door. He peered inside and found it empty. Then he heard voices coming from behind the building. Ethan followed the sounds and found a group of five or so people. With this being a volunteer station, he assumed the rest of the crew were at their day jobs.

The chief was at the front of the group. When their eyes met, the chief gave him a quick nod before continuing to speak to the firefighters.

Ethan didn't want to interrupt. Maybe stopping by wasn't such a good idea. After all, what was he expecting to come of this visit? He already had a good job waiting for him back in the city.

He'd just turned to walk away when he heard his name called out in a deep gruff voice. Ethan paused and turned to see the chief headed toward him.

The man was shorter and a bit round in the mid-section. His face was also roundish with flushed cheeks. His bald head was ringed with a bit of short silver hair.

"I was hoping you'd stop by." Chief Campbell smiled as he extended his hand to him. The chief's meaty hand engulfed his own in a firm handshake. "It's Ethan, right?"

"Yes, sir. I didn't mean to interrupt anything."

"You didn't. I have to get something inside. Walk with me." As they moved to the front of the station, the chief said, "You know, we're always looking for new members."

"Thanks. But I already have a job in Brooklyn."

The man's bushy brows rose. "And yet you're still here."

It wasn't a question but somehow it felt like one. Ethan wondered if the man forgot their prior conversation outside the bakery. Ethan cleared his throat. "I'm only in town long enough to help my aunt."

Chief Campbell nodded. "As long as you're in town, you're welcome to run drills with us."

"I'd like that." The words slipped past his lips before he even gave it some thought. But maybe this was his way to ease back into work. "Thank you, sir."

Because at most he only intended to spend a couple of more weeks on the island. And then he'd be back in Brooklyn. He was certain once he got back to his normal work routine, the nightmares would pass.

CHAPTER EIGHT

Picking up the pieces.

That was what Hannah felt like she was doing ever since the water pipe broke almost a week ago. Luckily the emergency restoration company had everything well underway. By Tuesday afternoon everything was dry, the pipes were replaced, and the electrical wiring had been repaired as well as inspected. And only now could the kitchen ceiling be replaced. The work was moving along as quickly as possible. But would it be fast enough to open on time?

The one negative was the insurance company would not budge on what work would be done to the building. They would pay to restore the building back to the condition it was in before the pipe broke. No matter how many phone calls she made or how much she pleaded, they refused to pay to finish the walls or floor.

And then there was the matter of the large deductible she'd opted for in order to reduce her annual premium, back when she thought she'd never need to use the insurance. Now paying the deductible would use up the funds she'd set aside to finish the work on the place. What was she supposed to do now?

Hannah mulled over her options. None of them were good. You couldn't open a business in a partially renovated bakery. The inspectors wouldn't stand for it. And she wouldn't want to do it. When she opened her own bakery, she wanted it to be spectacular. She wanted it to reflect the images she'd sketched in her notebook.

In order to save more money, she'd moved out of her apartment as soon as the utilities had been restored at the bakery and moved into one of the two apartments on the upper floor of the bakery. She'd taken the front apartment, facing the street.

Hannah made her way around the small apartment kitchen as she finished piping white buttercream frosting to the last double-chocolate cupcake. She added some pastel, flower-shaped sprinkles before placing the cupcakes in a large white box. These cupcakes were a special thank you. And now it was time to deliver them.

She rushed to the bathroom. When she gazed in the mirror, she groaned. There was flour on her face and in her hair. She was a mess.

As she worked to clean herself, her thoughts turned to Ethan. She hadn't seen him all week, not that she'd been expecting him to stop by the bakery. Still, she couldn't help but wonder if he was still in town. She hoped so...to properly thank him, of course.

She dried her freshly washed face and applied a light coating of makeup. With one more quick glance in the mirror and a fingertip of water to smooth an unruly strand of hair, she headed for the door with a box of cupcakes in hand.

One of the many things she loved about Bluestar was that everything was within walking or biking distance. The island was crescent-moon-shaped. A lighthouse marked each end of the six-mile-long stretch of land.

Before she knew it, she'd reached the fire station. It wasn't anything fancy—not like those massive-looking fire stations they showed on television. This was a small, one-story building made of red brick with two white bay doors and a gray shingled roof. And a whistle tower mounted to the roof. When it blew, there wasn't a soul in town that could sleep through the shrieking sound. Luckily, it rarely blew in the off-season. But when the tourists swarmed the island, anything was possible.

She'd visited this fire station countless times as a child. But not at all since her father died. She just couldn't bring herself to go there...until now. After almost two years since his passing, it was well past time.

It wasn't like she didn't know every single person who volunteered there. They were neighbors, old classmates, and the kindest people you'd ever want to meet.

As she stood on the sidewalk, staring up at the building that had been around all of her life, she was hit with memories—memories of her father. She'd been daddy's girl. And that meant she'd wanted to do what her father did. As a child, this fire station was like a second-home, as her father had been the fire chief.

She'd help clean and polish the bright red engine. She'd sat behind the wheel when she was so small her feet couldn't touch the pedals, just so she could see what it would feel like to control such an enormous truck. Back then she'd been certain that one day she would be a firefighter and drive a fire truck.

"Hey, you coming inside with that great big pastry box?"

She glanced over to find Greg Hoover. She craned her neck to take in his golden-brown face and short-cut dark curls. He immediately sent her a big friendly smile. He'd been a year ahead of her in school. Back in those days, he'd been tall and skinny—the star of the basketball team and popular with the girls. These days he was still the tallest man she knew at six feet seven inches but he'd filled out with muscles.

"Good morning, Greg." She flashed him a smile.

"You didn't say, are those treats in the box for us?" He waggled his dark brows at her.

She laughed. "Are you trying to tell me with that trim figure of yours that you have a sweet tooth?"

"Only when it comes to your baking."

"Aw...well thank you."

He held open the side door for her that led into the small reception area. "I'm not the only one that has a weakness for your baked goods. All of the guys were so upset when they learned your bakery had been flooded. We were all planning to send a lot of business your way."

74

Knowing it wasn't just her anticipating the grand opening meant a lot to her. "I still hope to open for business soon."

Greg looked at her. "You don't stop by much anymore."

She shook her head. "Just too busy these days."

That wasn't the whole truth, and she was pretty certain they both knew it. Coming here reminded her of the hole her father's untimely death had put in her heart—the deficit it'd put in her family.

Since they'd lost her father, things for her family had changed a lot. Her younger sister left the island—seeking fame and fortune in Nashville. Her brother rarely left the farm. And her mother had gone back to work at the visitor center. They weren't as tight as they'd once been.

As though the men and women could smell the baked goods, the firefighters migrated from the bay area into the reception area, which filled up quickly.

Hannah placed the box on the counter and knew she had to say a few words. "I came here—"

"Wait," Greg said, "I should get the chief."

He made his way to the office and tapped on the closed door. He immediately opened it. She was too far away to hear what was being said, but soon the chief followed him into the reception area.

Hannah made her way to Chief Campbell. He smiled brightly when he saw her. "Hannah, it's so good to see you." Instead of shaking her hand, he reached out and hugged her—just like he'd been doing for years.

When she pulled back, she returned his smile. "I brought a little thank you for what everyone did to save the bakery."

The chief's gaze moved to the counter where his crew were busy scooping up the cupcakes and devouring them. "You didn't have to do that—"

"Yes, she did," called out one of the men. "Just wait until you taste them."

Everyone laughed.

"I hope I get to taste them," the chief said. "They're going fast."

"Don't worry," Hannah said. "I can make more. It's the least I can do."

Chief Campbell looked at her. "We didn't do much."

"Sure you did." And she would be eternally grateful. "The restoration people said it could have been much worse if not for you pumping out the water and running the fans. So thank you."

He shook his head. "The real praise belongs to the young man who acted quick and shut off the water main."

Her thought turned to the handsome stranger who'd come to her rescue. She'd thank Ethan, if she could find him. She'd stopped by his aunt's a couple of times but he was never home.

"Your father would be so proud of you," the chief said, interrupting her thoughts.

"Thank you, sir. I'd like to think so."

"When are you planning to have the bakery up and running?"

"I had planned to open before Easter, but now with the flood damage, I'm not sure."

The man's bushy gray brows drew together. "You're still going to open, aren't you?"

"That's the plan." She failed to mention a few key components such as, she could no longer afford her contractor, so he'd moved on to his next job.

"How's your mother doing?"

Hadn't he just talked to her at the flood? "She's doing good. Always busy doing this or that."

He nodded in understanding. "Tell her I said hi."

"I will." Why couldn't he do that? Bluestar was a small town. It was harder to avoid people than it was to run into them. But she would pass along the message all the same.

Chief Campbell cleared his throat. "Well, if you need help with anything, let me know."

A chorus of "Me toos" went up in the room. Their generosity filled her heart with warmth, but she highly doubted any of them knew how to renovate a bakery. Besides, it was up to her to fix things.

Hannah thanked them all once more and then excused herself. She had a lot to do that day, including a meeting at the bank to see about an extension on her first loan payment or perhaps a supplemental loan. As she departed, she passed by the table where the cupcakes had been placed. She was pleased to see only a couple of cupcakes remained in the box.

When she opened the door, the mayor was coming up the walk. Mayor Banks smiled when he saw her. "Good morning, Hannah. How are things going with the bakery?"

"Morning." She wasn't so sure it was a good day. "Things are moving along."

He glanced down at the pavement as he shifted his weight from one foot to the other. "The thing is we need to finalize the tourist brochure soon for the printers." He lifted his gaze to meet hers. "Do you know yet if we should include the bakery?"

Yes teetered on the tip of her tongue. Without a listing in Bluestar's tourist pamphlet, the bakery would lose a ton of advertising that would turn into revenue. But she bit back her answer.

Instead she asked, "How soon do you have to know?"

Sympathy reflected in Mayor Banks's eyes. "That bad, huh?"

She shrugged and then nodded. "But I will figure it out. I just need a little more time."

"I can hold out for a few more weeks but no longer. We need the pamphlets by the first of May."

"I understand. I'll let you know as soon as I have something certain."

He nodded. "Sounds good. And if I can put you in touch with anyone to help, let me know."

"I will. Thank you."

She continued along the sidewalk when she glanced up and saw a familiar face. It was the man who'd helped her during the flood. Her heart skipped a beat. *What was that about?*

Sure, Ethan was kind of cute—okay, very cute. But she didn't have time for anything remotely romantic. Her time was all spoken for.

He stopped in front of her and sent her a warm smile. "Good morning."

"Good morning." There was that funny sensation in her chest again.

When she gazed into his warm brown eyes, her heart definitely stuttered. There was something about him, as though he could see straight through her and see her deepest fears and her wildest dreams. She glanced away.

What was up with her? None of that was possible. Her gaze strayed back to him. She took in his handsome face with its strong jawline, his straight nose, and once more her gaze settled on his eyes, which reminded her of chocolatey goodness.

If she wasn't so focused on salvaging the bakery, she might be tempted to ask him to join her for a lobster roll and milk shake at The Lighthouse. Nothing too serious, just a chance to get to know each other better. The idea was so tempting. And yet she hesitated.

Words tangled and caught in the back of his throat.

Ethan hadn't been expecting to see Hannah here. Sure he'd wanted to see her—wanted to check on how she was making out. And yet with her standing in front of him, he was at a loss for words.

Every time he saw her, she grew more beautiful—from green eyes that sparkled with gold flecks to her full, pouty lips. If he were in the mood to date, he'd definitely ask her out. But after being dumped by his long-time girlfriend and his subsequent on-the-job injury that left him questioning himself and his career choice, he was certain he was better off on his own.

But they couldn't just stand there on the sidewalk quietly staring at each other. He cleared his throat. "Hi."

She smiled. "Hi. How's your aunt doing?"

"She's as feisty as ever and anxious to come home. She wanted me to tell you how bad she feels about the flood."

"That is so sweet of her to worry about me when she has so much going on in her own life."

"She's worried about the Spring Fling."

Hannah nodded. "The festival is popular with young and old alike."

He arched a brow as the wheels in his mind started to turn. "You seem to know a lot about it."

She nodded. "I should. I've been attending all of my life. It's a Bluestar tradition. If you're still in town, you should check it out."

He shifted his weight from one foot to the other. "I'll be doing more than that."

Hannah's fine brows drew together. "I don't understand."

"My aunt is all worked up and insisting on coming home against the doctor's advice because she's in charge of organizing Spring Fling." He hadn't meant to tell Hannah all of this and yet the words kept rolling out of his mouth. "She can't come home yet. She isn't ready." He shifted his weight once more. "So I made her a deal. If she stays at physical rehab, I'd take over organizing Spring Fling."

"That's so sweet of you." Hannah beamed at him with an approving smile. And then the smiled slipped from her face. "You don't look happy. Didn't Birdie agree to the deal?"

"It's not that. She agreed."

"But there's another problem?"

He shook his head. "Don't worry about it. You don't want to hear about my problems—"

"I'm happy to listen. It'd be nice to focus on something besides my own troubles."

His gaze met hers. "I had a look at the tentative plans for the festival, and it's a lot more involved than I ever imagined."

Hannah gave a nod of understanding. "Sounds like you have some learning to do."

He raked his fingers through his hair. "Tell me about it."

"I can try and answer your questions."

He liked the idea of turning to her—for answers about the festival, of course. "You might be sorry you made the offer."

"May I have your phone."

He readily handed it over. Her finger moved rapidly over the screen. In no time, she was returning it to him.

"Now you have my number. Feel free to call me any time."

If this were another place and another time, he might have taken her invitation in a more personal way. "Thanks. I'll keep it in mind."

"I should be going. I have some errands before I decorate a birthday cake."

"It's your birthday?" If it was, he'd insist they go out to celebrate.

She shook her head. "No. It's for a client."

"Oh, I see." He couldn't deny that he was a bit disappointed. He didn't want her to go. Not yet. But in order to get her to stay, he had to think of something to say. "How are things going with the bakery?"

Her eyes widened as though she'd just remembered something important. "I've been meaning to thank you. I really appreciate all you did to keep me safe and saving the building from further damage."

He glanced down at the sidewalk as he rubbed his neck. He'd never been comfortable with praise. He was just doing his job. And then he realized he hadn't been on the job. Still, it was instinct for him to dive in and help.

He cleared his throat. "You're welcome. I hope the damage isn't too extensive."

"The front room isn't bad. The kitchen on the other hand, needs a lot of work."

"But your insurance should cover everything."

"To a certain extent." When he didn't say anything, she continued, "The policy says they have to put the bakery back to the condition it was in before the flood."

"Well, that's not so bad, right?"

"Except for the fact that the large deductible I have on the policy will eat up most of the cash I have allocated to complete the bakery renovation." Her face crumpled into a frown as worry reflected in her eyes.

"Oh. I see."

"The only good news was that the furnished apartments upstairs weren't damaged. Since I've already given my notice on my other place, I could have ended up homeless. Not really. I have my family, but you know what I mean."

He nodded. "How much work do you have left to do on the bakery?"

"Too much."

"For example?" Part of him was asking because he was curious, and the other part of his brain was concocting an outlandish plan.

Her eyes narrowed as though she was confused by his need to know the details. And as the silence stretched on, he didn't think she was going to confide in him. But then she started naming off the items from sanding and painting the walls to putting in the floor to adding the trim work and the final touches.

He had an idea that just might work for the both of them. "Would you be up for making a deal?"

"What sort of deal?"

"I can finish the bakery for you."

She immediately shook her head. "I don't think so."

"Why not?"

"Because...because I don't even know you."

"But you know my aunt. She will vouch for me."

Her fine brows drew together. "Do you even know anything about construction?"

"My grandfather put a hammer in my hand as soon as I was old enough to hold it."

"This is more than hammering nails. It has to be done properly. I...I have a lot riding on it."

"I've spent years donating my free time to building affordable housing." He liked to work with his hands and he liked being able to help others.

"But I don't have any money to pay you."

"You can pay me by helping me organize Spring Fling. It's outside my wheelhouse. You know all of the islanders and how the festival is supposed to work."

Her lips pursed together as though she was thinking up another reason this situation wouldn't work. He wasn't sure why she was resisting his help, but he had to cut her off before she talked herself out of accepting his offer.

"Listen, you need the help. And I could use yours. I don't want to let my aunt down and by extension the whole island."

Her gaze met his. "I'll need some references for your work. I can't just have anyone work on the bakery."

He saw her point. If it was his place, he'd be cautious of whom he let work on it. "Fair enough." He pulled his phone from his pocket. He selected three volunteers, who had their own contracting businesses. They'd all vouch for his capabilities. He forwarded her their contact information. "Feel free to talk to all of them. They'll tell you what I'm capable of."

"I'll get back to you shortly." She turned to walk away and then turned back to him. "Hey, are you even going to be on the island long enough to finish the job?"

"If needed, I can be here until Easter."

"That long, huh?" She smiled as though she'd just come up with a plan that he wasn't sure he'd like. "By the way, I was wondering if you'd be interested in attending a town function with me."

Was she asking him out? His interest was piqued. "Town function?"

"You know, a bunch of people get together. There'll be food and dancing. That kind of stuff."

His gaze narrowed on her. She was working too hard at being vague about this event. Disappointment assailed him. "It's a wedding, isn't it?"

She sighed and her shoulders drooped. "Yes."

He shook his head. "Sorry. I'm not into dating right now. And I don't do weddings."

"No. Not a date. I swear. I just can't show up alone."

"Why not?"

"Because..." When he continued to stare at her expectantly, she continued. "Fine. If you must know the town is working on setting me up, and I just can't go through that. I thought it might be nice to go with a friend."

"But we're not friends, are we?"

"I don't know. You saved me from getting electrocuted. That sounds like what a friend would do." She sent him a too-bright smile. She was desperate.

"Let me think about it," he heard himself saying. That definitely wasn't the turn down he'd been intending to say. But it wasn't a *yes* either. Hopefully with a little time she'd find someone more suitable to be her date—*erm, escort.*

"Great." She sent him a pleased smile. "I'll get back to you on the other thing."

And with that they went in opposite directions. He wanted to know why a beautiful woman like Hannah couldn't get a date of her own and instead the town felt obliged to set her up. Under those circumstances, how could he turn her down? There was nothing worse than being set up on a blind date.

He turned onto the sidewalk leading to the firehouse. Once inside, he noticed a couple of guys standing around eating chocolate cupcakes. Ethan had no doubt they were baked by Hannah. He'd love to sample her sweet creations, but as he strolled closer to the baker box, he noticed it was empty.

"Can I help you?" a young woman with a long dark ponytail, not more than twenty, asked him.

"I was looking for the chief."

The woman pointed over her shoulder at a closed door. "He's in his office. Go on back."

"Thanks." Ethan made his way to the door and knocked.

"Come in." When Ethan opened the door, the chief looked up from a stack of papers on his desk. Chief Campbell got to his feet and moved out from behind the desk. "It's good to see you again." He held out his hand and gave Ethan another firm shake. "I wasn't sure if you'd stop by again."

Ethan glanced down at the paperwork on the man's desk. "I hope I'm not bothering you."

"Not at all."

Ethan wasn't sure exactly why he'd taken the chief up on his offer to visit. It wasn't like he didn't have his own station house back in New York. That's where he should be working. But that would come soon enough.

And now that he'd struck up a deal with the beautiful baker, he was starting to feel more comfortable on Bluestar Island. Who knew that would happen? But there was something about this town—about Hannah—that drew him in.

CHAPTER NINE

"A great guy."
 "Very reliable."
 "Hard worker."

The praises for Ethan were plentiful and appeared to be earnest.

The next afternoon, Hannah thanked the last man on Ethan's list of references and disconnected the call. She'd spent the past half hour or so calling everyone on the list Ethan had given her. They were all friendly and chatty. According to Ethan's sources, she couldn't do any better than him. *"The best of the best."*

At this moment, she needed all of the help she could get to finish the bakery on time or as close as possible. Yesterday's meeting at the bank hadn't gone well.

Penny-A-Day Savings & Loan was a small-town bank that was privately owned by William Penny. His family was one of the island's original residents. She'd been informed that the bank felt awful about the incident, but there was no way they could extend or otherwise modify her loan payment. Hannah had pleaded but it had still been the same answer. Desperation seeped into her bones. She couldn't lose her dream.

Feeling cooped up in her apartment, Hannah made her way downstairs to the bakery. It was abuzz with activity. And at last, she'd received some good news. The work on the front room was complete.

She rushed to the front of the bakery and came to an abrupt halt. Her definition of complete and theirs was quite different. The walls consisted of freshly hung drywall with crevices between each board. And the floor was nothing more than sheets of plywood screwed down. But the head of the restoration crew had given her the go-ahead to resume her renovations in the bakery showroom.

She glanced down at her notebook that held her drawings of how she'd envisioned the bakery when it was completed. Sadness enveloped her. She didn't think any of those visions would come to life, but she'd be grateful if this place ever got to the point where it could open for business.

She wanted to drop everything and fix it herself, but she didn't have a clue where to begin. A five-foot, six-tier *Alice In Wonderland* inspired cake with a tipping tea pot as well as tilting tea cups and saucers would be so much easier to create. Not that she'd ever attempted such an ambitious cake—at least not yet.

With a frustrated sigh, she stepped out into the sunshine. It was time to meet up with Lily and Josie at The Lighthouse Café to go over the wedding shower plans. She knew her friends were more than capable of planning the event, but she felt bad they were doing what she'd volunteered to do.

A couple of minutes later, she entered the café. It wasn't terribly busy. She waved to Fred and Martha Williams, newly retired and proud grandparents of Tommy and Susie. She knew most of the island's permanent residents and those she didn't know were friends of friends.

She joined Lily and Josie at a nearby table. "Hi." As Hannah sat down, she noticed Lily in a fitted purple jacket with a pink top beneath it. She had a notebook open and a pen in hand. "What did I miss?"

Lily spoke up first. "We picked a beach theme since they're having a nautical theme for the wedding. We thought it'd be fun."

"It's going to be a blast." All attention turned to Josie, who was dressed for work at the inn with a navy skirt suit and a white blouse with a gold name tag. "I've picked out some games and ordered decorations."

"And I've coordinated the dinner menu with the pub," Lily said.

They showed Hannah all of their plans. She couldn't believe how much they'd accomplished in such a short amount of time.

Hannah smiled. "Thank you. I don't know how I'll ever repay you."

"I do," Lily said. "Tell us how things are going with the bakery."

"Yes, tell us about that and what's up with you and Birdie's nephew." Josie waggled her brows.

"I don't know what you're talking about." Heat rushed to her face. "Nothing's going on."

There was a simultaneous, "Uh-huh," followed by twin looks of disbelief.

Hannah ignored their implications about Ethan and instead gave them a brief overview of how things were going with the bakery. But just as quickly, the conversation returned to Ethan. They peppered her with questions.

With a resigned sigh, Hannah told them about the deal Ethan proposed. "And now his references have given him glowing recommendations. So I'm not sure what to do."

"What's to be unsure about?" Lily said. "I've seen him around town, and oh boy, is he cute. And if he's willing to help you out, I'd jump on the offer."

"Leave it to you to consider his hotness quotient first." Hannah dramatically rolled her eyes and shook her head.

"Hey, you can't deny that he's some good eye candy," Josie chimed in.

"And if he's skilled with construction"—Lily steered the conversation back to the main subject—"I'd give him a chance. What could it hurt?"

"I can't take a handout," Hannah said. "I need to do this on my own."

"It's not a handout. You know a lot about the festival. Your mother used to plan it back before..." Lily's voice trailed off.

"You can say it, before my father died." It'd taken her a while to get to the point where she could speak of it without her emotions rising to the surface. "Everything changed after he died. But I know what you mean."

"You should take him up on the offer." Josie's voice drew Hannah's attention back to the conversation. "It gets you both what you want."

She knew her friends were right. She should readily accept Ethan's offer but still she hesitated. Why was she holding back?

"You're trying too hard to go solo," Lily said. "I know Brad tried to steer you wrong and almost ruined your deal to buy the bakery, but Ethan isn't Brad."

Hannah's ex had gone behind her back to talk to the former owner of the bakery, telling Mr. Hamil that she didn't know what she wanted. Just the memory of hearing it from Mr. Hamil filled her with anger. Brad had gone on to tell Mr. Hamil that when they were newly married, they'd be trying for a baby right away, and she wouldn't have the time to devote to the bakery. She'd immediately confronted Brad and asked him where all of those plans had come from because they hadn't come from her. Her plans had been focused on opening the bakery and then figuring everything else out.

She'd been angry that Brad would go behind her back. And Brad had been hurt that her first priority wasn't their wedding and family. It was in that moment she realized he was right. If she could put her business ahead of their wedding plans, they just weren't meant to be. She'd given him the ring back that night.

He'd been furious. He told her she would regret breaking things off. To this day, her only regret was not doing it sooner.

Josie's voice drew her from her thoughts. "Sometimes you need to rely on your friends—even new ones."

Hannah felt so lucky to have them as friends. But what would they think of her if she failed? What would her family think?

"There's something else bothering you," Josie said. "What is it?"

"What happens if I fail?"

"But what if you succeed?" Josie asked. "Take Ethan up on his offer. He knows what he's doing and you don't have to pay him. With you helping to coordinate Spring Fling in exchange for him working on the bakery, it's not a favor. It's bartering. In the end, you won't owe him anything."

Hannah's gaze met her friends. "You honestly think this is a good idea?"

"We do." Lily smiled and nodded enthusiastically.

"Do it," Josie said. "This is exactly what you need."

Hannah narrowed her gaze on Josie. "Why are you pushing so hard?"

"Because I'm hoping you'll bake donuts for the inn. Guests will love them."

"Are you serious?" This was the first Hannah had heard of this business opportunity.

Josie smiled and nodded. "I was planning to wait until the grand opening to bring it up, but it seemed like you needed the encouragement now. I talked Mrs. Barton into the idea. She said we'd start with an order of donuts and if they go over well, we might add to the daily order."

Hannah's mouth gaped. She'd had no idea Josie had been planning this. "That would be wonderful! We could figure out what flavors—maybe we could rotate them—" Hannah halted her excited rambling as she realized she still didn't have a functioning bakery.

"What's wrong?" Lily asked.

"I just realized I can't do it, what with the bakery the way it is."

"Then hire Ethan," Josie said.

"Speaking of which"—Lily gestured to the door—"he just walked in."

"He did?" Hannah's gaze moved to the entrance. There he stood. All six plus feet of him. Her heart picked up its pace as heat rushed back to her cheeks.

And then his gaze met hers. She knew she should turn away, but her body betrayed her and refused to move. It was as if there were a magnetic pull between them.

She wondered if he was there to see her. In the next heartbeat, she realized that was a silly supposition. This was a restaurant, and it was more than likely he came in for a late breakfast or early lunch. But was it possible he'd seen her through the window? Yes, that was possible. She halted her rambling thoughts. And then she realized she'd been staring at him for far longer than she should.

Lily cleared her throat. "I should be going."

"Me too," Josie said.

Her friends' voices broke the spell. Hannah looked at her friends as they got to their feet. "What about the wedding shower? What can I do to help?"

"You did the invitations," Lily said.

"And we've got the rest." Josie sent her a smile before following Lily toward the door.

Hannah watched as her friends passed by Ethan with a quick hi. His attention quickly returned to her. He was headed in her direction. Her heart beat faster. She should move. She should do something—anything but sit there—waiting for him.

♥♥♥

She smiled.

And then he smiled.

Ethan felt a warmth grow within his chest as he basked in Hannah's sunny glow. It wasn't like he'd stepped in the café just to see her. His life was complicated enough without

90

letting himself start something that had absolutely no chance of a future, especially with him in New York and her there on the island.

He paused next to her table. "Hi. Can I join you?"

"Uh, sure."

He sat down across from her and tried to think of some casual conversation, but his mind drew a blank. What was up with that? He never had problems speaking with women—not until now.

"Hi." Darla's voice drew him from his thoughts. The server approached the table. "What can I get you?"

"Um..." He suddenly didn't feel hungry. "How about some coffee? Black."

"Sure. Coming up." Darla turned to Hannah. "Ready for a refill?" Hannah shook her head and thanked her. Darla moved behind the counter where the coffee pots rested on a warmer.

"I hope I didn't interrupt anything," he said.

"What?" She momentarily looked confused. "Oh, you mean with Josie and Lily?" When he nodded, she continued. "They had to get back to work."

"I don't mean to keep you."

"I have a couple of minutes."

Darla returned with a steaming pot. "It's a beautiful day. I can't wait until my shift is over to get outside and soak up some sun." They both agreed about the weather as she turned over the cup on the saucer in front of him before filling it with coffee. "Can I get you anything else?"

He shook his head. "Not yet."

He knew by sitting there amongst all of the delicious aromas, he would undoubtedly change his mind. And it would give him an excuse to sit there longer and enjoy Hannah's company. He contemplated asking her if she'd had a chance to check on his references, but he knew she had because one of his friends had already texted him, letting him know some woman with a pretty voice was checking up on him. Now it was up to Hannah to broach the subject.

Instead he said the next thing that came to mind. "It's warming up."

Her perfectly plucked brows drew together. "Excuse me?"

"The weather." He nodded toward the sunshine streaming in through the window. "It's going to be a warm spring."

"Uh...yes, it is." She sipped at her coffee.

So much for her broaching the subject of them helping each other out. Maybe she'd decided against it. Maybe she found someone else to do the job. The thought deflated his mood.

His gaze strayed to her beautiful face as she returned her cup to the saucer. He noticed her smile as she waved to an older man that had just entered the café. Even though Ethan barely knew her, it was obvious there was something special about her just by watching her interact with others.

And then, realizing that he was staring, he glanced down at his coffee. *Ding.* He withdrew his phone from his pocket to find a message from his captain. It appeared Cap was getting anxious for a firm date of Ethan's return. His visit to Bluestar was taking longer—much longer—than he'd ever imagined.

Ethan: *I'm not sure. My aunt needs help until she can return home.*

Cap: *Your vacation runs out at Easter. Be here the following Monday ready for work.*

Ethan: *I'll see you then. Thank you, sir.*

There was no response. Ethan knew he was pushing things, but he was certain this time away was just what he needed because even though the nightmares still plagued him, they weren't as prevalent. That had to be a good sign, right?

"Is something wrong?" Hannah's voice drew him from his thoughts.

"No." He slipped the phone back into his pocket. "It was just my captain confirming my return-to-work date."

Her eyes filled with worry. "Do you have to leave already?"

He shook his head. "I still have time."

She smiled. "That's good. I mean so you have longer to enjoy Bluestar. Between you and me, spring is the best time on the island."

"Why is that?"

She fidgeted with a spoon. "For one, I like to refer to it as the calm before the frenzy." The smile reached her eyes and made them twinkle. "It's the time before the vacationers descend upon the island and life moves at warp speed."

"And what are the other reasons?" He didn't know why he'd asked. That wasn't true. He was itching to know more about this woman.

"You mean besides the fact that it's no longer freezing cold outside, that the days are longer, and the tulips fill the town with a rainbow of colors?"

The vision she painted made him smile. "Yes, other than that."

"It means if I figure out how to fix the bakery, I'll be in business for myself, doing what I love every day." Her face had become animated as she spoke of the bakery. Just as quickly the magic faded and a sadness reflected in her eyes.

He knew she was worried, and he wanted to make her smile once more. "Don't worry. It's all going to work out."

"I wish I was as certain as you." She finished off her coffee. "By the way, I called the numbers you gave me."

"Really?" He subdued his rising excitement. "What did they have to say?"

"That you're amazingly talented and I'd be a fool not to hire you."

Something told him she'd embellished those comments just a bit. "And what do you think?"

Hannah hesitated as though weighing her options. Maybe she already had friends who'd stepped up to help her out. Everyone in Bluestar seemed to like her and he could see why. Maybe he was out of luck. Maybe—

"It's a deal."

Her words caught him off guard. She'd been so hesitant that he was certain she was going to turn him down. "Are you sure?"

"Yes. But it sounds like you've changed your mind."

"No." He shook his head. "Not at all." He was looking forward to getting started. "When will they be finished with the restoration work?"

"They're finished with the front room. I talked to them and you can start working on that room while they finish up in the kitchen."

"Then I'll plan on getting to work tomorrow. Have you decided on all of the details?" When she didn't answer, he added, "You know, the paint colors? The flooring?"

"I have most of it figured out."

He nodded in understanding. "Are you available tomorrow morning?" Then realizing how that might sound, he said, "To go over the plans for the bakery."

"And the plans for Spring Fling?" When he nodded, she said, "We could meet at the bakery."

"Sounds good. I'll bring my aunt's binder."

"And I'll bring my notebook. How about we meet up at seven? Or is that too early?"

"It's perfect. I'll see you there."

"See you then." She slipped some money under the edge of the saucer and then made her way toward the exit.

He just had to make sure he was able to complete all the work before he headed back to New York. He wouldn't leave Hannah in an awkward position. She'd been through enough.

With his aunt and Peaches to look after, he was going to be one busy man. Just the way he liked it. No extra time to contemplate the fiery images of the past. He could concentrate on the here and now.

♥♥♥

She was healing quickly.

Birdie smiled as she took a seat in the chair next to the bed. It was a recliner so the leg rest had been raised as not to put undue stress on her pelvis. It felt so good to be out of that bed. But she was warned that she couldn't sit in the chair for long. They didn't want her to overdo things and undo any of the progress she'd made.

The truth of the matter was that she was healing much faster than anyone had anticipated. She chalked it up to her healthy diet full of leafy greens and her daily walks around town. She'd watched some of her friends kick back and take it easy as they grew older. Once they lost their mobility, they didn't get it back. She didn't want that to happen to her. And so she'd keep moving as long as God allowed her. This incident was only a minor setback. She'd be out and about in no time. There was something so rejuvenating about the fresh sea air and the sun's warm rays.

She just had to keep pushing and she'd get released soon. She was hoping to be out next week. Spring Fling wasn't far off. And she'd started to feel guilty about pushing Ethan to take over the coordination. He didn't know how it all worked.

She should call him and have him bring her notes to the hospital. At this stage, she should be able to do most everything remotely. Yes, that sounded like a plan.

"Aunt Birdie?" Ethan stood in the doorway to her room with a surprised look on his face.

She smiled, so happy to see him. "Didn't I just see you yesterday?"

"Yes. But this couldn't wait. I have something I want to discuss with you."

95

Oh no! This sounds serious. She suddenly worried that he'd been called back to the city. And poor Peaches would have to be uprooted from her home.

"Well, don't stand all the way over there. Come in." She gestured toward the foot of the bed. "Have a seat."

Once he was perched on the edge of the bed, he said, "I did something and I don't want you to be upset."

She sat up straighter. Worry pumped through her veins. She'd definitely been away for too long. "Tell me what it is and we'll figure out how to fix it."

His eyes widened. "It's not like that. Nothing's broken." He raked his fingers through his hair. "The thing is that I have no idea what I'm doing with Spring Fling."

"Oh, is that all?" She waved off his worry. "Don't worry. I'm planning to get out of here soon. You won't have to do it alone."

"Wait. The doctors said you were being released early?"

"Well, no." She averted her gaze. "Not exactly."

He nodded. "Then don't worry because I found someone to help me with Spring Fling."

Her astute gaze zeroed in on him. "Who would that be?"

"Well, she needed someone that's good with their hands, and I needed someone that's familiar with the festival. And well, we made a deal."

Birdie was more confused now than she was when they'd started the conversation. "You made a deal with whom?"

"Oh, I forgot that part—Hannah Bell."

Inwardly she cheered. Outwardly she maintained a calm expression. "And you'll be working on the bakery for her?"

He nodded.

Birdie resisted the urge to grin and rub her hands together. Instead she continued her nonchalant demeanor. She knew her nephew. He wasn't one for commitments and certainly wasn't one to be pushed into anything. She couldn't let him know this is what she'd been hoping would happen.

She nodded in understanding. "Hannah is a good choice. Her mother used to organize Spring Fling until the accident."

"What accident?"

Birdie shook her head. It wasn't her story to tell. "Doesn't matter." Actually, it did. Everyone in town could see how hard the loss had hit the Bell family, especially Hannah. If ever there was a daddy's girl, it had been her. "What matters is that you and the festival will be in good hands with Hannah's guidance."

"Really? I mean you're not upset that I asked for help?"

She waved away his worry. "Not at all."

"But soon you'll be home to take over."

She let out a deep sigh. "The truth of the matter is, I think I've been pushing myself too hard. I think I need to lie down for a bit. Would you mind pressing the call button next to the bed?"

"Um, sure." He did as she asked. "One more thing."

"What is it, dear?"

"I noticed you still have Uncle Gil's tools. Would you mind if I used them?"

"Not at all. Help yourself." Anything to make him feel more at home on the island.

With Ethan occupied, she could stay on at Sunny Days. Perhaps it wouldn't be so bad to slow down like that handsome PT guy kept telling her to do. After all, everything was now in good hands—Ethan and Hannah's. She did like the sound of their names together.

Maybe with a little more time on the island that frown and those worry lines on Ethan's face would be permanently wiped away. After all, Bluestar was known to wash away people's worries and to bring couples together. Perhaps it would work for Ethan and Hannah.

Oh, yes, she needed to slow down and spend some more time there at Sunny Days. She smiled as she climbed into bed. For the first time since she'd fallen, she was certain everything would work out just the way it was supposed to.

97

CHAPTER TEN

Her stomach shivered with nerves.

Early the next morning, Hannah told herself that it was her excitement over making her dreams come true and not anxiety over the possibility of losing her entire life's savings plus the money her father had so kindly left to her.

As Hannah stood in the front of the bakery, she reached into her backpack purse and pulled out her notebook. She gripped it with both hands. It was something she didn't share with people, but in this instance, Ethan couldn't create her dream unless he saw what she wanted.

"Are those your plans?" he asked.

"In a way." She worried her bottom lip and wondered if she was making a mistake. What if he thought her drawings were silly or too over-the-top?

"May I see them?" He held out his hand.

It was then she noticed the red, uneven skin on the back of his hand. She knew what it was—a burn scar. Her father had a couple of them, though none were serious. Ethan's scars, on the other hand, looked as though they'd been far more serious. What had happened to him? She wanted to ask and yet, she didn't want to know.

He tugged on his long shirt sleeve. "Don't worry. It doesn't hurt."

It was then she realized she was staring. Heat rushed up her neck and settled in her cheeks as she glanced away. "I...I'm sorry." She rushed to hand over the notebook. "Here you go."

She felt bad for him. It looked like whatever he'd been through had been brutal. And as he opened the notebook, she noticed the other hand had similar scars too. She made a point not to stare anymore by starting to pace around the bakery. She'd already embarrassed him enough and that certainly hadn't been her intention. Not at all.

After her father's death, she'd tried to stay away from anything that had to do with fire, whether it was the department, the firefighters, or even first responder TV shows. She didn't realize until that moment how much she'd been avoiding the subject. And now the reminder was right in front of her.

Ethan didn't say anything as he took in all of her hand-drawn plans. He turned page after page. Time seemed to go on forever.

She wanted to ask him what he thought. Was any of it even possible now that she was on a shoestring budget? Instead she remained quiet, letting him digest the information.

He finally closed the notebook and smiled at her. "You are quite a talented artist."

"I'm not that good." She had never been good with receiving compliments.

"I beg to differ. I now have a good idea of what you want. Do you mind if I hang onto the notebook for a bit longer?"

"Only if I can borrow Birdie's binder for the Spring Fling."

"You've got a deal." He moved to where he'd dropped his jacket by the door and picked up a big purple binder.

Hannah wasn't expecting such a large, full binder. *Oh boy!* Her friends were right; he wasn't giving her a handout. This would definitely be a fair tradeoff.

She accepted the hefty binder from him and moved to the other side of the front door. "I'll just set it over here until we're done."

"I need to take some measurements. Do you mind if I go in the kitchen?"

She shook her head. "Be careful. It's still a mess in there. It's taking them a bit to get the ceiling fixed."

"No worries. As a firefighter, I'm used to moving carefully through rooms."

"You're a firefighter?" She didn't know why this caught her totally off guard, but it did. After seeing the scars, she should have guessed.

He nodded. "Been one for years."

The thought brought her no comfort. None at all. It just drove home the dangers of his occupation—dangers she was intimately familiar with now.

"I'll be right back." He moved to the kitchen.

She welcomed the alone time. It gave her a moment to compose herself. She didn't want to say or do anything to make this arrangement awkward for either of them.

She waited in the front room and answered some texts on her phone about cake orders and a couple about the upcoming wedding shower. At this point, she felt like she was being pulled in a million different directions, but she assured herself it would be all worth it in the end.

And then Ethan returned to the showroom. When their gazes met, her stomach dipped. There was something about him that drew her in. She wanted to know him better. And that wasn't good with him having such a dangerous career.

She wasn't going to get involved with a firefighter and that included Ethan. The risk to her heart was just too great. She still had the scars from losing her firefighter father. She couldn't go through that again.

She was better off staying focused on the task at hand—getting her bakery up and running. It was what her father had taught her—stay focused. As a child, she was forever getting distracted by this or that. She'd start one project only to get partway through and go do something else.

When she was seven or so, her father would take her out to the vegetable garden. He would assign her a task and he'd give her so long to do said task. If she completed it in time without getting distracted, he'd give her a treat. Sometimes it had been money, sometimes it had been a prize of sorts, and other times it had been his praise. They were all worthy prizes because all she'd ever wanted was for her father to be proud of her. Would he be proud of her now?

She gave her head a mental shake. Now wasn't the time to contemplate things that were out of her control. What was in her control was helping Ethan figure out what was left to do to finish the bakery and calculate how much it would cost.

For what felt like the longest time, she followed Ethan around the room. With the windows papered over, only the newly installed can lights shed light on the room. He would measure and write. Measure and write. She felt as though she should be doing something, but she had no idea what that might be. And so she remained quiet and offered a helping hand when he needed assistance measuring or moving things out of his way.

When he at last sat down on the floor and leaned back against the wall, she couldn't take it any longer. "So what do you think? Is it doable? Can I open before Easter?"

He patted the dusty floor next to him. "Come sit."

She eyed up the dirt and resisted the offer.

He glanced down at the floor, swiped his hand over it, like that was going to do anything to clean up the mess. "Sit. And we will talk."

With great reluctance and an aversion to dirt, she sat down. "How long do think this will all take?"

His brown gaze met hers and he smiled. "Did anyone ever accuse you of asking a lot of questions?"

"All the time. I have an older brother."

He nodded in understanding. "I don't have any siblings. I always wanted a brother, but it wasn't in the cards."

"Strangely enough, while growing up I would wonder what it'd be like to be an only child. I guess people always long for whatever it is they don't have."

"You might be right about that one. Like sometimes I wonder if I picked the right profession for the right reasons."

"You don't like your job?"

"It's not that. Sometimes I just wonder what it'd be like if I'd made another career choice."

"What would you do if you weren't a firefighter?"

He shook his head. "I don't know. It's just with the time off, I've been doing some thinking. Perhaps too much thinking."

"Besides firefighting, what else do you like to do?"

He shrugged. "Work with my hands. Be a carpenter. Or maybe a contractor. But that's never going to happen. I come from a long line of firefighters on my dad's side of the family. So it is expected as a Walker that I would carry on the tradition. But on my mom's side of the family, my grandfather was a contractor. He built a lot of houses in and around New York City."

Hannah liked that he'd confided in her. And now she wanted to give him some helpful advice. "I'm sure your family loves you, and they'll understand whatever decision you make about your future."

He raked his fingers through his hair, scattering the short strands. "I don't know why I told you all of that."

"It is nice to know that I'm not the only one struggling with things right now." She reached out and gave his forearm a quick reassuring squeeze. "Change isn't easy. Maybe that's what scares you more than what your family will think."

Ethan turned to her. "What about you?"

She wasn't so sure she wanted to get into her family history. It was better to stay focused on the here and now. "My problem right now is figuring out how long it'll take to finish the bakery. And if I'm going to be able to afford anything like I have in my notebook."

His brows furrowed together as his gaze lowered to his notepad. "I can't give an accurate estimate without some investigation. I'd need to price out the supplies. And then we'll have to see how soon the orders will come in."

The frustration of more unknowns and more waiting welled up in her. Ever since the flood, there had been no clear-cut plan. No firm details.

"Relax," he said, as though he could read her mind. "It's not that bad."

"You don't understand what all of this not knowing is doing to me. I need a plan. I need to know that this is doable. I need to know that I can afford to finish the job."

He explained what steps needed to be completed before she could get the inspector in there for her certificate of occupancy. He answered her numerous questions to the best of his ability. She appreciated his patience. But in the end, it sounded like a lot of work.

"Therefore," he said, "I'd say it'll take at bare minimum three weeks to finish."

"Oh." She blinked back the tears of frustration. There was no way she would be able to meet the bank loan without the bakery being in operation. Her business was about to go belly up before she even made her first sale.

"Hey, don't look so sad. The good news is that you should be able to open just after Easter."

"Easter?" She thought about this.

It was two weeks later than she'd planned. Could she still make it work? Would she be able to make her loan payment?

"Do you still want to go ahead with the project?" The rumble of Ethan's deep voice drew her from her thoughts.

That answer she didn't have to think about. "Yes, I do." But there was another hurdle. "I know you can't give me an exact number, but I need to know roughly how much this is going to cost before we go any further. The deductible on my insurance policy was large and it wiped out a large chunk of my savings. If I can't afford to finish this, there's no point in even starting it."

He looked over the list and as he mentally tallied up the expenses while the seconds turned to minutes, she'd never been so anxious for anything in her life. She willed the number to be within her budget. Was that even possible now that her savings had dwindled so low?

And then he gave her a rough quote.

She didn't react at first. The number hit the top end of her revised budget, but it was within the bounds. So that was good. But on the bad side, it didn't allow for any incidentals. And she'd been doing this long enough to know that construction/renovations came with incidentals.

"Hannah, stop stressing." He rubbed the back of his neck. "Those were just numbers I made up. Give me a little time to get you some real numbers."

She nodded her agreement.

Just then the front door opened. Brilliant sunlight shone into the room, making Hannah momentarily squint.

"Hannah?" Her mother closed the door. Worry lines etched her eyes. "Is everything okay?"

Both Hannah and Ethan got to their feet. "Everything's fine, Mom." And then remembering Ethan, she said, "Mom, you remember Birdie's nephew, Ethan?"

"Sure, I do." Her mother smiled. "It's good to see you again."

"It's good to see you too." And then he turned to Hannah. "I should be going. I have a lot to do. I'll get back to you shortly."

"I'll be waiting."

"I hope we'll be seeing more of you," her mother said. Before Ethan was even out the door, her mother turned to her with a glimmer in her eyes. "Isn't he a cutie?"

"Mom!" Heat rushed to Hannah's face. She was certain Ethan had heard her mother as she'd done nothing to lower her tone. The door closed with a soft thud. Hannah frowned at her mother. "Why did you say that?"

Her mother arched a brow. "You mean you don't think he's cute?"

She wasn't going to answer that question. She didn't like to lie and if she did agree with her mother, it would just further her mother's cause. It was best just to change the subject. "Ethan is only in town to care for his aunt."

"I see. And how is Birdie doing?"

"Good from what I hear. She's anxious to get home."

"I can imagine. Still it was so nice of her nephew to drop everything to come help her. And word around town is that he's available—"

"Mom!"

Her mother waved off Hannah's shock at the flagrant attempt at matchmaking. "Okay. But you have to admit that it's been a while since you dated."

"I've been busy."

"Yes, you have. But maybe you should give him a chance. After all, he's a hero." Her mother beamed. "Your hero. Saving your life has to count for something."

"You act like he saved me from the jaws of a shark." She didn't want to encourage her mother where Ethan was concerned. "And you seem to forget that he's a firefighter."

Her mother grew quiet for a moment. "He's not your father. What happened to him...well, you can't think it's going to happen to someone else you love."

"I don't love Ethan. I hardly even know him. But with his occupation, he takes the same risks as Dad—risks that I just can't take."

"Even though he's a good guy?"

"Even then." And now it was time to change the subject. "I'm working on a plan to get the renovation back on track."

Her mother looked around at the unfinished walls. "I wish you'd let me help you."

"Thank you but I've got it."

She knew her mother would do everything possible to help her, but Hannah couldn't ask her to do it. After her father died, her mother had been forced back to work to make ends meet. She felt guilty for taking the small amount of money her father had left her. Her siblings felt the same about their similar inheritances. But their mother wouldn't hear of keeping it.

Her mother glanced around, not that she knew anymore about construction than Hannah did. "And how are things?"

"They're going good." Not exactly a lie.

"And Ethan, he's helping you finish the bakery?"

There was no way she would be able to keep that information from her mother. "Yes. Well, maybe. He's looking into things and he's going to give me a quote—"

"If it's money, I can help."

And there it was, the problem she'd been hoping to avoid. "Thanks, Mom. But you and Dad already helped me enough. I need to do the rest on my own."

Her mother smiled and shook her head.

"What?" Hannah asked.

"I was just thinking how you're so like your father. Stubborn to the core."

"And that's a bad thing?"

"Sometimes. When you're too stubborn to let those that care about you help out."

"I'm okay, Mom. Honest. I've got this. And Ethan is helping me."

"That can't be cheap."

"Actually, we did a bit of bartering." Hannah went on to tell her mother about their arrangement.

"And Birdie's okay with this?"

"I haven't personally spoken to her yet, but Ethan talks to her all of the time."

"Maybe you should talk with her before you two get too deep into this plan. I know how much the festival means to her. It must be so hard for her to be out of the loop."

"I'll speak to her as soon as possible."

Her mother looked around the bakery once more. "Well, if I'm not needed here, I have to get to the community hall for a quilter's guild meeting about our latest charity project."

Her mother gave her a hug and then headed out the door. Hannah loved her mother dearly but didn't want her emotionally or financially invested in the bakery. The risk of failure was too great. If she couldn't open on time—if she couldn't meet the bank payment—it would be disastrous. But hopefully her deal with Ethan would keep that from happening.

Hannah grabbed her phone from her back pocket and selected Ethan's number. The phone rang once, twice, and then a third time.

"Hi. What did you need?"

"I was wondering when you were going to visit Birdie because I'd like to go with you, if it's all right. Or I could just go alone." She wasn't used to inviting herself on outings. And the longer he was quiet, the more anxious she became. "On second thought, I'll just go on my own—"

"Are you busy at lunchtime today?"

"Today?" She hadn't expected it to be so soon, but she consulted the calendar on her phone. "Today would work."

"I'm leaving on the noon ferry."

"I'll meet you at the dock."

When she disconnected the call, she realized that some people in town might read something into her accompanying Ethan to visit his aunt. But she didn't care about the gossip. She knew the truth. It was business only. Nothing more.

Now that people knew she could talk on the phone, it was ringing off the hook.

Ring-ring. Ring-ring.

Birdie smiled. She wondered who it was this time. She set aside the blanket that was now a quarter of the way completed. She reached for the phone.

"Hello."

"Aunt Birdie, it's Ethan."

107

He never phoned her. Had something happened to Peaches? Or was he phoning to say that he had to return to New York earlier than he'd planned? The thought deflated her mood. It would ruin all of her plans.

"Aren't you coming to visit today?" she asked.

"About that. I was wondering how you'd feel if someone came with me?"

The more company, the better. "Who?"

"Hannah. You know how she agreed to help me organize Spring Fling? Well, I think she has some questions for you."

Birdie beamed. If they kept this up, they wouldn't need her matchmaking efforts. "I'd love to see both of you."

"Good. We'll see you in a little bit. And I might have another surprise for you."

Another surprise? What was her dear nephew up to? "You can't leave me in suspense."

He laughed. "I'll see you soon."

And then they hung up. All the while Birdie was wondering about this budding relationship her nephew had started with Hannah. She didn't know how those two were going to make things work as a couple. His job was in New York and Hannah's beloved bakery was there on the island. It wouldn't be easy. But when it came to love, there was always a way.

She remembered a similar couple. She had grown up in Brooklyn. Her entire family had lived there. On Sundays, they'd all get together at her parents' house for a big meal. Back then, she couldn't imagine ever leaving New York and her loving family. And then along came Gil.

They'd met on her family's vacation to Bluestar Island. It was love at first sight. But it took them a bit to figure out who was going to give up their home and join the other. She'd finally given in because the island was idyllic.

She was certain it was a location her family wouldn't mind visiting regularly. And they had vacationed on Bluestar Island for many years. Oh the happy memories...

Even so, giving up her home and family to move away hadn't been easy. Birdie knew the transition wouldn't be easy for Ethan or Hannah, but if they were meant to be together, they'd find a way to make it work. And once she saw them together, she'd see for herself if they were destined for each other.

Her smile broadened. She hadn't been this excited in a long time. She didn't know how she'd be able to concentrate on her knitting now. She couldn't wait for Ethan and Hannah to arrive.

CHAPTER ELEVEN

And Peaches made three.

Ethan navigated his pickup through Boston and then into the suburbs. Peaches sat next to him with Hannah in the passenger seat. On this bright and sunny day, they were on their way to see Aunt Birdie. The trip was extra special because he'd finally talked Sunny Day's administrator into letting him bring Peaches for a visit. Both dog and human missed each other so much that it was almost painful to watch at times.

Every time he talked to Peaches about Birdie, her tail would thump the ground. Other times, though, Peaches was sullen and her appetite was iffy. When he'd told Peaches where they were going today, he could have sworn the dog understood because she was so excited he had a hard time getting her to stand still long enough to put on her harness.

But now it was his other companion that had him struggling for what to say. The problem was he'd said too much earlier at the bakery. He'd caught himself before he'd told her about the fire—about the nightmares that troubled him.

He halted his thoughts. He didn't want to dwell on the incident. It was in the past and soon the nightmares would stop. He recalled what he'd been told in the hospital about how talking about the incident would help him. He just wasn't ready yet to put words to his nightmare—to admit how it rattled him to the core.

However, the silence as they neared Sunny Days wasn't good. It gave him too much time to think about things that were better left alone—things like potentially leaving his job—ending the Walker tradition of firefighting. He halted his thoughts. He needed to focus on something else.

Ethan cleared his throat as they waited at a red light. "I talked to some suppliers this morning. I was able to call in some favors and get a discount."

"Really?" Excitement rang out in her voice. "Thank you so much. That will definitely help my tight budget. But..."

"But what?" He chanced a glance at her, taking in her worried expression. All too soon the light changed, and he had to turn his attention back to the road as traffic surged forward.

"I feel bad that you had to call in favors because of me."

"Oh, that's no big deal. I'm happy to help." If she liked that, he wondered how she'd feel about his next cost-saving suggestion. "What would you think about using some end lots, you know"—he struggled for the right word—"discontinued items?"

"What sort of items?"

"Floor tiles for one."

"I was planning to put in wood floors. I already bought them." She paused. "But most of the boxes got ruined in the flood."

"I looked into wood and I'll be honest, it's expensive. I know tiles aren't what you planned but it could be used to add a pop of color to the place."

"I don't know." She grew quiet as though giving his suggestion some serious thought. "I pictured something elegant, not bright and colorful."

Ethan wheeled his pickup into the entrance of the Sunny Days Physical Rehabilitation Center. The visitor parking lot was full, which didn't bother him. A full lot meant lots of visitors for the patients. Who could object to something like that?

Once he located an available spot in an adjacent lot, he parked. He turned off the engine and turned to her. "What's your favorite color?"

"Blue."

He breathed a sigh of relief. It was a color he could work with. "They didn't have enough white tiles to do both rooms, but they had some other colors in the same tile. Blue was one of them. I don't know if it's elegant or not, but we could do a white and blue check design."

She didn't immediately reject the idea, so that was something, but she hadn't exactly jumped at the idea either. "What other colors did they have?"

"They had gray and green. They were sold out of black." When she frowned, he said, "Or we can get the wood and try to cut costs from somewhere else."

She shook her head. "Flooring is a big-ticket item. We should do it your way. I'm sure it'll grow on me...eventually."

He pulled a picture of the tile up on his phone. "This is it."

When he handed it over for her to take a closer look, their fingers brushed, causing his heart to thump hard. There was just something about her that got to him. She pulled away, as though she hadn't noticed the electric charge between them. He told himself it was for the best, but he still felt disappointed about her lack of interest in him.

Hannah stared at the phone, swiping across the screen a few times. "It's not bad. It's a deeper blue than I was imagining, which is a good thing. And I like it better than the other colors. It helps that it's real ceramic tile."

"I'll let you know what else I find." He hooked Peaches's leash. "We should get going."

They walked across the parking lot in silence. When he reached for the door handle, he felt a hand on his arm. He glanced over at Hannah to find her staring back at him.

"I'm sorry," she said.

"For what?"

"Not being more excited about the great deal you've found. I'm grateful. Truly I am. It's just when you've had a certain image in your mind for so long, it takes a bit to modify it."

"Believe it or not, I understand. I've seen your beautiful drawings, and I promise to make the bakery as elegant as I can while still saving money."

"Thank you for everything." She smiled.

His heart beat faster. "Happy to help."

"Does your aunt know I'm coming with you?" Hannah asked as she clutched the purple binder to her chest.

"Yes. I told her. She was excited, as Sunny Days is far from Bluestar, making it a haul for her friends to visit. And a lot of her friends no longer drive."

"That's rough."

"I know. That's why I've been making plans to bring some of her friends with me."

"You're an awesome nephew."

He glanced to the side, catching Hannah smiling at him. His heart once more picked up its pace. He wasn't used to people praising him. He tried his best to stay in the background when they were on the job. After all, it wasn't one man that fought a fire; it was the whole crew.

But this was different. Hannah was different. Still, he felt uncomfortable with the compliment. "I haven't done anything that anyone else wouldn't do."

"I don't know about that. Not everyone would drop their lives to come to a small island in order to look after their aunt's dog while she was recovering. And you're doing an amazing job." She glanced down at the dog. "Huh, Peaches?"

As though the dog knew what she'd said, Peaches barked in agreement.

Not sure what to say, he remained quiet. He changed directions and led them around to the side of the facility where there were shade trees, picnic tables, and benches near a small pond.

"Aren't we going inside?" Hannah asked.

"We can't take Peaches inside. It's why I had to wait for a warm day to bring her." Ethan held out the leash to her. "Can you hang onto Peaches until I get my aunt?"

113

Hannah took the leash. "Sure. No problem. We're becoming fast friends." She knelt down next to the dog and ruffled her fur. "We'll be fine."

He took long, swift strides toward the double glass doors that led to the indoor lounge area. His gaze scanned the area for his aunt. He knew she didn't like being cooped up in her room all the time. She was a social creature who was used to taking daily strolls along the streets of Bluestar.

He greeted the now-familiar nurses by name as he made his way to her room. And there was Aunt Birdie resting in a chair with her legs up, an open book on her chest, her reading glasses on and her eyes closed. He paused. He didn't want to wake her.

He turned to leave when he heard, "Where exactly do you think you're going?"

For just a moment, he felt like a kid again. He smiled as he turned. "I didn't want to wake you."

Aunt Birdie made a "humpff" sound. "I wasn't sleeping. I was resting my eyes."

He didn't want to argue the point, but that was some serious deep breathing she was doing for being awake. Instead he decided to share his surprise. "Peaches is here to see you."

Her gaze looked past him, as though searching for her beloved companion. "Where is she?"

"She's waiting outside with Hannah."

A big smile lit up Aunt Birdie's face. "Well, let's not keep them waiting."

Aunt Birdie insisted she could walk. He didn't agree. It was a long way for her and once outside, the path would be a bit uneven. In the end, the nurse insisted his aunt use a wheelchair if she was going to go outside. Ethan resisted the urge to say I told you so.

Once seated in the wheelchair, Aunt Birdie said, "Let's go."

"Your wish is my command." He pushed her down the hallway.

"Is this all the faster it will go?"

He merely laughed. He hadn't seen his aunt this excited, well, ever. His footsteps came quicker.

When they were outside, Aunt Birdie called out, "Peaches!"

Immediately the dog turned. When Peaches's gaze landed on Aunt Birdie, she barked as her tail rapidly swished back and forth. She set off at a run. Hannah wisely let go of the leash or she would have been dragged across the lawn.

Aunt Birdie looked ten years younger as she fussed over her four-footed buddy. "I've missed you." Peaches licked her cheek. "Yes, I have. I'm so sorry to have left you. But Ethan appears to be taking good care of you." His aunt glanced up at him. "You aren't giving her too many treats, are you? She's a beggar but we don't want her gaining weight." She turned back to Peaches. "No. We don't."

Ethan joined Hannah on the bench. He was glad he'd looked into bringing Peaches for a visit. It was like the visit had breathed new life into his aunt. The worry lines framing her eyes and mouth smoothed out. And her smile went the whole way to her eyes and made them sparkle.

Aunt Birdie turned to them. "I'm sorry. Where are my manners? Hello, Hannah. Thanks so much for coming to visit me."

"It's so good to see you," Hannah said. "You're looking good."

"Tell that to my doctor." Aunt Birdie frowned. "I've been telling him that I can do my exercises at home, but he says I'm still not good enough to be discharged. And I have so much to do—obligations to fulfill."

"And that's why I'm here," Hannah said.

"It is?" Aunt Birdie sat up straighter. "How so?"

Ethan was more than willing to sit back quietly and let the women talk. Hannah seemed quite at ease with his aunt, but then again they lived in the same small town. Living in Bluestar so different from what he knew growing up in a big city where neighbors would move in and move out without him catching their names. But it wasn't that way on Bluestar Island, where everyone knew everyone and from what he could tell it was virtually impossible to keep a secret.

"Ethan mentioned that you had a lot planned for Spring Fling," Hannah said. "And I'd be more than willing to take over until you're able to do it."

Aunt Birdie's brow arched as her gaze moved to Ethan. "You're having poor Hannah do *all* of the organizing when she already has her hands full with starting a new business?"

"It's not like that—"

"We're helping each other out," Hannah interjected.

"Really?" Curiosity reflected in Aunt Birdie's eyes. "Tell me more."

Hannah explained what happened at the bakery and neither he nor his aunt stopped Hannah to let her know he'd kept his aunt updated on the situation with the bakery. To his surprise Hannah touted him as a hero for stopping her from stepping in the flood water with the electricity still on. He didn't feel like a hero, but this was her story so he kept quiet.

"I'm so sorry that happened to you," Aunt Birdie said.

"Thank you." Hannah held up the purple binder. "I brought this along. I was hoping we could go over some of my questions."

"Certainly." All the while Aunt Birdie petted Peaches, who'd made her way onto his aunt's lap.

Hannah hadn't been kidding when she said that she had questions for Aunt Birdie. She pulled her notebook from her backpack and proceeded to ask question after question.

Once Aunt Birdie answered all of Hannah's questions, she said, "With you two working together, I know it'll go smoothly." Aunt Birdie reached out and gave Hannah's arm a brief squeeze. "Thank you. You're a sweetheart for volunteering to help. Now before I forget, in my desk is a map from last year. It shows all of the places where I hid the eggs in the park. Afterward I was able to go back and find the ones that were left. You might want to do the same things this year."

"That's a great idea." Hannah smiled as she continued to write more notes.

Aunt Birdie subdued a yawn, but Ethan noticed the exhaustion written across her ivory face. "We should probably get going." He checked the time. "If we hurry we can catch the next ferry."

"If you have any questions," Aunt Birdie said, "I'll be right here."

"Thanks," Hannah said. "I'm sure we'll need your input. There's a lot to do. And we have a lot to learn."

A smile pulled at his aunt's lips. "Just trying to do my part. I know the younger people are so busy with their families and work that they don't have time to plan these types of special events. Spring Fling was always my favorite festival. It meant that spring was here and soon everything would bloom." A faraway look came over her face, as though she were recalling those happy memories. "But I won't keep you any longer."

Aunt Birdie fussed over Peaches a little bit more, and then Ethan escorted her back to her room. He helped her into bed at her request.

It appeared the visit had taken a lot out of her or perhaps it was the physical therapy before they'd arrived. Either way, she didn't have to worry about anything. With Hannah's invaluable help, Spring Fling would be a success.

CHAPTER TWELVE

This was so much more work than she'd been expecting.

Saturday evening, Hannah stood in Birdie's house. After Ethan had finished working at the bakery for the day, he'd invited her over to work on Spring Fling plans. Hannah knew they had to get started on the details for the Easter egg hunt, that they were woefully behind since Spring Fling was in a few weeks.

"Why don't we eat first?" Ethan's deep voice drew her from her thoughts.

They'd picked up a large pepperoni pizza from the Pizza Pie Shoppe on the way to his place, well, Birdie's place. It was the first time Hannah had been inside the house. When she'd visit with Birdie it was always during warm weather. They'd have lemonade out on her sweeping porch with an amazing view of the ocean.

As she glanced around, she noticed the place was well-kept, but it was a bit on the small side. Still, how much room did one person need? Her gaze moved to the French doors. And with that amazing ocean view, it was picture perfect.

"Here we go." Ethan handed her a plate with a couple of slices. "We can sit on the couch."

She turned, finding a pillow and blanket on it. "You sleep there?"

He shrugged as he placed his plate on the coffee table. "I'll just move those."

She couldn't imagine why he'd sleep on the couch. It didn't look that big. And when she sat down, she found it wasn't comfortable. No wonder she'd noticed him more than once rubbing his neck.

Then she thought of the vacant, furnished apartment across the hall from hers. Should she offer it to him? With him leaving the island soon, it'd be available for summer rentals. Still, she hesitated.

When he sat next to her, the cushion sagged in his direction. She had to quickly adjust herself so as not to fall into him.

"Sorry," he said, looking uncomfortable. "It's an old couch and the springs have seen better days."

"So why do you sleep here?" Once she'd uttered the words, she wished she could take them back.

He cleared his throat. "I tried my aunt's bed, but it's too small and soft. So it's either the couch or the floor. I tried the floor, but I could barely move in the morning."

Awe... Sympathy welled up in her. At the same time, her respect for him spiked. He was going out of his way for his aunt. Only a good guy would go to all of this bother.

"You could stay in my apartment," she blurted out. When his eyes widened in surprise, she realized how that might sound—wrong, very wrong. Heat engulfed her face. "Not in my actual apartment. Not with me," she stammered. "I have another apartment. It...it's across the hall."

His brows knitted together. "You're offering me the extra apartment above the bakery?"

She nodded, not trusting her words.

"I don't think so." He took a bite of pizza.

Wait. He was turning her down? He'd rather sleep on this lumpy, sagging couch? What was she missing?

"Why?" She had to know the answer.

"You should rent it to someone else."

"But I'm offering it to you. And you need it. You can't keep sleeping on this couch." When Peaches moved to his side to beg for food, she realized why he might be hesitant. "And you can bring Peaches."

His hesitant gaze met hers. "Are you sure? Most apartments don't allow dogs."

"Of course I'm serious." Her gaze moved to Peaches. "We're buddies. Aren't we, girl?"

"Arf!"

"Problem solved." Hannah smiled at her ability to fix one problem.

"I don't know what to say, but thank you. That's generous of you."

"You're welcome. Now we better eat so we can get some planning done."

"Agreed."

And so Ethan turned on the television while they ate. She was surprised when he turned on a home renovation show instead of the sports channel.

When the show ended and the dishes were cleared, it was time to go over the plans for the egg hunt. Hannah reached for her backpack and pulled out a notebook where she'd written a bunch of notes about the festival.

"Where do you want to start?" he asked.

"How about we find all of those order forms that she said were in her desk?"

Ethan nodded in agreement.

She followed him to the aforementioned desk. He sat down in the small, short chair that made him look like a giant. Hannah couldn't help but smile at the way his knees stuck up as though he were sitting in a kid's chair.

"What's so funny?" he asked.

"Oh, nothing. Except that chair was definitely not made for you."

"Tell me about it." He pulled open the first desk drawer. It was crammed full of papers and recipes his aunt had clipped from the newspaper or a magazine. *Oh boy*! This was going to take some time.

"Why don't you start on one side," Hannah said, "while I search the drawers on this side."

"Sounds like a plan to me because we don't have all night."

"That's right. We have to get you moved into the apartment."

"And I have to get up early. I have a supply order to pick up and some walls to mud."

"Hmm...that sounds fun. Why do you throw mud at the walls?" She sent him a teasing smile.

"I wish it was that fun. No, I have to cover the seams in the drywall. And then when its dry, hopefully in a day or two, it's going to need to be sanded."

"That sounds like a lot of work."

"It is. But if you want smooth walls, it's what needs done."

"Maybe I can help you. After all, how hard can sanding be?"

He shrugged. "But won't you be busy with your baking and then working on the festival plans?"

"I've read your aunt's entire binder and been on the phone with the event coordinators for the Bloomin' Tulip Contest and the jelly bean relay. They've told me Birdie got them everything they needed before her accident."

"Oh. Okay. You can help in the bakery, if you want. I can show you what to do."

And then a thought came to her. "What if we help each other? That way it'll keep things from getting too monotonous." When he opened his mouth to argue, she added, "And I recall you telling your aunt that you'd help me with the festival."

His lips pursed together as though he were trying to think up an excuse to get out of it, but then he surprised her by saying, "Okay. You've got a deal."

Just then Peaches, who was sitting beside them, barked her agreement. And they both laughed.

"I guess it's unanimous now." Hannah withdrew a stack of clipped pages. "I think I found some of the papers we're hunting for."

Ethan was already in the second drawer down. "And I think I have some flyers."

"Things are looking up."

When Ethan sent her a reassuring smile, her heart tumbled in her chest. Yes, things were definitely looking up. But what would happen when Birdie was home again and Ethan returned to his life in New York?

It was then that her grandmother's words of wisdom came to mind, *Don't trouble trouble until trouble troubles you.* She used to think her grandmother's sayings were silly but now she was finding comfort in them.

♥♥♥

He felt great!

It was amazing what a decent bed could do for one's outlook on the day.

Monday afternoon, Ethan moved rapidly through his tasks and even when he'd realized he'd picked up the wrong sandpaper that cost him precious time, it hadn't doused his good mood. He'd merely moved onto the next task on his list. With the restoration work now complete, he was able to work in any part of the bakery.

Ethan noticed Hannah wasn't around. In fact, he hadn't seen her once that day. Not that he was anxious for her company. He knew she had a cake to deliver that morning, and she was making a detailed list of what needed to be done for Spring Fling. And then there was the wedding shower for—what was her name? He stopped and thought for a moment because he'd been in Bluestar Island for more than a week and little by little, he was learning to put names to faces. It was something he'd been challenging himself with each day.

He paused from where he'd just finished mudding a wall in the showroom. He knew the name. It was on the tip of his tongue. He struggled to recall the name. It was an easy name.

And he refused to give up. Amy? No. Amber? No. A...

"Amelia!" He smiled at his accomplishment.

"What about Amelia?"

He turned. Hannah stood in the doorway. She looked as beautiful as ever with her long auburn hair pulled back in her customary messy bun. A few strands of hair had worked free and framed her face.

And then he realized he was staring and glanced away. "I was just trying to remember her name is all."

Hannah arched a brow. "Any particular reason?"

He shrugged, feeling a bit awkward. "I've been trying to put names to faces."

"And Amelia just happened to pop into your mind?"

He shrugged once more. That bit of awkwardness had now morphed into distinct discomfort. "It's no big deal."

She didn't say anything for a moment. Instead, she stood there staring at him as though trying to figure out what was up with him. He was starting to feel the same way.

He cleared his throat. "Thanks for the use of the apartment. I had a good night's sleep."

"You're welcome."

Trying to lessen the weirdness of the moment, he went back to moving to a new section of the wall. At this point, the new display cases and counters hadn't been delivered, but they were due to arrive next week, so he wanted to get these walls primed, prepped, and painted before the delivery date.

Hannah moved about the large room, dodging his tools and supplies like a fine dancer. "Do you honestly think it'll be completed before Easter?"

"Are you saying you doubt me?"

She shook her head but her gaze didn't meet his. "I was just beginning to think with the flood and then the insurance company giving me a hard time, that it wasn't meant to be."

He felt bad for her. This was supposed to be one of the most exciting times in her life, and now it was marred with additional stress and worry—none of which was any fault of her own.

"That's all behind you," he said, continuing to work on the wall. "Now you just have to envision this place finished."

"I'm trying to, but it's not going to look how I'd originally imagined."

He paused, worried he wasn't doing something right. "What's wrong with it? If you tell me, maybe I can fix it."

"Oh no. It's nothing that you've done. It's just that originally I wanted to put some history back into the place. This bakery has been here for at least a hundred years. It just feels weird to make it totally modern."

He smeared more mud on the wall. "So what were you thinking? Some old photos on the wall?"

"No. But I like that idea." She reached for her phone, and her fingers started moving over the keypad.

"Did you just write that down?"

"I did. With this place, my work, the upcoming wedding shower and Spring Fling, my brain is leaking information." She laughed. "So I've started making notes for myself on my phone. It's helpful. You should try it sometime."

"Maybe I will." It would definitely help him with this remodel. "As for the bakery, you have a lot of ideas in your notebook. Is there anything it's missing?"

"I had picked out some antique fixtures online. You know like switch plates and light fixtures. I even found an antique cash register and was going to see if someone could strip out the guts of it and replace them with modern-day technology."

He was impressed. "Sounds like you've given this a lot of thought."

"Trust me. When you've been dreaming of something for nearly half your life, you have a lot of time to envision just what you want." She sighed. "But those were dreams and this is reality. I need to be happy with what I have and stop wishing for something different."

He gave it a little thought. It didn't take much. With a mother that prided herself on being the best shopper in all of New York, perhaps the country, he knew how to get Hannah what she wanted without breaking the bank.

"What are you doing this weekend?"

124

She turned a wide-eyed gaze his way. Her pouty lips were slightly agape as she stared at him. What in the world had he done to create such a reaction? He glanced down to make sure he hadn't knocked over his bucket, but it was standing right where he'd put it.

And then it was like the clouds had cleared and he realized his mistake. He inwardly groaned. He was usually better around women, but he was a bit out of practice.

He cleared his throat. "I didn't mean that as in you and I...that we would, uh...what I meant was that if you don't have plans, we could go to an estate sale."

Her stunned expression turned into one of puzzlement. "And why would we go there?"

"Because you would be surprised at the history you can find at estate sales."

"And you would know this how? For some reason, I just don't see you as the antique collecting type."

"It's my mother's fault."

"Your mother?" The confused look remained.

"Yes, when I was young, she would drag me along on her outings. It didn't matter if it was a yard sale, an estate sale, or any other sale you can imagine. I bet even as we're talking that she's negotiating a better price on an antique in France."

"But what does she do with all of the stuff?"

"She says she finds them new homes where they'll have someone to appreciate them. I think she loves the hunt. She gets so excited when she finds a nice piece that's been lost in the clutter of estate sales."

"Interesting. And your father, he's a firefighter, like you?"

"Yes. But he's higher up in the chain of command. He's the chief of department. And he wants me to follow in his footsteps." And then he admitted something he'd never told anyone before. "Not only that but he wants me to become the fire commissioner." This time Ethan did rake his fingers through his hair without thinking of the mess it might make.

"That's a lot to live up to."

"Tell me about it. And the worst part is I don't want to do it. I don't want to keep climbing the chain of command. I don't want to fight politicians over the budget and push paperwork. I'm happy being out in the community helping people."

He didn't know why he'd dumped all of that out there in the open. What was it about Hannah that had him peeling back the layers of his life and letting her see what was inside him?

"Then don't do it." She made it sound so easy.

"I can't."

"Sure, you can. Just tell your father. He'll understand."

Ethan shook his head. "No, he won't. His father's father was a fire chief. His father was a borough commander. And he's chief of department. I'm expected to continue the Walker tradition."

"But if it doesn't make you happy—"

"Never mind. I shouldn't have brought it up." He didn't know whom he was more upset with: her for making it all sound so simple or himself for even entertaining the notion. "I know it sounds silly that a man of my age is worried about disappointing my parents, but we've always been close. They've done their best by me. And I'm not sure what I want to do with my future." His gaze met hers. "Sorry. I'm sure that's more than you wanted to know."

"Not at all. If you ever want to talk more, I'm a pretty decent listener." She eyed up his work. "Can I help you with that?"

"How are you at sanding?"

"I know how to move sandpaper back and forth."

"Good you're hired." He smiled at her, hoping to lighten the mood. "But not until tomorrow evening. This needs time to dry. And then we'll start over there." He pointed to the other side of the room that had already been prepped.

Hannah took the moment to look around the big room. Her beautiful face creased with worry lines. "There's so much to do."

"Stop worrying. It'll get there. And it's going to look great when it's finished. Tonight I'll do a little research for estate sales in the area. If I find one, we could go Saturday morning if you're available."

She worried her bottom lip as though considering the offer. Then her eyes widened as though she'd thought of something. "The wedding shower is Saturday."

He wasn't willing to give up yet, because they didn't have time to waste if she was going to open before Easter. "What time?"

"Not until the evening."

"The sales are in the morning. We could be back in plenty of time."

"Aren't you visiting your aunt that day?"

"We'll just make it one big trip. Shopping. Visiting. And some lunch in there somewhere. How does that sound?"

"As long as we're home by four, count me in."

"It's a date." The words slipped out before he could stop them.

Had he meant to say those exact words? No. Definitely not. Still he couldn't help wondering, did he secretly want to date Hannah? He'd just had a bad breakup. Did he want to go down that road again?

"I better get going." Hannah's voice drew him from his thoughts. Her face was flushed as her gaze avoided his. "Will you be all right here? I mean, um, do you need anything?"

"I'm good. Thanks."

And with that she was gone. There wasn't so much as a goodbye.

And now the bakery seemed so empty without her presence. Not that he wanted her company or anything. Still, it was nice not to be alone. He'd spent a lot of his off hours alone in New York. Not because it was his choice, but rather because it worked out that way. But here in Bluestar Island, everything was different.

Peaches stared at the door that Hannah had just walked out.

"Seems I'm not the only one she's made an impression on."

Peaches barked in agreement.

CHAPTER THIRTEEN

Had she made a date with Ethan?

Surely not. It was just work. Friends being friendly.

At noon on Tuesday, Hannah sat in a quiet corner of The Lighthouse Café, trying to digest this information. In front of her was her laptop, and next to it was an uneaten lobster roll, her favorite.

The computer screen was open to a website selling small kid's toys, the kind you win at carnivals. The toys needed to fit the festival's budget and be small enough to fit inside plastic eggs. So far Hannah had picked out miniature animals, bouncy balls, and candy.

Her thoughts kept straying back to yesterday and Ethan's invitation to spend Saturday morning with him. It definitely wasn't a date. No way. Even if Ethan was easy on the eyes— very easy—she wasn't going to date him.

And Ethan, well, he wasn't in a good place to start a relationship. He was confused to say the least. He didn't even know if he wanted to continue to be a firefighter or not. How did that happen? Did he just wake up one day and question all of his life choices? Or did it have something to do with those angry red scars on his wrists and hands?

She'd noticed that he never mentioned them or what had caused the injuries. Not that she could blame him. Whatever had happened must have been awful. Her heart ached for him.

"What has you so deep in thought?"

The familiar voice had Hannah glancing up to find Lily standing there, studying her. Hannah quickly glanced down, as though if she looked at Lily too long, she'd be able to read her thoughts—thoughts about Ethan.

Heat rushed to her face. "I...I was just going over plans for the Easter egg hunt."

"Uh-huh." Lily took a seat next to Hannah. "Looked more like you thinking about a certain someone."

The warmth in her cheeks intensified. "I wasn't thinking about Ethan." As soon as the words were out of her mouth, she realized she'd made a big mistake. "I wasn't."

"Really?" Lily grinned at her. "Funny how his name popped right into your mind."

"I...uh..." She floundered for a reasonable excuse. And failed.

"Sure looks like you and Ethan have hit it off."

"We're helping each other. Nothing more." Why did it feel like the temperature in the café had climbed dramatically? Hannah reached for her iced tea and took a large gulp.

"Uh-huh." Lily grinned at her.

"Would you quit saying that?"

"I'm sure you've noticed that he's good-looking."

How could I not notice? He's the most handsome man I've ever laid eyes on.

"And he's a good guy," Lily said. "Look at how he dropped everything to help his aunt."

He's certainly gone above and beyond.

"And look at how Peaches has bonded with him. You know what they say about animals being good judges of character."

It's true. Peaches adored Ethan. And it appears the affection goes both ways.

"And—"

"Stop." Hannah didn't need Lily spouting off all of the reasons Ethan was a good catch for some lucky lady—just not her. "Sounds like you should be dating him."

Lily waved off the idea as she shook her head. "Oh no. Not me. He only has eyes for you."

"He does not." She frowned at her friend. "It isn't like that."

"Okay. Relax. I was just giving you a hard time."

It was time to talk about anything but her relationship with Ethan—*erm, their business relationship.* "I have all of the RSVPs for the shower this weekend."

"Oh good. I need the number of guests in order to sort out seating and everything." Lily removed her digital tablet from her purse and started making notes for the upcoming celebration.

Darla stopped by the table and took Lily's order. Hannah still had her lobster roll and if she didn't eat it soon, it wouldn't be any good. She took a bite.

By the time Lily's salad was served, they'd covered the guest lists and started on the seating chart. Hannah had insisted on baking the cupcakes for the party. She had to do something because this party had been her idea.

"I think Amelia is going to enjoy the party, and it'll give her a chance to get to know some of the island's residents better." Hannah ate another bite of her roll.

"It can't be easy moving to a place where you only know one person." Lily sprinkled black pepper over her salad.

"Agreed. But it's amazing what people will do for love. Not that we'd know."

For a bit, both Hannah and Lily were lost in their thoughts as they finished eating. She couldn't help but wonder if Ethan's use of the word *date* hadn't been a mistake but deliberate. Was she that out of practice with men that she couldn't tell if he was interested in her? Her heart picked up its pace. Was it possible?

"And what are you thinking about?" Lily's voice drew Hannah from her thoughts.

"Um...nothing."

"Is nothing the reason you're blushing?"

"I am not." But her cheeks were definitely warm.

"Want to talk about it?"

Just then the server approached their table. She topped off their iced teas and cleared their dishes. All the while, Hannah thought about confiding in her friend.

Though they could tease each other, they knew whatever was said between them wouldn't go any further. But it was like once she said the words, it would make what transpired between her and Ethan a fact—something not easily dismissed.

Hannah's mouth grew dry. She sipped her tea. And then she whispered, "I think Ethan might have asked me out?"

Lily's eyes widened. "That's awesome!"

"Shh..." She glanced around to make sure no one had overheard their conversation. Thankfully no one was close by. She didn't want to stir up any small-town gossip.

"Wait." Lily spoke softly. "You said he might have. Does that mean you're not sure?"

In a hushed voice, Hannah said, "It was supposed to be work-related, but then he used the word *date*."

"Men don't throw that word around lightly. Did you ask him to clarify things?" When Hannah vehemently shook her head, Lily asked, "Do you want it to be a date?"

Yes. No.

She was so conflicted, but the fact she was torn didn't go unnoticed by her...or by Lily. Maybe she was just blowing this out of proportion.

"Sorry, I'm late." Josie's voice drew Hannah from her thoughts. Josie sat down next to Lily. "There was a problem at the inn and I just couldn't get away. What did I miss?"

"Nothing," Hannah said.

"Everything," Lily replied.

The simultaneous and conflicting answers had Josie's brows drawing together. "Looks like I got here just in time. What did I miss?"

"Wait until you hear what happened with Hannah." Lily grinned.

"Does it have to do with the bakery?" Josie asked. "Because I've been giving the situation some thought."

Lily shook her head, all the while Hannah glared at her friend as her face once more grew warm. "It's way better."

"Better than the bakery?" Josie asked.

Lily grinned and nodded.

Hannah couldn't take this agonizing build up any longer. It was best to just get it out in the open. She waved at Josie to lean in close and then she whispered, "Lily thinks Ethan asked me out."

"Oh!" Josie's eyes filled with excitement. "That's awesome. Wait. Why did you say she thinks? And why are we whispering?"

"Because I don't need the gossips to get wind of this and make a thing of it. As for Ethan, well, we have plans to go to an estate sale this weekend on the mainland. But it is all business," Hannah said firmly. "Nothing more."

Josie looked confused. "Why does Lily think it's a date."

"Because he said, 'It's a date.'" Lily smiled triumphantly.

Josie's lips formed an *O*.

"It's a figure of speech," Hannah insisted. "Besides, don't we have more important matters to discuss?"

"I agree with Lily," Josie said. "Men don't say date unless they mean it."

Hannah remained quiet and eventually the conversation shifted to the preparations for the wedding shower. All the while Hannah's thoughts circled around both Lily and Josie's assessment that Ethan had asked her out. That wasn't what she wanted to hear. Or was it? She was so conflicted.

Before opening his eyes the next day, Ethan stretched. When he lowered his hand, his fingers brushed over soft fur. His eyes sprang open and he turned his head to find Peaches's face right next to his.

"Morning, Peaches."

He ran his hand over the pup's head and down her back. He was rewarded with a swipe of her tongue over his cheek. Ethan sat up and slung his legs over the edge of the bed. His fingers raked through his hair. It was good to have his own place. Well, technically it wasn't his place. It was only temporary.

Buzz. Buzz.

He wondered who that could be first thing in the morning. He grabbed his phone from the bedside table. The number wasn't one he recognized. Still, it could be something about his aunt.

He pressed the phone to his ear. "Hello."

"Mr. Walker, it's Chief Campbell. How are you?"

"Uh, good." He didn't recall giving him his number.

"You sound a little confused. If you're wondering how I got your number, it wasn't hard."

"Let me guess, you were talking to my aunt."

"As a matter of fact, I was. When I mentioned that I needed to speak to you, she readily gave me your number. I hope that's not a problem."

"No. Not at all. What did you need?"

"I was hoping you could stop by the fire station this morning."

Ethan couldn't help but wonder what the chief had on his mind. This was so unexpected. "The thing is I don't have any free time. I'm working on the bakery."

"This won't take long. I'll see you in a few minutes." And then the phone went dead.

Had the chief hung up? "Hello?"

More silence.

Ethan sighed. What was it the chief had on his mind? It must be awfully important. Ethan jumped out of bed with a bounce in his step. He rushed through his morning routine and then with Peaches fed and now leashed, they headed out the door.

The fire station wasn't far from the bakery. In fact, it was a short walk. Along the way, everyone he passed greeted him and most paused to fuss over Peaches. It was so different

134

from his life in New York. And he had to admit it was nice—it made him feel at home, even if this wasn't his home.

When he guided Peaches in through the front door of the fire station, he didn't see a soul. "Hello?"

"Back here."

He followed the voice to the back of the firehouse and found the chief in his office. "Hi. I hope you don't mind that I brought Peaches."

The chief smiled. "Not at all. Hey, girl."

Peaches barked her greeting.

Ethan cleared his throat. "What did you need?"

The chief waved him farther into the office. "I just need your signature on a couple of papers."

"My signature? For what?"

"I thought while you were in town that we'd set you up so you can hang out with the crew and go out on some calls."

Ethan shifted his weight from one foot to the other. "But, sir, I already have a job."

"I know. But when you're here, we could use your help."

Ethan glanced around at the empty station. *Help with what?* But he kept his thought to himself. "What papers are these?"

"Just adding you to the roster for legality reasons." The chief explained each document to him. "Don't worry, you won't be signing your life away." The chief held the pen out to him.

Ethan hesitated. The chief's expectant look spurred him into action. He read over the papers. They were exactly what the chief had said they were. After reasserting that he wasn't staying on the island permanently, Ethan signed his name.

He'd just walked out the door when he ran into Greg Hoover. They'd previously run into each other here at the firehouse and a few times around town. Greg was an easy guy to be around. His talkative nature made Ethan feel immediately at ease.

Being tall, Ethan wasn't used to craning his neck to look into someone's eyes but Greg's imposing height was the exception. "It seems like we keep running into each other."

Greg smiled. "Is that your way of saying you were hoping to avoid me?" Greg sent him a teasing grin.

"Not at all." He suddenly felt awkward and not sure what to say. "I..."

"Relax man." Greg smiled. "I was just giving you a hard time."

Ethan breathed easier. "You had me there."

"It's my day off, so I figured I'd check in with the chief and see what needed to be done around here."

"Your day off and all you can find to do is come here?" But then again, who was he to complain? When he was in New York, he spent most of his time at the fire station unless there was a building project that could use his help.

Greg turned his attention to Peaches, who was sitting next to Ethan. Greg fussed over the dog and she happily lapped it up. He straightened. "What can I say, I like it around here. The guys are the best and I know this is getting to be a lot for the chief."

"So you're planning to become the next chief?"

Greg held up his hands. "Not me. No way. I don't mind the work, but I don't want to do the paperwork and let's not mention dealing with the mayor." He shook his head. "I wouldn't be good in that position. But I know the chief is hoping to find someone to fill his boots so he can retire."

"Well, he's lucky to have you around to help him out."

"So what are you up to? How's your aunt doing?"

And so Ethan filled him in on what was going on with the bakery and his aunt's condition. It felt good to have another guy to hang out with and shoot the breeze. That was one thing he missed about Brooklyn was his friends at the firehouse.

Not that he didn't enjoy talking with Hannah. Perhaps the problem was that he enjoyed talking to her a little too much.

And then what would happen when his time was up on the island? He didn't want to set either of them up to be hurt.

Maybe what he needed to do was put some distance between them. After all, he was hired to do a job. It didn't mean they had to spend a lot of time together. He would treat her just like any other client.

"Ethan?" Greg sent him a strange look.

"What did you say?"

"I was asking if you need any help at the bakery."

He could use some help if he was going to meet Hannah's deadline, but he didn't feel right about imposing on their new friendship. "Thanks. But I'm good right now."

"We should hang out sometime. Do you watch hockey?"

"I do."

They named their favorite teams. They moved on to comparing their favorite players and finally the teams' records.

Ethan shook his head. "I guess we'll find out whose team is better when they play each other."

"You're on. Well, let me know if you need help at the bakery." He sounded as though he meant it.

"I will. I should get to work. I'll be seeing you."

As he made his way back to the bakery, he couldn't help but notice how quickly he was being drawn into this tight-knit community. He hadn't meant for that to happen and yet it had.

He had become a regular at The Lighthouse Café for breakfast. So much so that when they saw him come through the door, they started his order. He even had a regular seat at the counter. And if that wasn't enough, he was co-coordinating Spring Fling. And now the ink was drying on the papers making him an official Bluestar firefighter. He didn't even recognize his life anymore.

When he stepped inside the bakery, he was surprised to find Hannah sitting in the middle of the showroom floor. "What are you up to?"

She scurried to her feet and brushed off her jeans. "I was just trying to envision this place as something more than it is now."

Ethan released Peaches from her leash, and she went to curl up in the bed he'd made for her. "And what do you think?"

Hannah's face lit up as her eyes reflected her anticipation. "That I can't wait until it's finished."

"It's not going to happen overnight, but it's getting there little by little."

She shoved up the sleeves of her long-sleeve T-shirt with *Bluestar 5K* emblazed over the front. "And I'm here to help."

His eyes widened. "Are you sure?"

She nodded. Then she bent over to pick up a white pastry box. "And I brought breakfast."

"Breakfast?" He smiled. It seemed there wouldn't be a need for him to visit the café that morning.

She stepped up to him and opened the lid, revealing two big muffins with a crumble topping. Immediately his mouth watered.

"Are both of those for me?" he asked.

She laughed. "I thought we'd share. But if you want them both, that's fine. I have more upstairs."

"What are they?"

"Blueberry crumble muffins. I hope you like them."

"I'm sure I will."

If she kept baking for him, he'd never want to leave. When his gaze shifted from the sweet treat to her, he found her smiling at him. It filled his chest with a warm fuzzy sensation. Oh yeah, it was going to be hard to leave when the time came.

CHAPTER FOURTEEN

What was it like to live in a grand estate?

Hannah pondered the possibilities.

Early Saturday morning, the sun's rays shined down over the earth, making the dew glisten like fine jewels. If she didn't know better, she'd say the owners of this sprawling estate had strategically placed crystals throughout their manicured lawn to have this dazzling effect.

Yet, the morning's beauty couldn't compare to the excitement Hannah felt at being a guest here at this grand estate. When Ethan had first mentioned a sale, she'd thought he meant a yard sale. This was definitely not a yard sale.

In the center of the perfectly green carpet of grass was a slight grade and at the top sat a white stately mansion, which looked as though it had been around for centuries. Each of its many windows were adorned with black shutters. Behind its towering columns stood double red doors that beckoned to her.

Just for a moment in Hannah's imagination, she pretended she was an invited guest to a prominent gathering. Oh, how exciting those events must have been. The mansion would likely have been the highlight of the social circles.

"What has you smiling?" Ethan's voice intruded upon her daydream.

"Oh, I was just wondering what it might have been like fifty or a hundred years ago, when people were invited for grand parties. Do you think movie stars and politicians visited here?"

His dark brows furrowed together.

"What?" She didn't think it was that strange to wonder about the people who used to live there.

"Nothing. I just didn't take you for one of those who were into hype and glamour."

"I'm not." She glanced around at the people there for the sale. Some of the women were dressed in slacks and heels while others were dressed casually like her. The men were also a mix of business casual or jeans. "Have you looked at me?" She gestured to her dark pair of boyfriend jeans with the cuff at the ankles and her Boston Red Sox jacket. "What part of this outfit says glamour to you?"

"You look good in anything you wear."

It was like a blast furnace had just opened and set her face aflame. He thought she looked good. Her pulse raced. This outing was starting to sound more like a date all of the time.

But it couldn't be—she wouldn't let it. As nice and as handsome as Ethan was, he was still a firefighter. He put his life on the line most every time he went to work. And...and she couldn't lose someone else she cared about.

"We should be able to find you something for the bakery that has a lot of history." His voice drew her from her thoughts.

"I hope so. Shall we head inside?" Hannah was anxious for this date or whatever it was to be over. "We don't want to be late and miss getting a seat. There are a lot of people here today."

Ethan leaned over to her and said softly, "Don't worry. We have time to look around."

She inhaled the spicy scent of his cologne mixed with his own masculine scent, and she momentarily forgot what she'd been about to say to him. She breathed in again, deeper this time. She didn't think she'd ever smell that wonderful scent again without thinking of Ethan.

It took her a moment and some serious concentration. "It doesn't matter," she said. "We both know I don't have the budget to bid against these people."

"What you don't know is that they aren't here to lay out a lot of money. Most of these people are looking to score a good deal. So we have a chance. Trust me." He sent her a reassuring smile.

And she instinctively did trust him. She knew he would never intentionally do anything to hurt her. It'd been a long time since she'd felt that way about any man. Wait. She'd never felt this way about any man. She was in trouble—big trouble.

♥♥♥

Ethan couldn't think of any place he'd rather be than there with Hannah.

He had a good feeling about today. He smiled. It was going to be a great day.

As they waited to enter the mansion, he chanced a glance her way. He got a warm sensation in his chest. He wasn't willing to examine what it meant. Because he wasn't staying in Bluestar. And there was no way Hannah would leave her brand-new bakery—her dream. And he couldn't blame her.

He glanced away, turning his attention to their objective for today: finding fixtures for the showroom that added character to the bakery. He hadn't been sure exactly what Hannah had envisioned for the décor, but from the doorway, he could see inside the house and there appeared to be some beautiful things.

As they neared the entrance of the mansion, they had to register for the auction. Hannah insisted that she would register herself as these purchases were for her bakery. Ethan worried that the bids might go higher than she could afford and as a backup plan, he also registered. When Hannah questioned his actions, he said he might see something to bid on for his mother, which was a possibility.

Buzz. Buzz.

There was no one he wanted to speak with at the moment—except Hannah. Still, a sense of responsibility had him checking the caller ID. It was his mother. He considered calling her back but it might be something about his aunt.

"Sorry," he said to Hannah, "I have to get this. It's my mother."

"No problem."

He stepped away and pressed the phone to his ear. "Hey, Mom, I can't talk."

"So it's true. You're on a date."

His mother never used to know anything about his social life that he hadn't told her. It would seem that had changed since he'd been on the island.

He lowered his voice. "And who told you that?"

"A little birdie." His mother's tone carried a note of amusement.

He wasn't so amused with everyone knowing his business. "I do need to go."

"I hope you have a great time on your date."

"It's not—" He stopped himself in time. He didn't want Hannah to overhear and read too much into what he said. Because he wasn't quite certain what to call this outing. Was it a date? More importantly, did he want it to be a date? He had no answers.

He ended the call and returned to Hannah's side. "Sorry. It was my mother checking in."

There were unspoken questions reflected in Hannah's eyes. "Is everything all right?"

"Uh-huh. Just Mom being Mom."

Slowly the people in front of them moved inside. The auction had garnered a big turnout. That wasn't necessarily a bad thing. It all depended on what everyone was interested in bidding on. He just hoped it wasn't the same items that interested Hannah.

Stepping into the spacious foyer, Ethan craned his neck to look around. The owners had definitely seen to its upkeep. The ceiling consisted of intricate and ornate plasterwork. And in the center was a giant chandelier. As his gaze slid down the wall, he took in the brass and crystal wall fixtures.

He hoped there would be something there that would fit Hannah's definition of elegant.

"How did you get us in here?" Hannah interrupted his thoughts. "This place is amazing. And I overheard someone mention that the estate sale was by invitation only."

"My mother is well-connected when it comes to antiques."

"Please thank your mother. This is amazing." Hannah's gaze continued to take in every detail of the estate.

He failed to mention that he might have persuaded his mother with a bit of begging to get a most-sought-after invitation. It had certainly piqued his mother's curiosity as he usually avoided these things by using every excuse known to man. So when he'd written it off as needing some specific pieces for a project he was working on, she quickly put it together and assumed that it was for Hannah. It appeared his mother and Aunt Birdie had been talking—a lot. Perhaps too much. Definitely too much.

They walked through the spacious rooms. They were quiet for the most part, unless something caught Hannah's attention. Then she'd tap him on his arm and lift up on her tiptoes to whisper in his ear. It was much like touring a museum.

In the dining room, Ethan noticed Hannah was no longer beside him. He stopped and turned. The dining room was crowded with people. Thankfully the furniture had been removed, allowing for greater mobility.

He had to lift up on his toes to peer over all of the people. Where could she have wandered off to? And why hadn't she said anything to him?

And then he spotted her standing in the center of the room. She hadn't meandered off at all. She'd merely stopped. He followed her gaze to the ceiling where there was a crystal and brass chandelier. Not nearly the size or impressiveness of the chandelier in the foyer. But this six-candle structure with all the crystal dangling from it had certainly caught Hannah's attention. By the way she was looking at it, he'd hazard a guess that she was in love with it.

He'd seen similar looks on his mother's face when she'd find a certain piece at an auction and just couldn't bear to leave without it—no matter the price. He'd also spent enough of his youth at auctions to know the piece would go for a much higher price than Hannah's lean budget could afford, even if she was to cut everything to the bare minimum.

It took time to work his way back through the crowd that was moving in the opposite direction. It was much like he imagined a fish felt trying to swim upstream. And yet with a bit of patience as he squeezed past a number of people, he was once more by her side.

"Find something you like?" he asked.

Hannah blinked as though she'd been lost deep in her thoughts. "What?"

"The chandelier—I take it you like it."

"Oh yes. It's beautiful." Her gaze moved back to it. "I think I'll bid on it."

He didn't want to ruin her good mood to let her know it would probably sell for a four-figure price. Instead he said, "Let's see what else we can find."

"Oh yes. We should keep moving," she said as though she wasn't aware of how long she'd been standing there or that he'd had to backtrack to reach her.

"Are you enjoying yourself?"

"I am." As they fell in step with the people around them, she said, "Thank you for bringing me here. I've never been to an auction before. But I wouldn't mind going to more."

"I'll have to put you in touch with my mother." He said it more as a sort of joke than anything else.

"I wonder how your mother would feel about having a tag-along. I could keep adding to the features of the bakery, a little at a time."

She liked the idea of hanging out with his mother? He swallowed hard. He never thought she'd take him up on the

144

offer. Mary had gone one time to an auction with his mother and afterward swore she'd never go again. His mother was quite fine with that decision.

"But of course, it'd never work, what with your mother living in New York and I'm in Bluestar."

He let out a pent-up breath. "Yeah, that's quite a commute."

"Still, if she were on the island visiting Birdie and had a local auction, you can count me in."

"I...I'll let her know."

All of this time he'd been thinking that once he returned to his life in New York that he'd never see Hannah again, but that wasn't quite true. Aunt Birdie would keep drawing them back into each other's orbits. Not that it changed their circumstances. But still he liked the thought of having Hannah in his life, even if it was only occasionally.

She tapped his arm. "I think it's time to take our seats."

He glanced around, finding people rushing to the expansive living room where the auction was to be held. "I think you're right."

By the time they got to the room, there was only seating left in the back of the room. "I'm sorry."

Hannah's fine brows drew together. "For what?"

"Not thinking about grabbing our seats while you looked around."

"It's not like I thought of it either."

"So did you see anything you want to bid on?" He already knew the answer just by watching the expressions on her face as they'd passed through the various rooms.

"Oh yes. More than I can possibly afford. But thanks to you and your cost-cutting suggestions for the renovations, I'm hoping I can afford a couple of things." She held up her hand and crossed her fingers for luck.

Just then a man in a dark suit and tie stepped up to the podium in front of the room. Next to him was a giant screen displaying the auctioneers company name.

He welcomed everyone and then he got straight to business. The items were displayed on the screen as well as listed in the brochure they were given upon registering for the auction.

There were so many items from the twenty-one-room mansion. Numerous times Hannah started to bid on an item, only to drop out as the price quickly escalated. He felt bad for her. He knew what it was like to want something so much and not to be able to afford it. Ethan thumbed through the brochure, looking for the dining room chandelier. He had some savings. He'd hoped to own his own house by now, but with the real estate prices in New York, he was still saving money. Perhaps he'd spend a bit of it today.

"I won the bid on some ornate vintage brass plate covers." She smiled, looking pleased with herself. "That was so fun. I want to bid again."

He laughed softly. "That's awesome. They'll look amazing in the bakery."

"Now I need something else to go with them. Like that chandelier. I have a little bit of money I made from a couple of cake sales the past week. I could add that money to what I have in the bakery budget."

He nodded in agreement. He just had this sinking feeling it wouldn't be enough.

"It would look amazing in the center of the room. And with the bakery's high ceilings, there would be plenty of room to hang it without having to worry about anyone bumping their heads on it. Right?"

He gave it some thought. "I'm not sure without actual measurements. But you could always put a display table beneath it."

"Oh, I love that idea. It'd be a real show piece." Her smile made her eyes twinkle like jewels. "I can already imagine it. This is going to be so much better than the images I sketched in my notebook."

A pang of guilt started in his chest. He shouldn't be getting her hopes up. She had no chance of having the winning bid on such a fine chandelier. But he couldn't help but get caught up in her excitement. It was contagious. And she was right. It would give the bakery some flair.

He was beginning to envision Hannah as some sort of princess baker and the bakery would be her palace. He smiled at the image of her wearing a tiara with a smudge of flour on her cheek and a spatula in her hand as some sort of scepter. He wanted this all to work out for her—for her dream to come true. At least one of them knew exactly what they wanted and was going after it.

He focused back on the brochure. At last, he found the chandelier. It was a dozen or so items down the list. Not long now. And so he patiently waited, which was unusual for him. In the past, he'd never had the patience for these sales that could go on for hours. He'd rather be out doing something physical. Sitting around just wasn't something he was good at but seeing the joy this event brought Hannah was changing his mind...just a bit. Maybe accompanying her to auctions once in a while wouldn't be so bad.

And then at last it was time to bid on the chandelier. Hannah jumped into the fray right from the start. Her bid sheet with her number went up and down. Sometimes her hand didn't even make it the whole way down to her lap before it shot back up in the air.

Then just as he'd predicted the price started climbing into the four figures. At first, Hannah kept bidding into the low four-figures, but he knew even that was too much for her. And then with a distinct sigh, her bid sheet came to rest in her lap. When the auctioneer prompted her to bid some more, she reluctantly shook her head. Her eyes reflected her utter disappointment.

Without thinking Ethan raised his hand. The auctioneer accepted his bid. And moved on to the other bidding parties of which there were now two.

"What are you doing?" Hannah asked. "You can't bid on it. I don't have that kind of money."

Before he had a chance to answer her, he was raising his hand again. There was this driving need within him to do this—to win the auction. Because Hannah was right. It would be the show stopper in the bakery.

"Ethan, stop. You can't do this."

And yet he kept bidding. And bidding. They were now down to him and one other party. He just wanted it to be over.

Ethan called out a substantial increase in the price, hoping it would be enough to knock the other bidder out of the running. The auctioneer turned to the other party. He called once, twice, three times.

"Sold!"

Ethan breathed his first easy breath since the bidding had begun. Quite honestly it was the first time he'd ever bid on anything, and he had to admit that there was a bit of a rush to it.

He turned to Hannah. "We did it."

She had her arms crossed as her distinct frown doused his exuberant mood. "No. You did it."

"But I did it for you."

"And I told you I can't pay you for it. I hope you and your chandelier will be happy together."

She was mad at him? His elated mood quickly deflated. He hadn't meant to overstep. He'd let himself get caught up in her vision. Surely she wouldn't stay mad at him. He hoped.

CHAPTER FIFTEEN

She couldn't believe what he'd done.

Hannah was still upset with Ethan for stepping in and bidding on the chandelier.

They now sat quietly in Birdie's room as Ethan visited with his aunt. They'd previously planned to stop by on their way back to the island. And though she was upset with Ethan, she wouldn't deprive Birdie of seeing her great-nephew just because Hannah was anxious to put some distance between herself and Ethan.

As Birdie and Ethan discussed Peaches, Hannah sat quietly by. She tried to figure out why his action had upset her so much. Some women would be over-the-top excited to have a handsome man make an extravagant purchase on their behalf.

But the thing was Ethan hadn't even talked to her about bidding on the chandelier before he'd done it. He took it upon himself to decide what would make her happy, just like her ex used to do.

Brad had decided in what manner she should spend her money. He said the beach house would make her happy. He'd decided they should marry immediately. It would make her happy. He'd decided they should start a family right away. She'd love being a mother. And through it all, he hadn't discussed it with her.

Just like her father had decided many years ago that being a firefighter wasn't for her. He didn't discuss it with her. He'd just said that there were a lot of other things she could do with her time.

She didn't need another man in her life to decide things for her. But what was done was done, and she was pretty certain Ethan couldn't use a big, beautiful chandelier. And so now she had to figure out how to come up with enough money to pay him back.

As it was, she'd bid on one other thing. It was something that only one other person wanted. It was an old mirror that had been cracked. The gold paint on the frame was worn and chipped. In other words, it was a mess. But she could see the beauty in it. And when the bidding started so low, she just couldn't resist bidding on it. She got it for less than a hundred dollars. Not too shabby.

If only the chandelier had been that cheap, she wouldn't be worrying about how to pay Ethan back. She'd had to scale back her baking orders in order to make room for planning the Spring Fling, but at this point most of it was now planned. Maybe it was time to put word out that she was open for more orders—a lot more orders. That chandelier was far from cheap.

Chime. Chime.

Everyone grew quiet at the sound of a cell phone going off. Aunt Birdie sent Ethan a disapproving look.

"It wasn't me," he said.

"It's me. Sorry." Hannah reached into her purse and withdrew her phone. "I'll mute it." When she glanced at the screen, her mouth gaped.

Ethan grew concerned. "What's wrong?"

"Nothing." Hannah smiled. "Awe... My niece's goat just had a baby. Nikki sent a picture." Hannah turned her phone for his aunt to see. "It's a black pygmy goat. It's a little boy. And she named it Dash."

"It's so tiny," Aunt Birdie said. "And totally adorable."

"It'll grow quickly." Hannah moved the phone so he could look too.

"I take it this isn't the first baby goat." He gazed at the photo of mother and baby.

Hannah moved her finger rapidly over the screen messaging her niece back. "My brother probably wishes those were his only two goats. Why? Are you looking to adopt?"

Ethan held his hands up. "Not me. I don't think my landlord would approve."

"You don't know what you're missing. They are so cute. My brother's late wife loved animals. So they have a menagerie of animals including miniature goats. Who knows what they'd planned to get after that, but then Nikki came along. Not long after that we lost my sister-in-law."

They offered their condolences.

Hannah was anxious to move on from that sad subject. She focused on Birdie. "I should have brought the plans for Spring Fling. I was in such a rush this morning that I forgot them. I'm sorry."

"No worries, dear. I'd rather hear the details from you than to look at a bunch of papers." Birdie sent her a reassuring smile.

And so Hannah filled her in on the plans. Birdie offered some helpful pointers here and there. But she seemed to like what Hannah had done—what she and Ethan had done.

"There's only one problem," Hannah said.

"What's that?" Birdie asked.

"The prizes. I know in the past you've offered some lovely gift baskets and a weekend at an exclusive B&B in the mountains, but two of the companies that you ordered from are out of business."

"Oh, I see." Birdie frowned. She turned to Ethan. "What do you think we should do?"

"I, uh, would need to think about it." Ethan's brow scrunched up as though he were hard at thought.

"Good. You think about it," Aunt Birdie said. "You're in charge of the prizes."

"I...I am." Ethan shifted uncomfortably in his chair. "I don't think that's a good idea."

"The way I see it," Birdie said, "Hannah has done more than her share of the planning. You don't want to dump all of the work on her, do you?"

151

Hannah wasn't so sure how she felt about putting Ethan in charge of something so important to the festival. But who was she to argue with the woman who was technically the head of the festival?

"No. Of course not." He had the decency to look a bit sheepish.

But if he was getting lectured about letting her do the bulk of the festival planning that meant she needed to do more around the bakery. After all, she knew how to sand and paint. The only problem was that she'd have to spend more time with Ethan. And right now, that was the last thing she wanted to do.

In fact, maybe they just needed to part ways. Surely, he was far enough along with the renovations that she could take over. Mentally she listed all of the things that still needed to be done at the bakery—the floors were missing, the walls weren't painted, and the new display cases needed to be installed. She kept ticking off things on the ever-growing list. It was quite intimidating. Maybe taking over the renovations wasn't such a good idea after all.

"You'll need to get those prizes to Lily so she can print up some new flyers ASAP. It'll help stir up some excitement for the festival," Hannah said.

He had this deer-in-head-lights look. "I...I'll do that."

"Oh good." Birdie clapped her hands together. "Things are coming together. I want you to know how much I appreciate this. With you two taking care of everything back home, I can concentrate on healing."

So much for going her separate way from Ethan. Like it or not, for the time being they were stuck together.

There was something wrong.

There was a distinct undercurrent of tension in the room.

Aunt Birdie frowned. Usually she was good at ferreting out problems, but Hannah and Ethan were being mum about what was going on between them. Had she been wrong about them?

She didn't think so. They'd make a great couple, if they'd just let down their guards. And there was still time for that to happen. Spring Fling wasn't for three weeks. Anything could happen in that time.

"Ethan, there's something else," Birdie said.

"What is it?"

"It's my tulips." She currently had Betty looking after them, but she clearly needed to get Ethan more engaged with the festival. "I'm worried about them."

"Your what?"

"My tulips. Weren't you listening?"

He nodded. "I was but I'm not sure what you're trying to tell me."

"The Bloomin' Tulips Contest is coming up soon. And I'm determined to beat Agnes Dewey this year. She's won the contest for the past four years." Birdie frowned. Bragging rights in Bluestar were extremely important. Because listening to Agnes brag for three hundred and sixty-five days was just not right. "Agnes makes sure everyone knows she has the best tulips in town."

"There's a contest for tulips?"

She frowned at him. "I thought you were working on the plans with Hannah."

"I am. Well, kind of." His gaze lowered. "I've been a little busy with the bakery."

So she noticed. Maybe that was the problem. They weren't spending enough time together. Maybe if she was home, she could push them together more. But she just as quickly dismissed that idea because if she was home, she'd have to take over the festival plans.

"Ethan, the Bloomin' Tulip contest is a Bluestar tradition. It's been going on for years. And this year I was hoping to

153

win it. I've been working hard to have the biggest and brightest blooms. I even have a secret ingredient."

"A secret ingredient?" Ethan's brows scrunched together. "It sounds more like you are baking the flowers rather than growing them."

She pursed her lips together. He wasn't taking this seriously. She needed him to take the festival seriously or he wouldn't invest himself in the plans—in spending more time with Hannah. "Are you listening?"

"Yes. I'm listening."

"Good. Then when you get home, this is what I want you to do." And then she started to tell him about her watering schedule. Then she waved them both closer, afraid that someone in the hospital might overhear them. "I add coffee grounds once a week. And not just any coffee grounds." She went on to tell them exactly what coffee grounds to buy and how much to add to the ground. "Don't forget."

Ethan nodded. "Don't worry. I'll take care of your tulips."

"Thank you." She smiled at both of them. "I don't know what I'd do without both of you."

"You'll never have to find out," Ethan said. "I'm only a phone call away."

"And I'm just down the road from you," Hannah said. "When you get home, I can be there to help you out."

"That's so sweet of you both."

Already her mind had moved on. The tulips and the prizes were not enough to pull these two together. She would need a little time to think of another way to open their eyes. They were both so stubborn. Why couldn't they see what was right in front of them?

"I have one other thing." Birdie waved them toward her. Then she lowered her voice so as not to be overheard. "I'd like to bring a little springtime cheer to everyone here at Sunny Days. But it's a big ask so it'll need both of you to make it work."

Ethan looked a bit hesitant. "What do you have in mind?"
"Easter baskets." She smiled.

CHAPTER SIXTEEN

It was party time.

And yet Hannah lacked enthusiasm. Things with Ethan were still tense. And she didn't know how to fix it. She wasn't even sure she wanted to fix it.

She pushed the troubling thoughts of Ethan to the back of her mind. Tonight was about celebrating her new friend's upcoming nuptials. She was so happy for Amelia. Just because Hannah's engagement to Brad hadn't worked out didn't mean she'd give up on true love—at least not for others.

But right now, she had a big decision to make. What to wear to the party?

She'd messaged both Lily and Josie. Both let her know they were wearing dresses and heels. To be honest, there weren't a whole lot of reasons to get dressed up on the island. Bluestar was known for its casual, relaxed atmosphere. Usually the only reason for getting fancy was for either weddings or funerals. Thankfully this was the former.

Hannah examined her small collection of dresses—twice. She wanted to wear her newer pink shimmery dress, but she didn't want to outdo the bride. She placed it back in her closet. Instead she pulled out an aqua dress. The hemline stopped a couple inches above her knees. It had a wide shimmery belt, a V-neckline and cap sleeves. It was fun but modest. Perfect for the wedding shower.

She had to get moving. She'd already delivered the cupcakes but she'd promised Lily and Josie that she'd return early and help them with the final touches.

Hannah yawned. Maybe she should have another coffee, but as she checked the time, she realized it was much too late to make one. She'd be fine.

She grabbed her purse and coat and slipped on her black heels. Pulling the door shut behind her, she turned and rushed down the stairs. She rushed into the bakery to make sure everything was turned off before she left and came to an abrupt halt.

There was Ethan sanding the wall. He didn't seem to notice she was standing there watching him. He moved the hand sander with smooth strokes up the wall. He didn't deviate. Each stroke was in the same direction. She found herself incapable of turning away. She continued to stare. When he lowered the sandpaper to his side, the silence jarred her back to reality. She wasn't ready to deal with him. Not tonight.

She just needed to quietly back away.

He turned. "Hannah wait."

She froze. Not sure what to say, she remained silent.

His mouth opened but no words came out. His widened gaze skimmed down over her dress. Heat swirled in her chest before rushing up her neck and settling in her cheeks.

"Wow! You look nice." His gaze finally met hers.

"Thanks." She momentarily forgot she was still upset with him. "I...I didn't think you were working tonight. Don't you have plans with Greg?"

He nodded. "We're going to watch hockey, but that isn't until a little later. I thought I could get some work done before then." He set aside his hand sander. "Listen, about earlier today at the auction, I'm sorry. I saw how much you wanted the chandelier and I thought I was helping. I didn't mean to overstep."

His apology meant a lot to her. It was so much more than Brad had ever done. Perhaps she'd been a bit defensive.

She eyed him warily. "You won't do it again?"

He held up his hand. "I swear not to overstep again."

She breathed easier as the tension in her neck loosened. "Thank you. I appreciate it. And honestly I'm thrilled to have the chandelier." Her gaze moved to the spot where it would hang. "It will look so fancy in here."

"So I'm allowed to hang it?" His gaze searched hers.

"As long as I can pay you for it."

He nodded. "But there's no rush."

"I appreciate it. I'd feel better if I could pay you back before you leave town. I'm taking on more baking orders." It wouldn't be enough money, but it was a start. "Are you sure I can't do anything to help you before I leave?"

He smiled. "With you dressed like that? I don't think so."

She glanced down at her dress. He did have a point. "I just feel guilty—"

"Don't. Go have a good time. I won't be here that long."

"If you're sure—"

"I am."

"You aren't going to need the cart tonight, are you?" Since she rarely drove it, she'd made her golf cart available to him while he was working on the bakery.

"I'm good."

"Okay. Just make sure everything is turned off before you leave."

"I will, Mom." He sent her a big teasing grin. "Hey, I'm not that bad, am I?"

"No. You're just right. Now go before you're late."

She checked the time. He was right. She had three minutes to get there. "Okay. Bye." She bent over and fussed over Peaches again. "Goodnight, girl."

She rushed out the door. The golf cart was parked behind the bakery. Thankfully, she didn't have far to go as the Purple Guppy was on Surfside Drive just across from Beachcomber Park.

The outside of the pub was painted purple with big plate glass windows in the front, giving the passersby a glimpse of the purple, black, and white décor with the massive aquariums that were placed throughout the dining room. Cartoon fish were painted on the walls. It was a fun and popular spot for regulars and visitors alike.

By the time she arrived, there was one parking spot left. She slipped her golf cart into the space and rushed inside.

They'd rented out the party room in the back of the pub. Lily and Josie were already there.

"What can I do?" Hannah asked.

When both of her friends turned to her with grins, she immediately glanced down to make sure her dress hadn't ridden up. Nope. Everything appeared to be in its proper place.

Hannah glanced up to find her friends rushing over to her. *Oh no.* This wasn't going to be good.

"So tell us," Josie said.

"Yes, tell us everything." Lily's eyes lit up with interest. "And don't leave anything out."

"Tell you about what?" Hannah knew exactly what they were talking about, but she needed a little time to sort her thoughts.

"About your date with Ethan," Josie said. "How was it?"

"It wasn't a date." Hannah's voice was firm, but inside she had to wonder if that was the truth. Because there were points during the day when she'd certainly felt like it was a date. But perhaps that was just a bit of an overactive imagination. And then she recalled how he'd overstepped with the chandelier. Her mood dimmed.

"Sure it wasn't." Lily's sing-song voice let everyone know she didn't buy Hannah's denial.

"Okay, just between us...maybe it was a little like a date." Hannah couldn't keep it from her best friends. She needed their input. "Maybe it was a lot like a date."

"Did he kiss you?" Josie asked.

Hannah shook her head.

"No biggie. I've seen the way he looks at you," Josie said. "He's totally into you. He's just not rushing things."

"But it wasn't all good." She told them about their tense moment.

"He was just trying to do something nice for you," Lily said. "It was sweet of him."

159

"He definitely overstepped," Josie said. "It wasn't like he bought flowers. It was an expensive chandelier."

As her friends debated the situation, Hannah sighed. "It's okay. We worked things out."

"You did?" Josie looked surprised.

Hannah nodded. "He meant to do something nice for me and I overreacted, thinking he was making decisions for me like Brad used to do. But we talked about it."

"And we can still like him?" Lily asked.

Hannah smiled. "Yes, you can. Enough about me. We have a party to set up."

They got to work, placing the beach decorations that included colorful sunglasses and seashell-shaped chocolates for favors, as well as some beach balls to bounce around the room. It should be a fun evening for all.

"How was your date?" Hannah's mother rushed into the room.

Hannah's heart lodged into her throat. Had her mother overheard their conversation? Surely not. Her mother wasn't the type to eavesdrop.

Hannah turned to her mother. "What are you talking about?"

"The whole town is abuzz about your date with Ethan. You didn't know?"

"No." Heat scorched Hannah's cheeks. "The whole town?"

Her mother nodded. "Hank from the ferry told Agnes and well, Agnes told everyone and anyone who would listen."

"Of course she did." Hannah frowned. She wasn't sure what was going on between her and Ethan, but she didn't know how they were supposed to figure it out if all of Bluestar were watching them. There were a few drawbacks to living in a small town. This was one of them.

The excited voices of arriving guests and the bride-to-be echoed through the pub. Through the open doorway, Hannah spotted Amelia in a short white lacy dress. But it was her

160

sunny smile and the sparkle in her eyes that gave her a warm glow of happiness. Every bride should look that way before their wedding.

Hannah didn't recall ever looking that happy with Brad. That should have been her clue that the relationship hadn't been right for her. It might have taken her a while to figure it out, but at least she'd done so before saying *I do*.

Ethan made her happy—most of the time. She'd been impressed with his earlier apology. As her thoughts rewound in time back to the way he'd looked at her—like she was the most beautiful woman in the world—her heart beat faster. No one had ever made her feel that way before. But where did they go from here?

It was a good evening.

Not as good as spending it with Hannah, but it wasn't bad at all.

Ethan lounged back on the couch in Greg's living room. A hockey game played on the big screen television. And a big red and white pizza box sat on the coffee table.

It was nice to hang out with a friend. He might not have known Greg for years but they had an easy rapport—as though they'd always known each other.

"You know," Greg said, "if you were planning to hang around the island for a while, I could use some help remodeling the kitchen."

"You think?"

"You can't open the fridge and the dishwasher at the same time. And some of the cabinet doors are coming off the hinges."

"I'd like to help but as soon as the bakery is completed. I've got to get back to work."

"I'm just saying I've seen what you've done at the bakery, and I'm not rich or anything but I could pay you something."

The thing was that the idea of starting over as a contractor was tempting. His mind already conjured up a new layout that would make the kitchen a lot more functional. But the logical part of his brain said that stepping out on his own without benefits was a risky proposition—not to mention how disappointed his father would be in him.

"I'll keep it in mind." Ethan finished off a third slice of pizza. "This is good."

"You mean you've been here all of this time and haven't tried the Pizza Pie?"

"Is that the little shop on the edge of town?" When Greg nodded, Ethan said, "Hannah got us a veggie pizza from there."

"They make the best food in all of Bluestar." Greg lounged back in his recliner.

"I don't know about that. The Lighthouse is good."

"But I'm talking pizza. Theirs is the best pizza on the island. Probably the best in all of Boston. If you don't believe me, ask your girlfriend."

Immediately Hannah's image came to mind. He dismissed it. "I don't have a girlfriend."

"That's not what I hear."

Ethan wasn't one to listen to gossip, but if it involved him and Hannah, perhaps he should know what rumors were circulating around town.

He swallowed hard. "What have you heard?"

"That you and Hannah had a date in Boston. And that you're permanently moving to Bluestar."

Wow! How do these things get started? He had one guess: Agnes Dewey. He'd only had to meet that woman once to know what she was like.

"It's not true." Ethan forced himself to lean back on the couch and not let the unfounded rumors get to him.

162

"So you didn't take the ferry this morning with Hannah?"

"Well, yes but—"

"And you didn't spend the day with her?"

"Yes but—"

"And did you enjoy your time together?"

"Yes but—"

"Then it sounds like a date to me."

"But it was work. I mean we went to an estate sale together to find things for the bakery."

"And?" Greg arched a brow.

"And...it wasn't a date."

"What is a date?"

"You know." Why was Greg being so difficult? He'd expect this from one of Hannah's girlfriends but he hadn't expected it from Greg. "Dates are dinner and a movie and that kind of stuff."

"I don't know. I kind of think a date is spending time together and enjoying yourselves. And that sounds like it's what you and Hannah shared today."

It was true. They had had a great time. It was so good he wouldn't mind doing it again. But was it the beginning of something? He wasn't so sure about that. And he wasn't ready to examine it too closely right now because his life felt like one big question mark.

"Anyway"—Greg's voice interrupted his thoughts—"I just wanted to let you know that my offer still stands to help out at the bakery. If you can show me what to do, I can do it. In fact, the whole fire department wants to help out. Between you and me, I think they're anxious to get the bakery open so they can get some more of Hannah's cupcakes on a regular basis."

"Thanks. I'll let you know if I need the help." He appreciated the offer, but he felt like he was cheating on his agreement with Hannah if he was to take outside help. After all, she was doing most of the Spring Fling plans on her own. But he tucked the offer in the back of his mind.

His thoughts turned to Hannah. He wondered how the shower was going. She sure looked radiant tonight. He wanted to rush back to the bakery in the hopes of running into her again, but that would be rude to his new friend, and besides he'd see her tomorrow. Why did that seem so far away now?

CHAPTER SEVENTEEN

Lunch at the farm.

An unexpected invitation.

After the debacle at the auction, Ethan had been worried that he'd permanently messed things up with Hannah. But then she'd surprised him by accepting his apology. Mary had never been that quick at forgiving him.

And then this morning, Hannah had surprised him with an invitation to join her at her brother's farm to meet the baby goat and have lunch. He didn't have the time with so much to do at the bakery, but when he opened his mouth, he uttered his agreement.

Pre-accident him never would have agreed to a leisurely morning and lunch when there was so much work awaiting him. Mary used to accuse him of being a workaholic. He'd denied it. To him a workaholic was someone who constantly found things to do. He didn't seek out his obligations; they'd somehow always found him.

But now post-accident him was finding that obligations didn't have to consume every minute of every day. There was time to enjoy life—to enjoy his time with Hannah.

There was one catch. On this Sunday morning, Hannah was planning to ride her bike to the farm. He hadn't ridden a bicycle in years.

Ethan had worried he wouldn't remember how to do it. But it appeared the saying about riding a bike is true, he picked it up right away. And thanks to Greg, he was able to borrow his bike in order to accompany Hannah to the farm.

The sun shone brightly overhead, drying up the dampness from the showers overnight. Ethan pedaled around on the road in front of the bakery, missing the puddles as he waited for Hannah to join him.

Who'd have thought a small New England island would have a farm, but it actually had more than one farm. The farms surrounded the town of Bluestar with a lighthouse at each end of the crescent-shaped island.

He learned all of this from the informational pamphlet at the visitor's center by the dock. You had to do something while waiting for the ferry, and so he read the pamphlets they offered tourists.

Speaking of waiting, it was time to leave. What was taking Hannah so long?

And then as though his thoughts had conjured her up, Hannah came around the side of the building with her perky pink bike. By the smile on her face, she either loved riding her bike or she was anxious to see her family. Probably it was a bit of both. But there was a part of him that wished the brilliant smile lighting up her eyes was all for him.

"Are you ready to go?" he asked.

"Of course." She took off on her bike. "I thought you were never going to get here," she called over her shoulder.

Wait. What? He took off after her, easily catching up to her. "I was the one waiting for you."

"No. You're the one that had to drop Peaches off at Betty's and then go to Greg's place to borrow his bike. And while you were gone, I was able to get the last judge we needed for the Bloomin' Tulip Contest."

"That's great, who did you get?"

"The pastor's wife. She was more than willing to do it."

"Good. But I've been out here riding around in circles waiting for you."

"I had to wait first. You were gone so long that I got distracted with your project." Hannah led the way south out of town. She pedaled along at a modest pace. "You were gone forever."

He kept pace with her as he consulted his fitness watch. "I was only gone fifteen minutes, sixteen tops."

She sent him an impish smile. "More like a half hour." She flashed him a teasing smile. "Here's a bit of Bluestar trivia—this is the main road that stretches from the northern tip of the island to the southernmost point."

"I bet it makes giving directions easy."

"It really does." She was quiet for a bit. Then she glanced his way. "I think you and Sam will hit it off."

"We already did when we met at the..." He hesitated, not wanting to mention the flood and ruin her good mood.

"It's all right. You can say it—at the flood. I've moved on and am looking forward to the grand opening. Everything is starting to come together, thanks to you and the estate sale. We found some great pieces that should add some character to the bakery."

He was relieved to hear her so upbeat. "Yes, we did." He thought of her drawings in her notebook. "Is it okay that it won't look exactly like you imagined?"

She nodded. "It's going to look better."

He suddenly felt some serious pressure to get this remodel just right. He swallowed hard. "Don't get your hopes up too high."

She glanced over at him. "Are you worried you aren't up to it?"

She was daring him? Him? He was never one to turn down a challenge, whether it was on an obstacle course or a marathon. He was always pushing himself to do things better and faster.

"Not at all. Let's do this." The words were uttered before he realized he was only succeeding in raising her hopes and if he didn't pull it off, she'd be crushed again. And this time, it would be all his fault.

"Don't look so worried." She sent him a reassuring smile. "I know you can do it."

Not wanting to think of the bare walls and floors awaiting him back at the bakery, he turned his thoughts back to their adventure on this sunny spring day. "So this farm we're going to, is it big?"

Hannah nodded. "It used to belong to my grandparents. Now my brother and his daughter live there."

Ethan wondered how her niece's mother had died, but he didn't want to overstep. Instead he went in another direction. "Who'd have thought a small island like this would have a farm on it?"

"The majority of the island is farm land."

"And beautiful land it is." He gazed out at the Atlantic as the two-lane road snaked its way closer to the shoreline.

"I totally agree. And so do a bunch of vacationers who return here year after year."

They rode along in the warm sunshine. And then he heard something. He listened closer. It was then he noticed it was Hannah and she was humming. The sound was catchy.

"What's that you're humming?"

She glanced over at him. "Oh. Sorry."

"No. I like it. Really."

Her cheeks pinkened. "There was a song on the radio this morning, and now I can't stop the lyrics from playing over and over in my mind."

He nodded in understanding, though he could honestly say he'd never had a song stuck in his head. He actually preferred silence when he was working. "Don't stop on my account. I liked it."

"You did?"

He smiled and nodded. She had the sweetest voice. But he noticed that as they continued to ride on, she remained silent. He'd made her self-conscious and for that he was sorry.

A little way down the road, Ethan slowed his bike. "Do you mind if we stop?"

"Not at all."

They both climbed off their bikes and left them at the side of the quiet road. They made their way over to the bluffs that looked down upon the rocky shoreline as the ocean came crashing against the rocks before rolling back out to sea.

Ethan moved to one of the large rocks and sat down. Hannah joined him.

He drew in a deep breath of fresh salty air. And then he slowly blew it out. "You know it wasn't until I came to Bluestar that I could take an easy breath."

"The island does have healing qualities." Hannah's voice was soft but the ocean breeze carried her words to his ears. "I've spent a lot of time staring out at the water, wondering why bad things happen."

"Did you find any answers?"

She shook her head. "Only that time helps lessen the pain."

He'd noticed a plaque at the fire station for Chief George Bell, Hannah's father, who'd died in the line of service. "I'm sorry for your loss."

"My father was out on a call. It started as a brush fire but by the time the fire department arrived, the barn was on fire. There were horses inside the barn—they were crying out for someone to save them. My father was that someone. He went in to save the horses and..." Her voice cracked with emotion. "He got all of the horses out but before he could get out, the roof caved in..."

Ethan reached out, wrapping an arm around her shoulders and pulling her to his side. This explained why she'd been such a stranger around the firehouse. He wasn't sure how long they sat together, staring out at the power of the sea.

He had some idea of what her father had gone through, but luckily, Ethan had made it out of his near miss but not without the scars both inside and out. And this was just one more reason why it was best not to get caught up in a relationship. He didn't want to hurt someone the way Hannah's father's death had hurt his family.

She pulled back and gazed into his eyes. "Thank you. I don't normally fall apart like that. But then again, I don't normally talk about what happened to him."

"It's okay. I understand...probably more than most."

She nodded. "Because you're a firefighter too. How do you do it? How do you put your life on the line, time after time?"

He leaned on his hands that were stretched out behind him as he tried to come up with an answer that she wanted to hear. He was drawing a blank. He didn't think there was anything that would make this right for her.

"I can't speak for anyone else, but for me, it's a calling." When Ethan was trapped in the fire—when he thought he'd never make it out—the things he'd regretted were all of life's moments that he'd let slip by. Maybe that's why he was plagued with doubts about his career choice. Was firefighting still his calling?

"A calling?"

He shrugged. No one had ever asked him that question. And he wasn't quite sure how to answer her. "It always felt like I was where I belonged, doing what I was meant to do."

She frowned at him. "You don't sound convinced. I know you said you didn't want to be a paper pusher, but if you were to stay in your current position at the fire department, would you get restless? Or would you be content with the position?"

His thoughts turned to his latest on-the-job accident. It wasn't the only time he'd been hurt, but it was the worst. And he knew without his team's quick actions, it could have been so much worse. But he wasn't ready to discuss any of that. Not yet.

"I don't know." He got to his feet. He turned back to her and held his hand out to her. "We better keep going or we're going to be late for lunch."

Hannah hesitated for a moment, as though she wanted to continue their discussion, but then she placed her hand in his as he helped her to her feet. But when her foot landed on the uneven rocks, she lost her balance. He reached out to her. Both of his hands wrapped around her waist, and he drew her to him.

Their gazes connected and held. The breath caught in his lungs as he stared deeply into her green eyes. He was mesmerized by her. She was fiercely independent one moment but vulnerable in the next. And then there was her great big generous heart, not only for those she cared about but even for strangers like him.

He was drawn to her and he knew it was a mistake. He knew in the end they'd both get hurt. But as his heart beat louder, common sense was drowned out. His gaze dipped to her lips.

Would it be so wrong to kiss her? He'd been thinking about it for far too long. It wasn't like it would be the start of a relationship. It would just be a kiss. But was it possible to kiss Hannah just once?

And then in the next moment, Hannah extricated herself from his hold. "Sorry about that." Color filled her cheeks. "I'll have to be more careful in the future." She stepped away. "By the way, Amelia and Jake's wedding is coming up. Did you still want to go?"

Still? It took him a moment to vaguely remember agreeing to accompany her. He considered politely backing out. Weddings weren't his thing.

But when she looked at him with those pouty lips, how could he resist a chance to spend more time with her? "I guess so."

She grinned at him. "Don't worry. You'll have a great time."

Somehow, he doubted it.

He watched as she quickly made her way back to the bikes, as though worried if she lingered that he would change his mind. It took him a moment to gather his thoughts, and then he followed her. With her as his date, maybe the wedding wouldn't be so bad.

The rest of the ride was quiet...and a bit awkward.

Hannah was pretty certain Ethan had been planning on kissing her back at the bluff. And there was a part of her that wanted to feel the touch of his lips against her own. And there was this other part of her that was hesitant.

She felt as though once that door was opened between them, then there wouldn't be any going back. And she couldn't let herself get involved with a firefighter. But she'd noticed how Ethan didn't seem anxious to leave the island.

In fact, the longer he was there, the more he seemed to fit in. It was almost as though he'd always been an islander. But then again, that could just be her projecting her hopes onto him.

"We're here," Hannah called out as she turned her bike onto a gravel driveway.

"I don't see much." Ethan glanced around. "Wait. I didn't mean that the way it sounded. What I meant to say is—"

"It's okay. I know what you mean. The farm sits far back from the road. My grandparents liked it that way. It gave them a lot of privacy as quite a few tourists like to visit the lighthouse."

"Lighthouse? As in one?"

She nodded. "Only the lighthouse on the southern tip of the island offers tours. The northern lighthouse is privately owned and they don't offer tours."

The bike bounced over the dirt road until they pulled to a stop in front of a white two-story house with a sweeping front porch with a swing at one end. Hannah had spent many hours sitting on that swing next to her grandmother as they watched the sunset.

The windows were adorned with red shutters and the roof was red. When she was little, they'd been painted a bright aqua—her grandmother's favorite color. But when her brother took over the farm, he and his wife decided they wanted the house to have the same colors of the barn.

Off in the distance was the big old barn that was older than her. It was painted the opposite of the house as it was bright red with white trim. She'd always wanted to play in there, but her grandfather had insisted that a barn wasn't a place for little girls. He'd said that barns were for work, storage, and animals. She was forever being shooed away, but as she grew older, she understood the dangers that lurked within the barn.

Her brother made sure to keep the yard well-maintained, but she'd noticed that without his wife around to look after the flowers and shrubs, that he'd let those things go. The only thing that stood out in the yard now was the old oak tree with a rope swing. Her grandfather had put a similar one there for her. She remembered swinging on it for so long her fingers cramped, and she had a hard time straightening them.

"I take it you like it here." Ethan's voice drew her from her thoughts.

She blinked and glanced over at him. "What?"

"You're smiling. I take it this place has a lot of good memories for you."

"Yes, it does. Some of my best childhood memories were made here at the farm." Hannah honked her bike horn a couple of times. She noticed Ethan trying to smother a laugh. She feigned a frown. "Are you laughing at my horn?"

By now a smile was most definitely pulling at his lips as his eyes lit up with amusement. He shook his head as though he didn't trust opening his mouth or otherwise he'd break out into laughter.

When she glanced back at the porch with no sign of her niece or her brother, she honked the horn once more. "They must be out at the barn."

They parked their bikes. Hannah led the way to the barn. She wanted to head straight for the goat pen and see the newest edition, but she knew she had to wait for her niece to show her. She wouldn't do anything to intentionally disappoint Nikki.

173

As they rounded the corner of the house, she spotted Sam and Nikki heading toward them. A big smile pulled at Hannah's lips. Her family meant everything to her.

"Auntie Hannah!" Nikki ran toward her. When she reached her, she wrapped her arms around her. "I missed you."

"I missed you too." Guilt rained down over Hannah.

The truth of the matter was that while she'd been rushing to open the bakery, she hadn't spent time with her niece. She'd told herself that she would make it up to Nikki, but she was starting to wonder if her life would ever slow down enough for her to make room for everything and everyone she cared about.

The two men greeted each other and shook hands.

"Hey, Sam, thanks for the invitation," Hannah said, knowing her brother rarely entertained guests.

Sam stood there in his old baseball cap, flannel shirt, and work jeans, looking the same as always. "You know you're always welcome. Nikki could hardly sleep last night, she was so excited to show you her new goat."

"And I'm just as anxious to meet him." Hannah glanced around. "I thought Mom would be here."

"She is," Sam said. "She's inside making lunch."

Hannah nodded in understanding. Her mother loved to cook about as much as Hannah loved to bake. Between the two of them, holidays were an extravaganza of food.

Nikki moved to Hannah's side. She pointed to Ethan and whispered, "Who's he?"

"This is Ethan. He's visiting Bluestar to help his aunt. And now he's been generous enough to help me finish the bakery."

"Hi." Ethan knelt down to speak to Nikki on her level. "It's nice to meet you." He held his hand out to her.

Nikki hesitantly looked at Ethan's hand and then she turned to her father, who said it was okay. Only then did she place her petite hand in Ethan's. He gave her a big smile and a gentle handshake.

"So you're friends with Auntie Hannah?" Nikki asked.

"I am. Could I be your friend too?"

She didn't say anything at first. "Do you like goats?"

"Goats?" When she nodded, he said, "Yes, I do."

She smiled at his answer. "We can be friends." Then Nikki turned back to Hannah. "Can we have a sleepover?"

"I, uh, sure." It wasn't like she was capable of denying her niece anything.

"Soon?" Nikki's blue eyes implored her.

"Yes."

"Next week?"

Oh boy, her niece wasn't going to let this go without some firm plans. Between the bakery grand opening and planning Spring Fling, she didn't know how she was supposed to fit everything in.

"Nikki"—Sam stepped up to his daughter—"your aunt is busy. She doesn't have time for sleepovers right now."

Nikki's smile drooped. Is that how her brother saw her these days? She used to be the aunt who was always available for babysitting and fun days out. And now she was known for disappointing her niece. She had to do something to change things.

"We're going to have a sleepover," Hannah declared.

"Tonight?" Nikki's face looked hopeful.

"Not tonight." She watched as disappointment came over her niece's face. "Maybe in a couple of weeks when you have spring break."

"That's so far away," Nikki whined.

Oh, the difference between a child's perspective and an adult's. "It won't be that long and then we can have fun together."

Nikki looked at her hesitantly. "You promise?"

"Yes. I promise."

"Great. Let's go see the goats." Nikki took her hand and then she reached for Ethan's hand. "Come on!"

Ethan sent Hannah a surprised look over Nikki's head. She sent him a reassuring smile. They had to run-walk to keep up with Nikki. She was a bundle of excited energy.

Behind the house was a large fenced-in area that was surrounded by a split rail fence lined with chicken wire to keep the goats in. Inside the area was a field of lush green grass, trees for shade from the hot summer sun, and a couple of wood houses with ramps to the doorway for the goats.

There were a dozen or so goats inside the fencing. Hannah always loved visiting with them. They each had so much character. And if she didn't live in town, she'd have a goat or two of her own.

"There he is!" Nikki let go of their hands and rushed over to the fence. "Dash is the little black goat with the white spot on his forehead."

"He's so cute," Hannah said. "Can I hold him?"

Nikki smiled. "You can if you can catch him. He's fast."

"He earned his name," Sam said.

"He can't be that fast," Hannah challenged.

"Come on," Ethan said. "I'll help you get him."

"Okay, you're on," Hannah said because she wanted to hold that little baby.

"This should be interesting," Sam quipped.

Hannah led Ethan inside the fence while her niece and her brother leaned up against the fence, watching them.

"I've got him." Before Ethan could even lean over to reach for the baby goat, Dash rushed past him.

"I'll get him." Hannah tried to sneak up on him. She was just about to grab him, when he ran off.

From the fence, Nikki giggled and Hannah's brother let out a hearty laugh.

"We told you he earned his name," her brother called out.

She turned back to see Ethan tiptoe up behind the baby goat. He was almost there. He almost had the goat. But then

176

Dash sprinted away. Ethan ran after him. His foot hit a patch of mud. He slipped. He landed on his knees in a mud patch.

Hannah tried not to laugh. She honestly did. But when he stood with a couple of spots of mud on his face, muddy knees, and a big frown on his face, Hannah let out a laugh that bubbled up from deep inside. Once she started to laugh, she couldn't stop. It felt so good.

She hadn't realized until now just how stressed she'd been over finishing the bakery and planning Spring Fling. She'd let it all take over her life. But from this point forward, she promised herself to remember to take time for the fun parts of life.

"It's not funny." Ethan frowned as he tried to wipe off the mud only to make a worse mess.

"Would you guys like me to get him?" Nikki asked.

Hannah shook her head. "I don't think that's good idea."

"It's okay." Nikki marched over to the gate.

Hannah sent her brother a questioning look. Sam shrugged but didn't make any motion to stop his daughter. If he didn't care if Nikki got dirty, who was she to worry?

Ethan gave up trying to clean his jeans. "I'm done." He headed for the gate. "You ladies are on your own."

Meanwhile, Hannah moved to the older goats—the ones she'd already made friends with during prior visits. She fussed over them when they came over to her to see if she had something good to eat. Sometimes she had snacks for them, but today she'd been utterly distracted with the thought of having Ethan get to know her family and vice versa. But she didn't know what she'd been worried about; so far it was going great.

"Dash. Here Dash." Nikki's sing-song voice called to the baby goat.

Hannah turned to tell her niece the baby goat wasn't like a puppy, but before she could form the words, she noticed the little black goat stopped running around to turn and stare at Nikki. Surely he wasn't going to march over to her. Was he?

In the background, she could hear the two men talking. So far, so good. A smile tugged at her lips. When she realized she was smiling, she stopped. It wasn't like she wanted Ethan to fit into her family. Did she?

No, of course not. She was just being nice to him because none of his family were around and...and because they were friends now. After all, you didn't spill your feelings to a stranger like she'd just done out at the bluffs.

"Come on, Dash," Nikki's sweet voice called out.

It was then Hannah noticed some new construction going on in the background. It looked like a barn—a much smaller barn than the big red one that already existed. She took the expansion as a good sign that the farm was doing well. Her brother wasn't one to talk about his business, so she could only ever guess at how things were going for him.

When Hannah's gaze returned to her niece, she noticed Nikki approaching the baby goat. Hannah waited for him to run away. Instead the baby goat stood still. The next thing Hannah knew, Nikki was holding Dash and fussing over him. *Wow*! Hannah smiled. Her niece definitely had a way with the animals.

Nikki carried the goat over to Hannah. "Do you want to pet him?"

Hannah smiled and nodded. "Definitely." She ran her hand over the baby goat's head. "He likes you."

Nikki hugged Dash. "I like him too. I wish Auntie Em was here to see him."

"Me too." Hannah remembered when they were growing up, how her and her younger sister used to share so many things. Now they were so busy with their careers they didn't talk that often. That needed to change soon.

Hannah walked with Nikki over to the fence line where the men were still chatting. Nikki handed Hannah the baby goat. After Hannah *oohed and aahed* over him, she turned to her brother. "So what are you building?"

178

"Nikki insists the goats need a bigger home than their little houses," Sam said.

"They do!" Nikki nodded.

"And I'm thinking of expanding the goat business. We can talk more about it over lunch." Sam's gaze moved to the goat in her arms. "That is if you're ready to give up Dash."

"I suppose." Hannah fussed over him a little more before setting him down. He took off, scurrying back to his momma.

And then they were off to lunch, just like they all belonged together. Hannah reminded herself not to get too used to this because before long, Ethan would be long gone. But for now she intended to enjoy their time together.

CHAPTER EIGHTEEN

Weddings were to be avoided at all costs.

And yet somehow Hannah had convinced him to be her date—*erm, escort.*

A week after having lunch with Hannah and her family, Ethan was wearing a borrowed suit. He tugged at the collar. He glanced around at the other guests. Yep, still too early. A frown pulled at his lips.

With Hannah by his side, they were sitting at one of the long white tables. If he didn't know better, he'd probably believe the rumors going around Bluestar about them dating. After all, they spent every afternoon and evening together. Granted there was a lot of sanding and painting going on, but there was also a lot of talking and laughter. For the first time in a long time, he was happy.

A wedding guest bumped into him, jarring him from his thoughts. The town's community center was crammed full of dressed-up people; even the mayor was in attendance. Amelia and Jake were now officially Mr. and Mrs. Wilson. If it made them happy, then Ethan was happy for them. But he didn't envision marriage in his future.

As it was he wasn't even sure what career path he wanted to take. The more he worked with his hands—the more he remembered how much he used to enjoy being his maternal grandfather's apprentice—and the more he was torn about returning to his job in New York.

He once again tugged at the collar of his borrowed white dress shirt. It wasn't that he didn't love firefighting. It was in his blood. But he wasn't sure it was all he wanted to do with his life. But was it too late for him to change? Should he stick with what he knew best? Or take a chance on being his own boss and starting his own business?

Not worrying about what everyone else was doing, he loosened his tie and unbuttoned the top button on his shirt. He could breathe a little easier now. Hannah had to borrow the suit from her brother or he wouldn't have had a thing to wear. Luckily or unluckily, depending on how you looked at it, they were the same size.

Ethan's gaze moved to Hannah, who'd just finished speaking with the woman seated next to her. He recognized the face but he couldn't put a name to her. When a slow song started to play, Hannah's eyes lit up as a big smile came over her. *Oh no!* She wanted to dance. *No way!* It wasn't happening.

It wasn't that he didn't want to dance with her. In fact, the idea was quite tempting. The only problem was once he held her in his arms, his thoughts would drift to other things...like kissing her. And he was leaving in two weeks.

He cleared his throat. "I'm going to get a drink. Can I get you something?"

"I'll come with you."

They both got to their feet when her mother approached them. "There you are." Mrs. Bell smiled at both of them. "It's good to see you here, Ethan. I hope you're enjoying yourself."

He forced a smile to his lips. "I am."

No, he wasn't. Who was he kidding? This wedding just reminded him of his failure at relationships. And he hated to fail at anything.

Her mother turned back to her. "It's a shame your brother couldn't make it. He claimed he didn't have anyone to watch Nikki, but I think it's still too much for him. Losing Beth, well, you know."

Hannah's eyes reflected her sadness as she nodded. "It's going to take him more time."

"I know. I just hate seeing him so miserable."

Hannah gave her mother a hug. "We're all there for him—as much as he'll let us."

Her mother pulled away. "I'm sorry. I didn't mean to bring you down. Go dance."

181

Just then a bouncy tune started to play. Both Hannah and her mother suddenly smiled. Apparently they both liked the tune.

"You have to dance to this," her mother insisted.

"So do you." Hannah gave her mother a pointed look.

Her mother shook her head. "Oh no. Not me. My hip is beyond shaking my bootie."

Hannah arched a brow. "But I did see you out there earlier with Captain Campbell."

Did her mother blush? It sure looked like it to him. Was there something going on between Hannah's mother and the fire captain?

"It...it's not like that," Hannah's mother said.

"Uh-huh." Hannah turned to Ethan. "What do you think? Will you dance with me?"

Both mother and daughter stared at him. He shook his head. "I don't dance."

"Oh please." Hannah's pleading voice tore at his resolve. "Just this once."

"Go on you two before it's over."

He had a feeling that no matter what he said he wasn't going to win. So he might as well get this over with. "Okay."

Hannah took his hand and led him to the crowded dance floor. For a moment, he stood there and looked around at all of the other people dancing around them. Some were slightly swaying to the music. Others were waving their arms about and doing footwork like they belonged on a dance show.

He turned back to Hannah and found her already dancing. She swayed side to side. And then he noticed her lip-synching.

He listened for a moment to the song. It sounded familiar. It took a moment but then he realized where he'd heard it before. It was the same tune Hannah had been humming on their bike ride to the farm. She liked this song.

He couldn't help but smile and then he moved to the music. They definitely weren't award-winning dance steps, but they seemed to gain Hannah's approval.

♥♥♥

It was such a great night.

A wonderful night.

Hannah felt as though she were Cinderella, at least for tonight. Her problems seemed far away and she was letting herself get lost in the beauty of the evening. It didn't hurt that her escort cleaned up really well. Who was she kidding? Ethan's hotness degree was off the scale no matter what he wore. Still, she was enjoying seeing him in a suit and tie.

When the song ended, they moved off the dance floor toward the refreshments. He turned to her. "You like that song."

"I do." She beamed at him. "It's my sister's song."

"Your sister likes this song too?"

Hannah laughed. "She does. But what I meant is she is the one singing it. It's her debut recording."

He paused as it all came together. "Your sister is Em Bell?"

Hannah nodded. "That's her. She's in Nashville making her mark on the world."

"I vaguely remember last autumn when the men at the firehouse all gathered around the television to watch a singing competition."

"You mean *Songbird*. Emma won it last year. She says that she's going to be a one-hit wonder, but I think she's a rising star."

"With a voice like hers, I agree with you. I had no idea your sister is famous."

Hannah opened her mouth to say something but she was interrupted by Agnes Dewey. "It's hard to believe you two have time for dancing the night away when the town's biggest event is on the line."

Hannah turned to the woman. "Excuse me."

"It just seems to me that you've been doing everything but working on the festival. And I don't want to see a Bluestar tradition ruined." Agnes pursed her thin lips.

"I'm trying my best," Hannah said. "Everything is under control."

"I've heard prizes haven't been sorted. There aren't any tablecloths. Nor are there baskets for the children's Easter egg hunt. What have you been doing?"

Maybe she was behind on a few things, but she still had time to wrap up the details. It would all get done...eventually.

Ethan stepped forward. "I'll have you know that my aunt gave me the responsibility for the festival."

"And all you do is work on the bakery for her." Agnes pointed accusingly at Hannah.

Is that what everyone thought? Hannah's gaze moved to the people who'd gathered around to hear what was going on. Did they all think she would let them down? The thought dug at a tender spot in her chest.

Her father had always been one to step up and volunteer. He thought to be a good neighbor that you had to do for others. Tears stung the back of Hannah's eyes. In some small way that's what she'd been doing by helping to plan Spring Fling. Obviously not everyone saw it the same way.

"We're working hard on everything." An angry tone threaded through his voice.

"Perhaps on the bakery," Agnes said, "but can we trust that you're going to get the festival, right? You haven't even attended the festival."

Hannah fisted her hands at her sides as she struggled to maintain her composure. She stepped up to Agnes. "You complain a lot, but I don't see you volunteering to help."

Suddenly the air felt as though it'd been sucked from the room. Hannah's head began to throb. She needed to get out of there before she said something she'd regret. She needed some fresh air.

She turned and headed for the door. She could hear Ethan calling out to her but she kept going. Her pace didn't slow down. She kept going until she reached the twin benches on either side of the walk. It was there she sat down.

All of this time, she'd been so caught up in her own drama she hadn't noticed how the people around her were doubting she could pull everything off. She'd been trying to do it all. Maybe she had taken on too many baking orders lately. She'd been trying to pay back Ethan as quickly as possible for the chandelier. Maybe she'd been too intent on being independent. Maybe she needed to slow down.

"Hannah"—Ethan sat down next to her—"are you all right?"

"I...I just needed some air."

His gaze searched her face as though making sure she was all right. "We could go home—maybe watch a movie or something."

She shook her head. "Not yet."

A rush of cool air felt good against her heated skin. Her head no longer pounded quite so hard. She didn't even want to think about what people were saying after that ugly scene. She inwardly groaned. Why did she let Agnes get under her skin? If she was honest with herself, she knew the answer.

Ethan gently nudged her with his elbow. "Hey, don't let that woman get to you."

Hannah's gaze met his. "Agnes is right. I've let myself get pulled in every direction. I need to slow down and focus. I can't let this town down."

He draped his arm over her shoulders and pulled her to him. "You won't."

"Did you see how everyone was looking at me in there?"

"They weren't looking at you. They were glaring at Agnes. When I walked away, there were a number of people jumping to your defense and letting Agnes know that they didn't agree with her."

"They did?"

He smiled and nodded. "Don't you know how much this town cares about you?"

"I..." She wasn't sure what to say. She was deeply touched to know that the townspeople had stood up for her. "I need to do something different. Obviously I have to finish my remaining baking orders, but once those are done, I'm done baking until the shop opens. That is if you don't mind waiting a little bit for me to pay you back for the chandelier." When he shook his head, she said, "I'll spend the mornings focused on the festival plans and making phone calls. In the afternoons, I'll help you in the bakery."

"You don't have to do that. I told you I'd get it done." The worry reflected in his eyes.

She wasn't the only one who had taken on more work than was reasonable. "I insist." She got to her feet. "I should go back inside." She rubbed her hands over her arms.

Ethan stood. He took off his suit jacket and draped it over her shoulders. "You don't have to go back in there. Everyone will understand."

"But I can't just walk away. What will they think?"

In the bright moonlight, Ethan stared deep into her eyes. He gently gripped her shoulders. "They will think you have the biggest heart and try to help everyone."

She should glance away but she was drawn in by his warm brown eyes. Her heart pounded in her chest. It echoed in her ears. Could he hear it? How could he not?

They'd been fighting this thing between them since they'd met. What would be wrong with giving into it just this once? After all, the whole town thought they were involved, why not live up to the hype?

With Ethan standing so close, it was hard to think straight. And with his jacket draped about her, she breathed in the scent of his spicy cologne. She inhaled deeper. Mm...

186

And then his gaze dipped to her lips. Was he going to kiss her? Her heart leapt into her throat, blocking any words she might say. Not that she could think of anything to say in that moment.

Did she want him to kiss her? Oh yes, she did. She'd never been so sure about anything in her life.

She lifted up on her tiptoes and then he was there pressing his lips to hers. It was better than she thought it would be—better than it had been in her dreams. Her feet felt as though they were no longer touching the ground.

"Hey, Ethan, are you out here?" a male voice called.

They sprang apart.

Hannah didn't know how to act or what to say to him. That kiss wasn't supposed to happen. And yet she didn't regret it.

"Ethan?" The familiar voice grew closer. And then Greg was standing in front of them. "There you are. Didn't you hear me?"

"Uh...sorry," Ethan said. "What did you need?"

Greg's gaze moved between her and Ethan. "Did I interrupt something?" His eyes widened. "I did, didn't I—"

"No." Ethan shifted his weight from one foot to the other. "It was nothing. What did you need?"

"You're positive?" Greg once more looked at both of them.

"Let's go inside." Not waiting for anyone to respond, Hannah started for the door.

It was nothing. The words pricked at her heart. Is that what he thought of their kiss? While she had been swept away, had he been unaffected?

CHAPTER NINETEEN

What did she do now?

Pretend the kiss never happened?

The next morning, Hannah was a nervous ball of energy. Sometime in the wee hours of the morning, she'd convinced herself that it didn't matter what he said about their kiss. The truth was that it'd been a mistake.

She'd been worked up over her scene with Agnes and not thinking straight, otherwise the kiss wouldn't have happened. Because if she'd been thinking logically, she'd have realized that he was all wrong for her. He was a firefighter. He took risks—risks she couldn't live with—risks that had killed her father.

But how did they rewind that moment and pretend it never happened? How did she forget the way it made her heart pitter-patter? How did she forget the sensation of floating above the earth?

She hadn't gotten a thing done that morning, except pace and move decorations around her apartment, only to put them back the way she'd had them originally. Needing to calm down before she spoke to Ethan, she opted to do the one thing that always made her feel better—bake.

After a quick trip to the market for blueberries and cream cheese, she baked a batch of muffins. It wasn't her best work but that hadn't been the purpose of the exercise.

By the time she made it down to the bakery, it was nearing lunchtime, and Ethan was hard at work. He was in the kitchen removing the old floor tiles that had been ruined during the flood.

"Hi." She paused in the doorway. "We need to talk."

He straightened. "Uh-oh. Those four words never precede anything good."

Her stomach shivered with nerves. How could he not know what she wanted to discuss? Was their kiss so easily dismissed?

She glanced down at the floor. "It's about last night." When she lifted her gaze, she noticed how his stance had grown rigid.

"I'm sorry about that."

Was he apologizing for kissing her? Heat rushed to her cheeks at the memory of his lips pressed to hers. She dismissed the thought. Or was he apologizing for acknowledging that it had meant nothing to him?

She opened her mouth to ask but totally lost her nerve. She told herself that it didn't matter. *Liar. Liar.* Instead, she said, "So we're in agreement that the kiss was a mistake and it shouldn't happen again?"

He was quiet for a moment—longer than was necessary—as though he was actually giving the question some serious thought. Finally, he said, "It won't happen again."

She nodded in agreement. "Can we pretend like it never happened?"

"If it's what you want."

"It is."

He pried up a floor tile, then he turned to her. His gaze lowered to the pastry box in her hands. "Looks like you've been busy. Who's the lucky person?"

"You. If you want them."

"What flavor are they?"

She lifted the lid and tilted the box so he could see inside. "Blueberry muffins."

"They look good." His voice lacked emotion.

She wondered how long this awkwardness would last. "I'll just put them here on the counter." As an ominous silence settled over them, she said, "What can I do to help?"

"I leaned the mirror against the wall in the front room, you could work on it."

Her heart gave an excited leap at the memory of the giant mirror she'd bought at the estate sale. She liked to think of it as a jewel in the rough. It was going to take a lot of work to make it look like new, but then again is that what she wanted? Something new? Or something with a story of its own written in each crack and crevice of the ornate frame?

Beauty is found in the flaws. It was something her grandmother used to tell her.

So perhaps there wasn't that much work involved. She could work on the large chips and cracks but leave the smaller ones to add character just like laugh lines added to a woman's beauty.

In the end, the mirror would complement the chandelier. But it was going to have to wait a little longer.

"I can start it after lunch," she said.

He paused and glanced at the time on his phone as though he couldn't believe it was lunchtime already. "It is noon."

She wanted to slip away and avoid him until he left town, but it was impossible. Aside from them living across the hall from each other, she'd promised to do her part to help with the bakery. She'd just have to pull up her big girl panties and get on with things.

"I'm going to grab something to eat across the street at Hamming It Up," she said. "Can I grab you something?"

"You don't have to bother."

"I don't mind." It was the truth.

He paused to give it some thought. "I'm not picky. Surprise me."

"A couple of sandwiches coming up."

"Sounds good. It's become my favorite deli. And could you get me a pickle spear?"

"Absolutely. I always get one with my order. I'll be right back."

And so she rushed across the street to the deli, which was busy as usual. But they had a few people working the counter while there were more in back making sandwiches, so the wait wasn't that long.

All the while she thought of Ethan. She told herself she had to forget about their kiss or the way she'd thrown herself

190

into his arms. Both were spur-of-the-moment things. Nothing that had been building or anything—at least not on her end. If she ignored those feelings, they would go away.

♥♥♥

It was awkward.

Ethan kept feeling Hannah staring at him when she thought he wasn't looking. What was she thinking? She was probably thinking about last night and the kiss—the kiss she didn't want to repeat. His ego took a direct blow—at least that's what he told himself was the reason he was feeling down.

But if Hannah was fine acting like he hadn't held her in his arms and she hadn't kissed him back, then so be it. He could pretend with the best of them.

Ten minutes later, Hannah returned to the bakery. She called Ethan into the front room where there wasn't such a mess.

"Mind if we pull up a piece of floor?" she asked.

He shrugged. It wouldn't be the first meal he'd partaken of on the floor. "As long as it's near the wall so I can rest my back. Pulling up all of those tiles has been rough."

"Sounds like a plan." Her gaze averted his.

She wasn't as good at playing pretend as she wanted to let on. He took some small comfort in that knowledge. It would seem she wasn't as immune to their kiss as she wanted to let on.

For a bit they ate quietly as they were both hungry. He still wondered what would have happened if he hadn't been called away by Greg to settle a light-hearted disagreement amongst the firefighters. Would she have felt different about their relationship now? As soon as the thought came to him, he pushed it away.

"This is good," he said, needing to break the silence.

"Yes, it is. Now that I'll be living across the street from the deli, I see a lot of sandwiches in my future."

"I don't blame you."

Is this what they'd come to? A bland, stilted conversation about food. He missed their fun, easy chats. Maybe trying to rewind the clock on their relationship was a mistake. It wasn't that he would bail on the remodel—he'd never do that to her. But they needed some space from each other.

He cleared his throat. "Hannah, this isn't working."

"You don't like lunch?"

"No. This." He waved back and forth between them. "Us." How did he say this gently? He couldn't think of any other way than just to say it. "We can't pretend to be friendly. It isn't working." It hurt him just to say the words. She had quickly become a good friend. And he already missed her fun, sunny presence. "I don't think we should work together."

Her eyes widened and her mouth opened but no words came out—not immediately. It was as if her mind had to take a moment to catch up with what had happened.

"But you can't quit. The bakery will never be finished in time. And the festival—the town is counting on us." Her rushed words practically ran together. "If this is about the kiss, we can pretend it never happened. We can—"

"Relax. I'm not leaving the island."

"You're not?"

He shook his head. "And I am finishing the work on the bakery."

"Then I'm confused."

"So am I." Earlier she'd acted like being around him was torture, but now she acted as though she didn't want to distance herself.

"Maybe we should start over." She set aside her sandwich.

"Start what over?"

"Us." She held out her hand to him. When he didn't move, she said, "Go ahead. Shake my hand." When he did, she continued. "Hi. I'm Hannah."

Her hand was small compared to his. He enjoyed the softness of her touch. A tingling started in his fingertips before rushing up his arm and settling in his chest with a warm sensation.

"Go ahead," she prompted. "It's your turn."

"Are you serious?" When she nodded enthusiastically, he laughed. "Hi. I'm Ethan."

She withdrew her hand. "See that wasn't so hard."

"Now what?"

She shrugged. "Why don't you tell me about where you live?"

"You don't want to hear about that." His life was pretty boring except for his job. And he knew that was a sore subject for her.

Still, she'd asked about where he lived. He told her about his apartment and how he lived ten minutes from his parents. She genuinely sounded interested. Wanting to keep the easy dialogue going, he told her about a bit of his childhood.

All the while he was careful to keep the conversation away from the fire department. And so when Hannah broached the subject, it caught him off guard.

"They must be anxious to have you back at the fire department," she said casually.

"I suppose."

"You don't sound anxious to go back."

He drew up a knee and rested his arm on it. If she was trying hard to have a meaningful conversation, he would do his part. "Honestly, I wonder if I'll ever be up for another fire call."

She arched a fine brow. "Does this have something to do with why you've been in Bluestar for so long?"

He nodded. "I had an on-the-job incident before I came to Bluestar." Now what had he gone and said that for? "I...I just needed some time away."

"I had a feeling it was something like that. If you don't want to talk about it that's okay."

He toyed with the straw in his drink. "For a long time, you would have been right."

"And now?"

"Now the memories don't have as much power over me. I'm even sleeping better."

"Bluestar is known for its curing ways."

He nodded. "If you could bottle it, you'd make a fortune. I don't feel like the same man who left New York."

"It must have been bad."

"It was." He paused, waiting for himself to shut down as he had in the past, but he didn't feel that cold wall of separation close in around him.

"You don't have to tell me. Not unless you want to."

He drew up the memories that for so long had played front and center in his nightmares. It had been a normal day. He could still feel the first rays of the sun shining through the window of the firehouse as he'd talked to his buddy about which football team was going to make the playoffs. "Nothing about the day said it was going to be life-changing, life-threatening."

It was true what they said about life changing on a dime and you just never see it coming. "Maybe I've been a firefighter for so long that I take the risks for granted. Maybe I got too confident that I could make it out of anything."

In his mind, he could hear the alarm blare throughout the station. All of their trucks were called out for a residential fire. "That call didn't start out feeling any different than any of the others. When I climbed in the truck, I was already thinking about kicking back that night and watching the game." His body tensed.

"As we pulled up to the house, the smoke was already billowing from it. I was one hundred percent focused on my job. It's like a switch inside gets flipped on." The images came rushing back to him, and his voice faltered.

He shouldn't have opened up this door into the past. There was a reason he'd never discussed all of the details of the incident with anyone. He'd only ever uttered what needed to go into his report.

When Hannah spoke, her voice was soft and soothing. "I can't even imagine what you faced."

Even though his pulse was racing, he had to keep going. He had to prove to himself that he was stronger than the memories.

"The air...it had an acidic smell. It wasn't good." In his mind's eye, he was back there. "There were flames in the back of the structure. Our team went in first. The smoke...it was everywhere. I made it upstairs. I found a little girl hiding in her closet. She'd been huddled there, sobbing for her dog." The memory of her frightened pleas for help echoed in his ears. "She wouldn't leave without her dog. I promised if she quit fighting me and came with me that I'd find her dog—at least I'd hoped to find him."

Hannah reached out and gripped his hand. She didn't say anything. Nor did she act as though his uneven burn scars fazed her at all. Just her touch said more than words could ever convey.

"After I'd handed the girl off, I searched for the dog. I didn't have much time. And then I spotted a small dog hiding in the corner of the living room next to the couch. I couldn't tell if he was breathing but I prayed he was alive."

Hannah's grip on his hand tightened. He wanted to glance at her but he didn't dare. He was afraid if he became distracted he wouldn't get the rest out. He had to keep going. The end was in sight.

He swallowed hard. He closed his eyes and the memories surrounded him. The smoke thickened. The fire was expanding. His stomach took a nauseous lurch.

"On the way out the door, part of the floor gave way. I fell." He heard Hannah's swift intake of breath, but he kept his eyes closed and kept going. "Later, I learned that there were a lot of painting supplies in the cellar. The owner is an artist. Anyway, the fire had started down there with a bunch of flammables. And then I...I got caught in a flash of fire."

Hannah gasped.

This time he did glance at her, finding tears streaming down her cheeks. He felt awful for making her cry.

He rushed on to say, "They resuscitated the dog."

"What about you?"

He cleared the lump in his throat. "I was trapped. My team got me out."

She swiped at her tears. "I don't know why I'm crying. I wasn't even there."

They both knew she was thinking of her father, who hadn't been as lucky as Ethan. He drew Hannah to him and held her for a moment.

She pulled away. "How bad was it? I mean afterward."

"I spent some time in the hospital with a broken ankle and some burns. It took me some physical rehab to be approved to return to work. Just when the paperwork came through, I found out about Aunt Birdie."

"Are you worried about going back to work?"

He shrugged. "It'll be different."

Her voice lacked enthusiasm. "So you're all set to go back home?"

He drank the rest of his cola. "Not yet. I have Spring Fling to attend and a bakery to finish." He hadn't intended to share any of this with her, especially when she wanted to keep distance between them. He swallowed hard. "Speaking of which, it's time to get back to work."

"That's right. I have a mirror crying out for some help." She quickly gathered their garbage. Then she turned back to him. "Thank you for sharing that. I know it wasn't easy."

"But it was worth it. If I'm ever going to make another rescue, I have to face what happened to me."

She nodded in understanding. "Are you good with us working together?"

"I wouldn't want it any other way. Do you know where to begin with the mirror?"

"I watched some videos online last night. I know how to strip the paint so that's where I'm going to start. I have to run out and get some supplies. Can I get you anything?"

He shook his head. "I'm good."

"I have my phone, if you change your mind." She deposited the garbage in a black bag and then headed out the door.

Ethan was still sitting there. He ran his thumb over the spot where her hand had once been. He missed the softness of her touch. He hadn't even left Bluestar, and he knew he was going to miss everything about this place—most especially Hannah.

CHAPTER TWENTY

Days had passed in a flurry of activity.

Ethan couldn't remember the last time he felt this exhausted. Or this driven. When he looked around at the work he'd accomplished, he felt a sense of fulfillment. The bakery was turning out better than he'd imagined.

The only problem was that all of the attention he'd paid to the details such as the trim work had cost him time. And right now, time was in short supply. He had to finish the bakery before he left town. He'd promised Hannah. But was that even possible? Especially now that Spring Fling was upon them.

With some help, anything was possible.

Right now, he needed to focus on helping Hannah with the final preparations for Spring Fling. Somehow they'd gotten past the awkwardness of the kiss. It didn't mean he'd forgotten it—not by a long shot. But he'd found he valued their friendship above all else. He could live with them just being friends—at least that's what he'd been telling himself.

"Did you get the Easter baskets sorted for Saturday?" Ethan asked Hannah as they stood in his aunt's kitchen. It was so early in the morning that the sun had just barely tiptoed past the horizon.

"I did." She smiled brightly as though she'd been triumphant. "Josie and Lily pitched in."

"I should have been helping more."

"You were helping by finishing the bakery. Stop frowning. It all worked out." She placed her bags of supplies on the floor near the table. "I'm the one who feels guilty for leaving you to handle the bakery on your own most of the week."

"And I told you not to worry about it."

He failed to mention that he had a lot of help from the fire department. They'd pledged to help him see that everything was done by Saturday—the last day of Spring

Fling. They'd all agreed to make it a secret for Hannah. The only problem was trying to keep Hannah out of the bakery until the big reveal that weekend.

"But I do worry," she said. "After we're done here, I can go help you."

"No! You can't." Even to his own ears his response came a little too fast. He cleared his throat. "I mean there are Easter baskets to deliver to Sunny Days."

She frowned. "You're right. We don't want to just drop them off and leave."

"That's right." He nodded in agreement.

"Then tomorrow I can help."

"When? Remember tomorrow is the first day of the festival."

She sighed. "That's right." And then her eyes grew shiny before she lowered her gaze. "It's just not going to work out."

"Hey." He walked over to her and placed a finger beneath her chin, lifting until their gazes met. "Remember our agreement?"

She moved away from his touch. "Ethan..."

"We agreed that you would take over organizing the festival while I worried about the bakery."

"But that was before when we both thought there was time to make this all work out. And now time is up and—"

"There's still time. Don't give up hope."

She sighed again. The dimness in her eyes let him know she had given up. "We need to get busy."

Maybe staying busy would keep them both from worrying about completing the bakery. "Yes, let's get to work."

Hannah unloaded the candy bags onto the table. "I got these for the baskets. Hey, did you fertilize your aunt's tulips?"

He nodded. "I did it just the way she wanted. I even switched brands of coffee I drink so it'd be the right grounds."

"That was so sweet of you. And what about the prizes?"

He smiled and nodded. "I took care of them last week."

"Awesome. I think everything is on track for tomorrow. Oh no!"

Ethan rushed over to her. His gaze searched her and then the table. "What's wrong? What happened?"

She let out a soft laugh. "Nothing. I mean I was worried I jinxed the festival when I said that everything is under control."

"That's all?" When she nodded, he said, "Then knock on wood."

She smiled and then rapped her knuckles on the wooden kitchen table. "Problem solved."

"Okay. Hopefully this won't take too long. When I saw Aunt Birdie yesterday, she said she had all of the dyes we'd need in her pantry. She'd also ordered the eggs and arranged to have them delivered this morning. I didn't think the local grocery store delivered food."

Hannah had her back to him as she stood on a stepstool, searching through the kitchen cabinets. "I don't think he delivers for anyone but your aunt. She has a way of getting people to do things."

"Tell me about it."

Ding. Dong.

"Looks like the eggs are here." Hannah closed the upper cabinet doors. Was that a joyful lilt in her voice? Surely not.

"I'll go get them." He headed for the front door.

"And I found the vinegar."

When he opened the front door, he was shocked to find a man standing there with a dolly loaded with two big boxes of eggs. *Wait. Boxes of eggs? What in the world?*

"I think there's been some sort of mistake."

The older man checked the paper attached to the clipboard. "Nope. It says two boxes of eggs."

This just can't be right. There's no way.

"Hannah?" He moved aside as the man rolled the eggs into the house. "Hannah! Hurry!"

She stepped out of the kitchen. "What's wrong?"

"There's a mistake with the order." He planted his hands on his waist. "We can't color all of those eggs."

Her gaze moved from him to the cases of eggs. "Two hundred eggs. Yes, that's right. We need them to take to the residents of Sunny Days. It was your aunt's idea."

The older man sent her a relieved smile.

Ethan did what he was told and moved the eggs to the kitchen. Hannah placed eggs in the bottom of pots and covered them with water. When she was done, each burner on the stove was filled. This was not going to be the short endeavor that he'd hoped. Luckily some of the fire crew were at the bakery keeping things going there.

They were done.

She blew out a sigh.

Hours later, Hannah placed the last colored egg in the crate to dry. It was after lunch now and the baskets still had to be delivered to Sunny Days.

She glanced across the table to Ethan. His hands were stained in a rainbow of colors. "It looks like you got more dye on you than on the eggs."

He looked at his hands. "At least they're festive now."

She smiled and shook her head. "Yes, they are."

"Your fingers don't look much better."

"I couldn't let you be the only one with rainbow hands. Now we better get the baskets put together. I have some cookies Nikki helped me bake last night to put in the baskets."

"You baked last night?"

She nodded as she rushed to the living room to get the plastic containers of cookies. "I thought I'd put a personal touch in the baskets."

"And dyed eggs aren't personal enough?"

"But you know I'm a baker." She opened the top container to let him see the egg and bunny shaped cookies.

"They look great. But when do you relax?"

"This from a man who spends every waking hour working on the remodel."

"Not every hour."

"Close enough. What you don't understand is that when I'm not on a tight deadline, baking is relaxing for me."

"What I know is that you're forever doing things for others." He sent her a smile that touched his warm brown eyes. "You're very special."

As he stared into her eyes, her heart pitter-pattered. She should turn away, but she was so drawn to him. And suddenly it felt like they were the only two people in the world.

The breath caught in her lungs. She hoped he would kiss her. At last. In that moment, she realized her aversion to his job hadn't diminished the spark between them. What did that mean for the future?

"Watch out—!"

She glanced down to see the cookie container was tipping to the side. "Oops."

He moved the cookies to the counter. "All taken care of."

She thought the moment had passed when Ethan stepped up to her again. "Hannah, I want to thank you."

"For what?"

"Being so good to me and my aunt. Without you none of this would have come together—at least not the way it's supposed to—not the way the Bluestar residents are expecting."

Heat inched up her neck and settled in her cheeks. "I just did what needed to be done."

"No." He gazed deep into her eyes. "You went above and beyond. You're amazing."

Their gazes caught and held much longer than was appropriate. Words clogged her throat. And all she could do was stand there totally lost in his chocolatey gaze.

He reached out to her. The back of his fingers lightly grazed her cheek. "I should stop now. I should walk away. But there's something special about you—between us. Hannah, I—"

"Ethan, there you are," his mother's voice called out.

He jumped back as though he'd just been splashed with boiling water. He swallowed hard and turned. "Mom. Dad. You're both here."

His mother sent him a big smile. "Well, don't just stand there. Give me a hug."

And so he did just that. All the while Hannah's mind raced to figure out what had just happened. Before his parents had interrupted them, what had he been about to tell her? She had the feeling it was something profound.

Ethan pulled back from his mother. "Mom and Dad, I'd like you to meet Hannah. Hannah, these are my parents Clara and Marshall."

As hands were shook and explanations were provided, she noticed a yawning distance looming between her and Ethan. Their moment had passed. Would they ever get it back?

What was going on?

Birdie didn't like to be so far away from the action. Sure there were phone calls from her friends in Bluestar filling her in on the goings-on, but it just wasn't the same as being there. And after that stunt Agnes pulled at the wedding reception, well, someone needed to be around to keep her in check.

And worst of all, Birdie's sources had told her that nothing appeared to have changed between Ethan and Hannah. If the festival didn't get them to reveal their feelings for each other, it would be too late. Ethan would head back to the city and who knew when he'd be back. And in the meantime, the island would fill up with vacationers—any of whom might catch Hannah's eye. That just couldn't happen.

Birdie picked up the phone and dialed. "Betty, I need your help."

Her friend didn't say anything at first. "Birdie, if this is about your nephew, I think you've done enough."

"No. I can't stop now. They are so right for each other. They're just too stubborn to see it."

"Did you ever think you might be wrong?"

"I know as sure as I'm sitting here that they love each other. I don't know why they're fighting it so much, but if we give them just one more push, perhaps a big shove—"

"Birdie, no."

"Betty, please. It'll be easy. I promise. And if this doesn't work, I'll leave you and them alone."

Betty didn't say a word for a moment, as though she was considering the idea. "What do you have in mind?"

And so Birdie told her best friend the plan. This just had to work. She wanted her nephew to be happy—just like she'd been with her dear Gilbert. Everyone should know that kind of love—at least once in a lifetime. It was her greatest wish for her nephew.

CHAPTER TWENTY-ONE

This morning was the Bloomin' Tulip contest.

Hannah yawned and then promptly gulped down some more coffee.

She'd been up late last night. After going with Ethan and his parents to Sunny Days to deliver the Easter baskets, they'd returned home much later than she'd expected. And there still had been some decorating to do at the community center before today's festivities commenced.

Her thoughts turned to the bakery. There was still so much that needed to be done to finish it. And she'd promised the mayor that the grand opening would be in a week. Her stomach shivered with nerves. What if they didn't make it? What if the bakery didn't open on time? How was she going to make the loan payment?

Where there's a will, there's a way. It's what her grandmother used to tell her. Hannah definitely willed this bakery to work out, but the way it would happen was a bit hazy at the moment. Especially when Ethan was due to leave town in just a couple of days. Would she be able to finish the rest of the bakery on her own?

She shoved the troublesome thoughts to the back of her mind as she rushed out the door. She'd knocked on Ethan's door not once but twice. He hadn't answered either time. And she hadn't heard Peaches. So where could he be?

When she headed to the steps, she thought she heard some noise coming from the bakery. It seemed he'd gotten an early start. She headed downstairs with her coffee cup in one hand and her phone in the other because message after message and phone call after phone call were coming in faster than she could deal with. The people of Bluestar were all abuzz with excitement for Spring Fling.

She moved to the interior door that separated the bakery from access to the private residences. She grasped the door handle and turned, but the door wouldn't budge. What in the world? She tried again. It was blocked. Had something fallen over? Or had Ethan left something in the way?

"Ethan?"

Nothing. That was strange. She could have sworn she'd heard activity down there when she was upstairs.

"Ethan, the door is blocked!"

Still, there was no reply. She must have been mistaken.

Someone needed to clear the blockage by the door. She'd just go outside and come in through an exterior door.

Chime. Chime. Chime.

And there went her phone...again. She wanted to ignore it. After all, she was on her way to the community center. Still, it might be something important. A sense of responsibility had her taking the call.

"Hello."

"Hi. It's Betty." The woman sounded a little breathless. "I wanted to let you know that Delores has come down with a cold. She won't be able to judge the Bloomin' Tulip contest."

"Oh, no. That leaves us with an even number of judges. That won't do." Her mind raced for a replacement.

She would ask Betty to do it, but she was already one of the judges. Who was she going to get on such short notice?

"I thought you'd want to know right away. I'm sorry about this."

"It's not your fault. It's not anyone's fault. Things happen. I'm on my way to the community center right now." The contest was due to kick off in less than two hours. "I'll figure something out and get back to you."

Hannah rushed out the door. Her mind was already abuzz with possible substitute judges. As she navigated her bike through the streets to the community center, she prioritized her list of candidates.

Once she reached the community center, she hopped off her bike and started making phone calls. The first was her mother, who was on her way to the community center. She politely declined because she'd entered the contest. And so did the next few ladies on her list. This was a disaster. Everyone she could think of had entered the contest this year. Bragging rights for the best tulips in town were apparently at a premium.

"Hannah." Her mother rushed over to her with Nikki beside her. "Were you able to find a judge?"

"Not yet." Hannah glanced around. "Where's Sam?"

"Oh, you know him. He said he has to work."

"I wish Daddy was here." Nikki frowned. "Why does he have to work?"

Hannah's heart went out to her niece. She knelt down in front of her. "Your daddy is working hard to buy you pretty yellow dresses like the one you're wearing and to take care of you and all of the animals. It's a lot of work for one person. I'm sure he wishes he was here with you."

Of that she was certain. Her brother had taken his role as single parent and sole breadwinner seriously—perhaps too seriously. He'd forgotten what it was like to have fun. She was going to have to set him up with someone and remind him what it was like to relax and have some fun.

Nikki crossed her arms. "I still wish he was here."

"Maybe he'll be able to come next year. But in the meantime, Gran and I are going to be here to cheer you on."

Nikki's blue eyes clouded with doubt. "You'll be too busy."

"Not for you. I promise." She made an *X* over her heart.

Nikki wrapped her arms around her neck. "I love you, Auntie Hannah."

Hannah hugged her back. "I love you too."

When they parted, Hannah's mother said, "We better go get you signed up for the contests."

"Okay." Nikki smiled as they headed for the signup tables.

Hannah turned and rushed inside the community center, happy to find both Lily and Josie already there, placing tulip entries on the table. And there was Ethan setting up another table for tulip entries. It was going to be a big turnout.

He was a big help pulling together all of the last-minute details for the festival. And the more she thought about it— the more a plan started to come together for her missing judge. She continued to stare at him as he bent over to secure a table leg.

"Hannah?" A familiar voice called to her. "Hannah?"

She turned to find Lily standing a few feet away. "Sorry. I was lost in thought."

Lily's gaze moved to Ethan before returning to her. "I guess I don't have to ask who you were thinking about."

"It's not like that."

Lily arched a brow. "It's not? Are you sure? Because it sure looks like you're into him as much as he's into you. And if you don't do something soon, he's going to be gone and he'll never know how you feel about him."

Her heart grew heavy as she thought of her life without Ethan in it, but she'd already made her decision. "I can't do it."

"What if he wasn't leaving? Would you take the chance then?" While Hannah quietly debated the answer, Lily continued. "Maybe he likes it here in Bluestar and he just needs a little extra incentive to stay."

She shook her head. "I can't do it."

She didn't know if it was because she was afraid to put her heart on the line again and have it get broken or if she didn't want to put him in the position of choosing between her and his firefighting career in New York. Or perhaps it was a bit of both. Either way, she intended to keep her feelings to herself—even though every time she looked in his eyes, it got harder and harder.

"Suit yourself, but I, for one, think you're making the biggest mistake of your life if you let him walk away." Lily gave her a pointed look. "Anyway, I came over to get you because we have a small problem outside."

With a smothered groan, Hannah followed her friend outside. All the while, she was busy thinking of every excuse for not revealing her feelings for Ethan. After all, she had the bakery to open and turn into a successful business. That wasn't going to happen overnight. Nor would it be easy.

But being around Ethan made her see that even a successful bakery wouldn't make her life complete—not without him in it. Over the past several weeks he'd become not just a friend but one of her best friends.

He was the person she wanted to tell when things went right.

And he was the shoulder she wanted to lean on when things went wrong.

Where was she?

Ethan stood off to the side of the community center. He scanned the growing crowd of now-familiar faces, searching for Hannah. No such luck.

Maybe she'd slept in. After all, she had been pushing herself to make sure everyone had a good time. He grabbed his phone from his back pocket. When he went to text her, he found his phone was dead. He inwardly groaned. He'd been so tired from working on the bakery that he'd forgotten to put his phone on the charger before falling asleep.

Oh, well, he had everything covered, didn't he...

"Ethan, just the person I was hoping to talk to."

He turned to find his father standing there. "Hey, Dad, what do you need?"

"Nothing. I just wanted to tell you how proud I am of you. I know you went through a lot with that accident. And then you stepped up to help your aunt. But you don't have to worry. Your mother and I are back now. You can go back to the city and get back to work. We'll look after Aunt Birdie."

This was the moment when he should tell his father that things had changed—that he was rethinking his future. Whereas firefighting had at one point been his main focus, now he was finding that his interests were more diverse.

"Dad, about that—"

"Yes, I know you've been here too long and need to get back to work. You stepped up when the family needed you. I'm so proud of you. You're a great firefighter and an even better son." His father hugged him.

His father was not the emotional type. Not that he was cold or anything but this outpouring was unusual for him. Ethan hugged his father back.

When they parted, Ethan looked at his father. "Is everything okay?"

His father laughed. "Looks like I should have said those things a long time ago if you're that caught off guard." His father shifted his weight from one leg to the other. "While we were away, I was able to slow down long enough to realize that I'd been putting off a lot of things in my life. I was always too busy for this or that. Now I don't want to keep putting off things I should do or things I should say. So I just wanted you to know how proud I am of you."

"Thanks, Dad."

What else did he say to that? How was he supposed to follow up his father's praises with the knowledge that he was thinking of quitting the fire department—quitting the Walker tradition? And then his father would want to know what he was going to do, and right now Ethan didn't have an exact plan, just a vague vision. That wasn't good enough. If he was going to do this, he needed a firm plan.

His mother approached them. "Isn't Hannah with you?"

She looked expectantly at him, like he should know Hannah's exact whereabouts. They didn't spend all of their time together—just most of it these days. But it wasn't like they were a couple or anything. He ignored how appealing that last thought sounded to him.

He swallowed hard. "I'm not sure where she is. My phone is dead."

Now why did he go and add that last part, like he would know where Hannah was, if his cell had been working? But it was the truth, wasn't it? Hadn't he just reached for it to text her? He stifled a groan.

"I'm sure she'll be along any time now," his father said. "In fact, here she comes."

Ethan glanced up to see Hannah headed straight for him. She wasn't smiling. In fact, her brows were drawn together with her forehead creased. Oh no, there's trouble afoot.

As soon as she was standing in front of him clutching her pen and clipboard, he asked, "What's wrong?"

"How do you know something's wrong?"

"Because your face always scrunches up like that when you're worried about something." It didn't go unnoticed by him that he recognized her expressions, but he refused to acknowledge that it meant anything.

"We're short a judge. You have to do it. If not, everything will be ruined."

"Whoa. Slow down. You're short a judge for what?"

"The tulip contest. Dolores Simpson is sick. And I can't find anyone who would be willing to judge that hasn't already entered the contest. We have an equal number of judges now and that won't do. So will you do it?"

He shook his head. "Hannah, I can't do it."

"But you have to."

No way. Not happening. He'd already seen how seriously these women took this contest. And he didn't need Agnes coming after him. That woman could be a bit intimidating, not that he'd admit it to anyone.

He cleared his suddenly dry throat. "Hannah, I can't do it. I know absolutely nothing about flowers."

Her face fell into a frown. That was not good. When she started to pout, his resistance always faltered.

"Pleeease..."

211

Ugh! He felt his resolve slipping away. And then a thought came to him. "But I entered the contest," he said as a last-ditch effort to get out of this. "Remember, I entered my aunt's flowers. She'd be so upset if I withdrew them. And I know which ones they are so I wouldn't be an impartial judge. I'm sorry."

"I'll do it." Ethan's mother stepped forward.

"You would?" Hannah's face lit up.

"That is if an outsider is allowed to judge."

"I don't know why not, but let me speak with the mayor and other judges. I'll be right back." Hannah rushed off.

"She's amazing," his mother said. "The fact that she would step up to help out with the festival for Aunt Birdie when she has so much going on in her personal life is remarkable." Confusion reflected in his mother's eyes. "But how are you two going to make things work? You know, when you return to New York."

It was the same question he'd wrestled with many times. "We're not. I mean it's not like that. We're, um, just good friends."

His mother looked at him in disbelief. "I think the only two people who believe that are you and Hannah. The rest of us can see what you two are denying."

Ethan's gazed dropped to the floor. "You must have been talking to Aunt Birdie."

"She's kept me updated on everything. I just had to see it for myself. And she's right. You two make a good match."

His father cleared his throat rather loudly. "Clara, don't you think our son needs to figure this out for himself."

"But, Marshall, you know how stubborn he can be. Remember when he—"

"Clara, leave him alone."

His mother sighed. "All right."

Just then Hannah came rushing back over with a big smile on her face. "They said it would be all right for you to be a judge. Come on. I'll introduce you to everyone."

And off they went, his mother and his...um, and Hannah. Because his mother wasn't right. How many times had Hannah told him she needed to focus on her business? She needed to make her business her priority. And there was the issue of him being a firefighter. Or was it possible she was growing more comfortable with his profession?

CHAPTER TWENTY-TWO

The Bloomin' Tulip contest was now underway.

Table after table showcased the colorful blooms from red and white to deep purple with many vibrant shades in between. Spring had definitely sprung.

Hannah was still mulling over Lily's suggestion that she tell Ethan about her growing feelings for him. She wondered what he'd do if she were to ask him to stay. Would he laugh at the suggestion of him giving up his successful career as a big city firefighter? Or would he look at her with pity reflected in his eyes because he didn't feel the same way for her?

"What event is next?" Ethan's father asked, drawing Hannah from her thoughts.

Judging the enormous amount of tulip entries would take some time. Hannah had decided to move the awards ceremony to the end of all the events in order to keep people from growing bored and drifting away from the festival.

She glanced down at her clipboard. "It's the egg-decorating contest. It's new this year."

"Was it your idea?" Marshall asked.

Hannah nodded. "I thought it would be fun for everyone. It's split into age groups and will replace the kid's coloring contest. This way the whole community can participate." She arched a brow at Ethan's father. "So what do you say? Want to decorate an egg?"

He shook his head. "I'd probably crack one."

"Don't worry, they aren't real eggs. We're supplying ceramic ones so everyone can take them home afterward."

"Good idea. But I'm afraid I don't have an artistic bone in my body."

Ethan came rushing over. "Hurry up. You don't want to be late."

He was looking directly at her, but Hannah didn't know what he was talking about. "Late for what?"

"The contest. You're entered."

She shook her head. "I didn't enter."

Just then Josie called out her name on the megaphone. "Hannah Bell, report to table two."

When she turned a puzzled look back at Ethan, she said, "What did you do?"

He sent her a grin. "Just go have some fun."

"I...I don't know. I'm the coordinator."

Ethan held out his hand and took the clipboard and pen from her. "Now I'm the coordinator."

"But Ethan—"

"Just go."

She had to admit that participating sounded like fun. Everyone else was having a great time; maybe it was time she relaxed and enjoyed the festival. She'd left everything in Ethan's capable hands.

She approached Josie. "Where do you want me?"

Her friend pointed to the last empty folding chair at the table. "That spot is yours."

Hannah lit up with a smile when she noticed the seat was right beside her niece. Nikki's face glowed with happiness as she waved her over. This was going to be fun. She treasured the time spent with her niece.

Agnes Dewey stepped in Hannah's way. "You can't participate."

"Excuse me." Hannah surely hadn't heard her correctly.

Agnes's face scrunched up with frown lines. "You organized this festival, therefore you can't take part."

"Says who?" Josie crossed her arms.

Hannah glanced past Agnes to see the wide-eyed stare on Nikki's face. She didn't want a scene to ruin this day for her niece. "It's okay. I don't mind sitting out."

"You signed up," Josie said, "you should get to participate. After all, if it wasn't for you, we wouldn't be having this wonderful day. That *everyone* gets to enjoy...even you, Ms. Dewey."

Agnes pressed her hands to her hips as she glowered at them. "This is not right. What if she wins?"

"What if she does?" Josie asked.

Just then Hannah noticed Ethan heading in her direction with sure and determined steps. Oh no! This was not good. Not good at all. People liked Ethan and slowly he was becoming a genuine part of the community. She didn't want him in the middle of this little skirmish.

When his gaze met hers, she gave him a little shake of her head. His steps slowed. Then she mouthed the *thank you*. He didn't look happy but he was willing to do this her way.

"What's the problem here?" Mayor Tony Banks strode up to them.

It was then Hannah glanced around and realized the entire community center was silent as all eyes were on them. Heat swirled in her chest. She wanted to sink into the floor and disappear. But most of all it was the worry reflected in Nikki's eyes that tore at her heart.

Hannah swallowed hard. "It's nothing. Can we please let everyone get on with the contest?"

"Oh, it's something," Agnes persisted. "Hannah thinks she can plan the festival and also participate in the events. It's not fair to everyone else."

Lily moved to Hannah's side. She was now flanked by her best friends. "How do you get that?"

"It...it's just not done." Agnes's face flushed. She turned to the mayor. "Tell them."

"I don't know what to tell them," the mayor said. "I don't think anything like this has ever happened with Spring Fling."

"I can back out," Hannah said. "There's no need to make a big deal if it." She turned to walk away.

"Not so fast," the mayor said. "Now that it's been brought to my attention, I think we need a decision."

Hannah stifled a groan as she turned around. "It's not necessary."

216

The mayor ignored her as he stepped up to the podium. "Excuse me, everyone. But it seems we have come upon an unprecedented predicament." As he continued to explain the situation in far too much detail for Hannah's liking, she struggled not to groan. "So I think what we need to do is vote on it. Can the festival organizer participate in the contests? Those who are in agreement raise your hand."

There was an overwhelming sea of hands that went up. Agnes frowned while Hannah struggled not to smile. It took what felt like forever to count the *yay* votes. Then it was time for the *nay* votes. That didn't take nearly as long. There was one vote—Agnes.

"Well, Ms. Dewey," the mayor said. "You've been overridden." He then turned to Hannah and her friends. "Well, what are you all doing standing there? Let's get on with it."

Hannah wanted to sneak off for a moment alone after that embarrassing moment, but after the town had her back, she couldn't let them down. And so she took a seat next to Nikki and stared at the egg, but she couldn't concentrate.

Out of her peripheral vision, she noticed that everyone around her was already hard at work decorating their egg. As she began to relax, she focused on her egg. When she attempted to come up with a design, she still drew a blank.

Then she knew what she had to do. She had to imagine it was a cake. When she thought of it that way, it was easy to think of the paints as frosting—okay, not exactly frosting as they had a much thinner consistency but it was now in her realm of skills. She hoped.

Except for one mishap by the name of Agnes Dewey, this was a great day.

The only thing that could make it better would be having Aunt Birdie here. Ethan wondered if perhaps he should have

217

persisted with his idea to spring his aunt for the day. But she'd been adamant about following the doctor's orders. In the moment, he'd agreed with her, but now he was wondering when his aunt's tune had changed. Since when was she so eager to do what she was told?

He had the feeling Aunt Birdie was up to something because she never complained about coming home like she had when she'd first arrived at Sunny Days. Ethan's gaze moved across the expansive community center to where Hannah was concentrating on her egg as she painted the final touches.

Was that it? Was his aunt hoping he and Hannah would get together? He'd never known Aunt Birdie to be a matchmaker before, but then again, he'd never been on the island long enough for her to make any grand plans.

But looking back now, he wondered if his fitting into this tight-knit community had been easy—perhaps too easy. Had his aunt been pulling strings from her physical rehab room?

Or maybe he was just exhausted from rushing to get the bakery finished and he just wasn't thinking clearly. Yes, that must be it. Because surely his aunt wouldn't sink to the depths of matchmaking. Not when she knew his whole life was back in New York.

Ethan helped place the painted eggs on the correct table to be judged by age category. With each person he assisted, he found something complimentary to say. Some were bright and cheery. Some had intricate designs. Some had drawings of flowers or animals.

And then Hannah approached him with Nikki by her side. As he watched her talk to her niece, he realized that someday Hannah was going to make a wonderful mother. He could just imagine her with a couple of kids of her own.

Just as quickly his vision filled in with a devoted husband and loving father. A frown tugged at his mouth as he pushed aside the troubling vision.

"What's wrong?" Hannah asked.

He blinked and glanced at her. "What?"

"You were frowning about something."

He replaced the frown with a smile. "You must be mistaken. How could I be frowning when I'm with the two most beautiful women in the room?"

Nikki giggled. "You're silly."

"I am?"

She smiled and nodded. "But I like you. Auntie Hannah likes you too."

"Nikki shush." Hannah's face filled with color.

"It's true," Nikki said. "She told me."

His gaze met Hannah's, and her face grew rosier. And then he glanced back at Nikki. "I like her too."

This made Nikki smile. Then she held out her egg. "I don't know where this goes."

He took the egg from her and turned it over. On the bottom was a number and letter. "The number is what identifies it as yours and the letter is the table it goes on for judging. Yours is table C."

"I see it." Nikki rushed over and added her egg to the table.

Ethan turned to Hannah. "It's your turn." He glanced around for her egg, but her hands were empty. "Did you already put it on the table?"

Hannah shook her head. "I don't think it's a good idea. I don't want to cause any more trouble."

"The only trouble today is Agnes. You saw the town. They are all behind you." He held out his hand. "Let's have it." He wiggled his fingers, anxious to see her creation.

She hesitated as she stared at him, but then she pulled the egg from her purse. It was wrapped in a napkin. He didn't know what he expected when she held up the egg, but it certainly wasn't the work of art in front of him.

He stared at Peter Rabbit, who appeared to be in a vegetable garden with a carrot in his hand. It wasn't so much

219

the scene itself but the delicate strokes that created such a detailed picture on such a small egg.

"This is amazing," he said. "I had no idea you were this talented."

Her cheeks filled with color. "It's what I do. I paint pictures but usually they're on cakes. It was fun to see if I could do such a small picture."

"I'd say you did an amazing job." He checked the bottom to see which table it should be placed on. "I'll just put it over here."

"Ethan, are you sure it's a good idea?"

"I think it's a great idea."

"Me too," Nikki chimed in. "I think it's the best." And then softly she added, "Even better than mine."

While Hannah and Nikki discussed all of the different styles of eggs from painted ones to others covered with glitter, his mind returned to the fact that Hannah liked him. When their gazes met and she blushed, was it the confirmation he needed? He desperately wanted to pull her away so they could be alone, but that was impossible now.

Because as the judges were allowed in the building to start their judging, Hannah had to make sure everything was arranged outside for the jelly bean relay. What he had to say to her would have to wait...for now.

CHAPTER TWENTY-THREE

The day was moving along quickly.

Perhaps too quickly.

For the most part, Hannah had loved the day. She frowned as she recalled the run-in with Agnes, but she refused to let that woman ruin this day. As Hannah glanced around at all of the people enjoying themselves, the smile tugged at her lips.

After the egg-decorating contest, they'd paused for lunch. The main part of the meal was catered by Hamming It Up Deli while the sides and desserts were all covered dishes prepared by the townsfolk. It was quite a delicious array of food.

But as good as it looked, Hannah only nibbled here and there. Her stomach was tied up in knots. She told herself it was the stress over finishing the bakery, but the truth was she wasn't ready to say goodbye to Ethan.

Her gaze settled on him as he spoke with his parents. He was so handsome. A dreamy sigh escaped her lips. He was nothing like her ex. Sure he might have gotten excited at the estate sale and overstepped, but once they'd talked it out, he respected her position and she realized his action had been well-intended.

She'd explained to Ethan that she needed to have a say in things and not be taken care of. He'd heard her. In fact, he consulted her a lot about the bakery —even about some of the minor things she didn't care so much about, like width of the trim work.

And somewhere along the way, he'd crept past the wall of her heart. All of the excuses she'd come up with to keep him at arm's length were failing her now. Because he'd shown her that he was someone she could count on— someone who saw her as an equal.

"A penny for your thoughts," Josie said.

"A penny? Seriously?" Hannah dramatically rolled her eyes. "With inflation, I wouldn't give away one thought for anything less than a dollar." And then she sent Josie a playful smile.

"Well, you certainly are in a good mood."

"You know what? I am."

"And I know what, or should I say who, has you in such a good mood." Josie sent her a knowing look.

"I wasn't thinking about Ethan." But the heat warming her cheeks was a dead giveaway.

"Are you going to tell him how you feel?"

Hannah shook her head. "There's nothing to tell."

"I don't even think you believe that."

"But he's leaving at the end of this weekend—"

"Maybe not. Maybe he just needs a reason to stay." And without another word, Josie walked away.

It wasn't the first time she'd heard that advice. Were Josie and Lily comparing notes? Or was it what they'd each observed? And were they right?

If she told him how she felt, would he stay? He certainly seemed happy in Bluestar. The island was one of those places where it was easy to fit in.

As though her thoughts had summoned him, Ethan appeared in front of her. When he smiled at her, her heart felt as though it had somersaulted in her chest. She swallowed hard, trying to maintain her composure and not let him know just how much his mere presence affected her.

"Are they finished judging the egg-decorating contest?" he asked.

She shook her head. "This year has the biggest turnout ever. Either the town is growing or we did a good job of getting people excited about the festival."

"I think you made the festival more family-friendly, and expanding it to include everyone in all of the contests was brilliant. I've heard people raving about how awesome the festival is this year and how they can't wait for it next year."

Hannah smiled brightly as she lightly clapped her hands together in excitement. "That's the best thing I've heard all day."

"But now people are getting anxious to get on with the relay. Are the judges going to be much longer?"

"I just checked with them and it's going to be a bit longer. That's why I've decided that we should have a combined awards ceremony at the end of today's events."

Ethan's brows rose in surprise. "I like the way you think."

She couldn't help but smile at his compliment. "Well, don't just stand there. Go tell everyone that it's time for the relay."

He sent her a tantalizing smile. It was one of those smiles that made her heart pitter-patter. Her gaze dipped to his lips just before he turned away and headed off to take care of business. And yet it was another opportunity that had slipped through her fingers. If she didn't work up the courage to tell him how she felt soon, she'd completely miss her chance.

"Ethan and Hannah report to the start line!"

The start line?

What were they talking about? Ethan glanced around for Hannah. Spotting her speaking with Betty, he approached her. "Did you do this?"

"Do what?"

"Sign us up for the jelly bean relay?"

She frowned at him. "Of course not."

"Someone did. They just called us to the start line."

"I should be moving along." Betty turned to walk away.

"Not so fast." He suspected that Betty knew what was going on. "Betty, who signed us up?"

She hesitantly turned to him but she averted her gaze. "I...I don't know. Why would you think I would know?"

"Because you can't look at me and you're flushed. So out with it."

"Okay. Okay. It was me." Her gaze met his. "I told Birdie it wasn't a good idea but she insisted."

"Last call," Mayor Banks called out on his megaphone. "Ethan and Hannah report to the start line."

"Come on." Hannah tugged on his arm. "Let's do it."

He couldn't believe he'd been roped into this. He'd narrowly avoided the egg-decorating contest, but his luck had run out now. He followed Hannah to the start line.

Ethan glanced around at all of the kids surrounding them. Little ones, older ones, and some in between. He shouldn't be there. He should be on the sidelines, cheering on the participants.

And then he glanced over at Hannah as she spoke with Josie and Lily. They all glanced his way, and he had a feeling he was the topic of conversation. He didn't even want to think about what they might be saying. Because if they were guessing that he wouldn't be any good at this relay, they'd be wrong.

After all, he was a firefighter. He may not be working now, but he would be soon. And he was agile. Though he'd never run with a jelly bean on the end of a spoon before. Still, how hard could it be?

Hannah approached him. "Are you all set for this?"

"It doesn't sound so hard."

"You think so?" When he nodded, she said, "Well, consider putting a spoon in your mouth and then scooping up a jelly bean. Then you have to race with it to your teammate and put the jelly bean on their spoon. Then they get to race back and place the jelly bean in the plastic egg.

"Are you sure you don't want to back out?"

He didn't like the thought of making a fool of himself in front of everyone. He'd never done anything like this. But he also wasn't one to back down from a challenge. "I'll do it, if you do it."

"I'm a pro at this."

"A pro?"

She nodded. "I've done the relay all of my life. Well, that is except for the last couple of years."

"Why not then?"

"Because my sister was always my partner and after she moved to Nashville, I just didn't bother to find a new partner."

"Are you sure you want to be my partner?" When her gaze met his, he forgot what he'd been about to say.

"I'd love to be your partner."

He wanted to ask her if they were still talking about the relay, but he resisted the urge. Whatever was going on between them would have to wait until they were alone.

♥♥♥

The sunshine warmed her face.

And the gentle sea breeze swept away her worries.

For the moment, Hannah relaxed and enjoyed the day. Win or lose, the relay would be fun. It would be a treasured memory of her time with Ethan—unless she convinced him to stay on the island.

The whistle blew. Hannah had the jelly bean for the first half of the relay. Even though she'd participated since she was a kid, it was still challenging.

The more the jelly bean fell from the spoon, the more she nervously laughed. The more she laughed, the harder it was to keep the jelly bean on the spoon. And it didn't help that Ethan was standing at the other end shaking his head in disbelief at her obvious uncoordinated efforts. What could she say? She was a baker, not an athlete.

By the time she passed the jelly bean to him, she was exhausted from laughing. And then he had the audacity to race back to the finish line without dropping the jelly bean—not even once. The nerve of him. When he deposited it into the plastic egg shell, he turned to her with a triumphant look. Her frustration immediately melted away. She smiled back at him. He'd done good, really good. But because of her blunders, it wasn't good enough to win. Not even close. They were something like seventh place out of seven entries.

"And now it is time to announce today's winners," Mayor Banks said, "but I think every entry was a winner, which is why I'm not on the judging panel." Laughter filled the air. Mayor Banks lifted a sheet of white paper and unfolded it. "And here we go..."

He started with the Bloomin' Tulip contest. You could have heard a pin drop as the many entrants shushed the crowd. One by one the names were called. And then the mayor called out Betty Simon's name. Birdie's best friend had won the blue ribbon and the bragging rights for the next year as the woman with the green thumb.

And then Mayor Banks moved on to the decorated egg contest. Nikki took first place. Hannah glanced over to where Nikki was standing with Hannah's mother. It was then that she noticed the man standing on the other side of her mother, Captain Campbell. He and her mother were talking and laughing. As her mother smiled, she looked years younger.

Hannah had to admit that seeing her mother enjoy another man's attention was strange for her, but after the initial shock of seeing her mother flirting with Captain Campbell subsided, Hannah realized she was happy for her mother.

Hannah turned her attention back to the mayor. He was now announcing the adult category of the decorated egg. "Third place goes to Agnes Dewey."

Above the applause there was an excited squeal from Agnes. Then the woman rushed to the gazebo to accept the white ribbon. The woman tore the mic from the mayor's hand.

She turned to the crowd with a huge grin. "I want to thank you all for this honor..."

226

"What is that woman doing?" Josie frowned as she crossed her arms. "She always has to make everything about her."

Ethan sent Hannah a puzzled look. She shrugged her shoulders, not sure why Agnes was rambling on about one of her cats.

The mayor wrestled the mic back from Agnes. Mayor Banks covered his fluster with a forced smile. "That's wonderful. Congratulations Agnes."

The woman was all smiles as she descended the steps and rejoined her group of friends.

"And now"—the mayor referenced the paper once more—"first and second place were very close. The second-place honor goes to Greg Hoover."

"Go, Greg!" Hannah didn't know he was so talented.

Without the need to make a speech, Greg took the red ribbon and prize money before returning to his position at the back of the crowd.

"And now for first place." The mayor held up the blue ribbon for everyone to see. "That honor goes to our very own Hannah Bell. Congratulations, Hannah."

I won? I really won?

Honestly, she'd never thought she'd win. She'd done it because she'd wanted to be a part of the community and to join in the fun. But winning, well, it made her feel like a kid again.

"Hannah?" The mayor prompted.

Ethan placed a hand on her back and gently pushed. "Go on."

Once she got in front of everyone, the mayor extended the blue ribbon, a white envelope with the prize money, and the mic. The mic? He expected her to speak.

She accepted the ribbon and envelope. But when she didn't readily take the mic, the mayor gestured for her to take it. "Say a few words. I'm sure everyone wants to hear from the person who helped plan this amazing day." And then the mayor turned to the crowd. "Ethan, why don't you come up here too?" When Ethan shook his head, the mayor said, "You aren't going to make Hannah do this all on her own, are you?"

That was all he needed to say to put Ethan in motion. Thankfully. Hannah loved interacting with the community, but she had a thing about speaking in front of large audiences.

Once Ethan was standing next to her, she backed away when the mayor handed over the mic to Ethan. "Um, thanks."

"Louder," Mayor Banks said.

Ethan cleared his throat. "Thank you. My aunt will be so excited. Birdie misses you all. And she can't wait to get home. Hannah and I were honored to be able to work on this amazing festival. We hope you all enjoyed it."

A loud cheer rose in the crowd.

Without another word, Ethan dropped the mic into the mayor's hand as though it were a snake that was about to bite him. And then Hannah walked away with Ethan by her side.

They meandered around Beachcomber Park where the outdoor games had been set up for the kids. There were a number of corn hole tosses, a couple of volleyball nets, a couple badminton nets, an obstacle course, and a mini-derby car race track. There weren't prizes for those games. They were just there so families could continue to enjoy themselves at their leisure.

They continued walking. They stopped now and then to talk to people. Some of them, Ethan knew. Others, Hannah introduced him to. It was nice that he was starting to recognize faces and actually be able to put names to the faces. She smiled. He was becoming a regular part of the community.

Nikki rushed up to hug each of them. She said she had the best day and hated to leave, but Sam was there to pick her up.

As Nikki went to meet her father, Mayor Banks approached them. "Well done, you two. I have to admit when I heard you were making changes to the original lineup for the festival, I had my concerns. But now that I've see it and watched the town's response, you both did a great job."

They both thanked him.

The mayor turned to Hannah. "I hate to put you on the spot, but I've delayed the printing of the tourist brochure as long as possible. Will the bakery be open at the beginning of May?"

"I...I don't know. There's still a number of things to do and Ethan has to go back to New York on Sunday." Hannah worried her bottom lip.

"Include it in the brochure," Ethan interjected.

The mayor's brows rose as his gaze moved between them. "Are you sure?"

Hannah turned to him. "You can't tell him it'll be done, if it's not."

"Trust me. The bakery will be open by May first."

Mayor Banks smiled. "That's wonderful news. We'll be looking forward to it."

When the mayor walked away, Hannah turned to him. "What are you doing?"

"Trust me."

"But Ethan—"

"Trust me."

"What aren't you telling me? And does this have something to do with the door being blocked this morning?"

"So many questions. Just give me a little more time and I promise I won't let you down. When I leave, you'll be able to finish what is left."

"Ethan, there's no way you can get all of that work done by yourself. I have to at least help you."

He shook his head. "What you need to do is concentrate on the rest of the festival. After all, the highlight is tomorrow with the egg hunt."

229

Uncertainty shown in her eyes. "But when it's over, you can show me what needs to be done at the bakery and I'll take over."

He gave it a little thought and then said, "It sounds like a plan."

"I just hope we don't both regret you making such a promise to the mayor." Her stomach knotted with nerves. So much was riding on the bakery opening on time.

They continued walking. Every now and then they paused to speak with friends. At last, they made it the whole way around the park. The fun was over for the day. And it was now time to clean up.

Hannah turned to Ethan. "You did great. Your aunt would be proud of you."

"She would be proud of you—you did most of this." He gazed deep into her eyes, making her heart pitter-pat. "I just did what you told me."

His compliment meant a lot to her. "I...I should get moving." But her legs refused to cooperate. She continued to stare into Ethan's dreamy eyes. Oh, she was falling hard for him. "Um...there's a lot of cleaning up to do."

"What do you need me to do?"

Pull me into your arms and kiss me.

She swallowed hard. "There's already a cleanup committee. So go. Enjoy the time with your parents."

"But we're still on for hiding the eggs, right?"

She'd asked him, as well as Josie and Lily, to help her hide the Easter eggs in the wee hours of tomorrow morning for the finale of Spring Fling. "Yes, we have a date tomorrow morning."

"Looking forward to it." He turned to walk away.

She thought about saying something to him about wanting him to stay here in Bluestar—stay here with her. As she thought of revealing her true feelings to him, her stomach took a nauseous dip. What if he didn't feel the same way? What if she made a fool of herself?

Or worse, what if he felt the same and neither ever said a word to the other? Her heart pounded harder. What if they missed their chance?

CHAPTER TWENTY-FOUR

He was falling in love.

And he was running out of time to tell her.

Ethan knew if he didn't tell Hannah how he felt, he would regret it, not just in the moment but for the rest of his life.

The thought of uttering those three little words made his heart pound. What if she didn't feel the same way? What if he'd been misreading her signals? But what if she felt the same?

This was it. This was his moment. He just had to claim it.

He turned to her. Her eyes reflected warmth and happiness, but was there something more? Did she love him too? He'd never know until he said something—

The shrill wail of the fire whistle filled the quiet of the evening.

The call to action silenced his words. Hannah blinked and the happiness disappeared. Instead her eyes reflected fear. He had no idea until now how deep her fear of his occupation went.

Before he could speak, Greg clapped Ethan on the shoulder. "We got called out. Didn't you get the message?"

"Message?"

"You're a Bluestar firefighter now. Let's go. We'll worry about setting you up in the system later." Greg rushed off.

"Hey, Ethan, let's go!" Captain Campbell called out.

"Ethan, don't go!" Her eyes pleaded with him.

"I have to. I'm sorry." The last thing he saw was the shimmer of unshed tears in her eyes. It tore at his heart.

More men fell in behind him. He lost sight of her. He turned and ran after Greg. Being an experienced firefighter, he knew that seconds could mean the difference between life and death. Hannah would understand.

This was his first official call with the Bluestar Fire Department. He had to stay alert and be ready for anything.

With red lights flashing and the siren wailing, Ethan rode in the Bluestar fire engine out of town. He felt so out of place, wearing turnouts and boots that weren't his. The men around him weren't part of his regular crew. And yet they hadn't questioned his presence. Instead they'd tossed him supplies and told him which truck to hop onboard.

His gut knotted up.

Fiery flashbacks crowded into his mind. His heart pounded. He wasn't ready for this—it was too soon. He needed more time.

And then things went from bad...to horrendous.

They were headed for a working structure fire. Not just any fire. It was at Hannah's brother's farm.

Ethan's mind crowded with images of Sam and Nikki as well as the farm animals. Nothing could happen to any of them. He thought of Hannah and how she was still working through the loss of her father. How was she going to take the news of a fire at the farm?

He longed to be there with her when she got the news. He wanted to be there for her to lean on—to do what she needed of him.

But he also knew with all of his years of experience that he would probably be of the most help right there on that truck. Because no matter what he'd been through, he wouldn't let the flashbacks stop him from doing what came natural to him. He would help Sam and Nikki any way possible.

As the fire truck rumbled its way along the winding two-lane road, his imagination conjured up an image of the big old farmhouse going up in flames. There couldn't be any mistakes. He had to do everything just right. Where a fire was concerned, there weren't do-overs.

The two fire trucks and one tanker truck rolled down the gravel driveway. Ethan craned his neck to see out the window. He focused on the big white farmhouse. He scanned the roofline. No signs of fire. Was it possible this was a false alarm? He certainly hoped so.

His gaze moved to the second floor and then lowered to the main floor. There were no flames and not even a plume of smoke. He breathed a sigh of relief to see the farmhouse was just as it had been.

The trucks rolled past the house into the back yard. He jumped out. There in the field sat the new barn—the one Sam and some men had been building. The smoke rose from it.

Nikki ran over. "Ethan, help!"

He knelt down. "Nikki, what's wrong?"

Tears tracked down her pale cheeks. "It's Dash. He kept running away. I...I put him in the new barn with his momma while I went to Spring Fling. They...they are trapped. Please save them!"

Ethan turned toward the new barn, which wasn't quite finished. As he studied it, he noticed the smoke was coming out the back. It didn't look like the whole barn was engulfed—at least not yet. Still, it didn't look good. Not good at all.

As he took in the scene, flashbacks of the past filled his mind. His pulse quickened. His breaths came quick. Fiery flashbacks filled his mind. His stomach churned. Could he do it again?

The entire fire crew had been called out.

That never happened unless...unless it was bad.

Even with the last remnants of the afternoon sun, a chill of apprehension inched its way up Hannah's spine. *Where were they all going?*

"Where's the fire?" she called out as one last man rushed past her.

He didn't answer. She wasn't even sure he'd heard her as he broke into a run.

234

The last fire on the island had been last summer. It had been a grease fire at The Lighthouse Café. Thankfully it had been minor with no injuries.

Please let this be minor.

She ran back inside the community center where cleanup efforts had commenced. Her gaze swung over the mass of worried expressions. At last, she located her mother. Hannah rushed up to her. "What's going on?"

Her mother's face was pale and her eyes glistened with unshed tears.

"Mom, what is it?"

"They said...they said your brother's farm is on fire—"

"What?" Her chest tightened. "Come on. Let's go."

She took her mother by the hand and rushed out the door. They headed straight for Hannah's golf cart. What she wouldn't do right now for a car. Her foot pressed the gas pedal to the floor. She didn't ease up on the accelerator as they whipped around a right turn.

"Hannah, slow down," her mother said.

"Slow down? This cart can only go twenty-five miles per hour." She inwardly groaned. "This can't be happening."

Her mother remained quiet the rest of the ride. Hannah couldn't tell if she was having a word with the big guy up above or if she was thinking of Hannah's father.

Her mother held on tightly as Hannah pushed the golf cart as fast as it would go. All the while, she prayed her brother and niece were safe. Any other damage they could deal with. But nothing could happen to Sam and Nikki. Their family had already gone through so much—they'd lost so much.

As the cart crested a rise in the road, Hannah spotted the glow of flashing red lights. It was a worrisome beacon. Part of Hannah wanted to turn around and pretend that none of this was happening. And yet she kept her foot pressed firmly to the accelerator.

Her family needed her. That was more important than painful flashbacks or the fear that had her white-knuckling the steering wheel. They'd all get through this terrible evening.

The sheriff stood in the driveaway, attempting to keep away gawkers. He waved for her to stop. As soon as he lifted the beam of his flashlight to their faces and recognized Hannah and her mother, he offered a quick word of comfort and then waved them through.

"I...I can't look." Her mother covered her face with both hands.

Flood lights illuminated the farm house. It had stood there all of Hannah's life as well as her mother's. Hannah remembered going there for Sunday dinners and holidays. It was within this very house where she'd first learned to bake. It was there where she'd gained a passion for creating delightful edibles.

"Mom, it's okay. The house is fine." Tears spilled over onto Hannah's cheeks.

"It is?"

"Yes. Look and see."

Her mother slowly lowered her hands. "It is." Her mother pressed a hand to her chest. "Thank God." She looked around. "Where's Sam and Nikki?"

"I don't know." Hannah gazed into the shadows.

Though the old farmhouse was still standing, there was still something terribly wrong. The heavy odor of smoke hung in the air. But if it wasn't the house on fire that must mean the barn was burning. Hannah's chest tightened as memories of her father's demise rushed to the forefront of her mind.

"I don't see Sam." Her mother's frantic voice drew Hannah from her troubling thoughts.

"I don't see Nikki." Hannah scanned faces, not taking time to speak to any of them. Everyone had a mission. Hers was to find her family.

Hannah noticed the firefighters were rushing around to the back of the house. She parked out of the way, near the house. She jumped out and rushed after them. Her mother was by her side.

"Keep looking. They have to be here." Her mother's tone, though determined, held a tremor of fear.

As they rounded the house, they were confronted with the sight of the fire. With the aid of the spotlights, they were able to see the smoke coming from the back of the new barn—the barn her brother had been building for their growing family of goats. Tears pricked Hannah's eyes. Was her family trapped in there? Her heart lodged in her throat. Were the goats in there? Was Dash in there?

"Auntie Hannah!" Nikki ran up to her.

Tears blurred Hannah's vision as she reached for her niece. She lifted Nikki off the ground into a big hug. She closed her eyes as the tears spilled down her cheeks. She'd never been so happy to see anyone in her life. With reluctance, she lowered her niece to the ground.

"Where's your dad?" Hannah's mother asked.

Nikki pulled back and pointed over to a group of firefighters. Sam was standing among them. His feet were planted on the ground with his hands pressed to his waist. His shoulders were rigid, as if they were holding up the weight of the world. As a firefighter said something to him, he nodded. She wanted to rush to him and hug him but she knew now wasn't the time.

The chief was calling out orders and another couple were putting on oxygen tanks. Hannah knew what that meant—they were going inside. And then the one man turned. It was Ethan. Their gazes caught and held for just a second.

In that precious moment, she begged him with her eyes not to go inside. Apparently he hadn't gotten the message, as he turned away and settled his helmet on his head.

Her gaze moved back to the burning building. Her stomach churned. Her mouth grew moist. And for a moment, she thought she was going to be sick right there in front of everyone.

Hannah closed her eyes and visualized her family, all safe and sound. Ethan was there smiling at her. Her breathing slowed. She swallowed once. Then twice.

The nauseous feeling receded. She opened her eyes. Still, the nightmare continued to unfold. She caught one last sighting of Ethan as he stepped inside the barn.

She couldn't stay there and watch him risk his life—just like her father had done time after time until his luck ran out. Grief and fear sent her heart racing. She couldn't stand there waiting.

Hannah looked around for her niece, who was now clinging to Hannah's mother. They were both watching in horror as the new barn burned.

Hannah reached out to her niece. "Come on. We're going in the house."

"No!" Nikki didn't take her gaze off the barn. "Dash and his momma are in there. They have to be all right." Nikki attempted to run toward the barn, but Hannah's mother pulled her back. "Ethan's gonna save them."

Hannah inwardly groaned as her gaze moved back to the barn. With all of the smoke and flames, she didn't think anything would survive. She needed to spare her niece from any additional trauma.

"Let's go inside," Hannah said.

Nikki fervently shook her head. "This is my fault."

Hannah crouched down next to her. "No, it's not."

"It is! Dash wasn't supposed to be in there. Daddy said so. But Dash kept getting lose. I...I wanted him to be safe." Sobs shook her slender shoulders.

Hannah's heart broke for her distraught niece. She scooped her up in her arms. Hannah leaned over to her mother, letting her know that they were going in the house—away from the smoke and growing flames—away from Hannah's worst nightmare.

She took one last glance in the direction she'd last seen Ethan. He wasn't there. She sent up a silent prayer that he and the others would be all right. And then she attempted to distract her thoughts by focusing on Nikki.

Once in the house, she placed Nikki on the couch before closing all of the blinds as though it would block out the nightmare ongoing outside. "What do you want to do?"

Her niece looked up at her with blotchy, tear-stained cheeks. "I want Dash." And then she started to cry in earnest again. "It's my fault. All my fault."

Hannah sat down next to her niece and pulled her close. She murmured whatever she could think of to soothe the girl. It was hard enough on Nikki to lose her grandfather and her mother at such a tender age, she shouldn't have to face anymore loss. It just wasn't fair.

After a time, Nikki calmed down. Hannah turned on the television. She selected one of Nikki's favorite movies from on-demand.

But Hannah couldn't sit there and watch a movie. She had pent-up energy. She got to her feet and paced behind the couch. What was going on outside? Where was Ethan? *Please let him be safe.*

Nikki stared at her.

Hannah stopped. "Sorry." She couldn't sit still, not until she knew everything was all right. She needed to do something—anything. "I know. Would you like some pancakes?"

Nikki's sad eyes said that she only wanted one thing— Dash.

Hannah felt utterly helpless. "I'll check and see if there are some bananas. You love banana pancakes with chocolate chips."

Not expecting an answer, Hannah moved to the kitchen. She gathered all of the ingredients she'd need for a batch of pancakes. And she even located some bananas.

She whipped together the batter and warmed the griddle. She was just about to pour the first pancake when there was a knock at the door. She paused and turned to it.

If it was her family, they wouldn't have knocked. Her heart clenched. Was it bad news?

Her mind rolled back in time to the fire that claimed her father. Fires were infrequent on the island. So when one happened, the news spread like a wave over the town.

That not-so-long-ago evening was so vivid in her mind. She'd gone to her parents' house. She'd wanted to check in with her mother and see if she'd heard anything about the fire call. When the firefighters hadn't returned quickly, they all knew it was bad.

Her mother had busied herself in the kitchen making fried chicken, mashed potatoes, and gravy. Her father's favorite meal. Hannah, needing something to do, had whipped up a batch of biscuits from scratch.

The biscuits had just come out of the oven when there was a knock at the front door. They'd both stopped and stared at each other. Friends knew to come to the back door.

But there was another knock that seemed to startle them out of their stupor. Her mother had dried her hands on a dish towel and made her way to the living room. Hannah followed as far as the doorway. It gave her a clear vision of the front door.

When her mother had opened the door, there stood then-lieutenant Campbell and the sheriff. Hannah's heart had sunk as her stomach took a nauseous lurch. It was bad, but at that moment, she hadn't any idea how bad—how much pain was going to tear through her close-knit family.

Knock-knock.

The sound brought her back to the present. It was then she realized her cheeks were damp. She swiped at them. She had to get it together. That was then. This was different. It had to be.

"Hannah?"

Ethan? She rushed to the door. She swung it open and saw Ethan standing there in his turnouts with his hair mussed up and a smile on his face. He was smiling, but why? And then she noticed Dash was in his arms. The goat was alert and appeared to be fine.

"You saved him." Tears rushed back to her eyes and she gave up trying to restrain them.

"And his mother."

"Nikki!" Hannah knew this was the medicine her niece needed. "Hurry!"

Nikki ran to the back door and came to a halt. Her eyes grew round as her gaze landed on Ethan holding Dash.

Then Nikki ran to them. "You saved him."

Ethan handed Nikki the goat. "He's been crying for you."

When Nikki turned to carry the goat into the house, Hannah said, "Outside."

Her niece didn't put up an argument. She was too happy to have her beloved goat back. And Hannah was just as happy.

She turned to Ethan, surprised to find him still standing there. She was so relieved to see him. Giving into her emotions, she rushed forward and threw her arms around him. For a second, he didn't move as though she'd caught him totally off guard. But then his arms circled around her and held her close.

She was so grateful he was all right. The pain of the past collided with the fright of the present. Tears ran unleashed down her cheeks. She was so relieved that life hadn't repeated itself.

"It's okay," Ethan murmured. "Everyone is safe."

She sniffled as she pulled away. She swiped at her cheeks and then she smiled at him. "You're Nikki's hero."

He shook his head as he shuffled his feet. "Not yours?"

She stood several feet from him with her arms hanging limply at her sides. Her gaze met his briefly, making her heart beat faster. Then she glanced away. "You should go."

"Hannah, I can't talk now but later—"

"No." She shook her head. "There's nothing to say."

"I disagree."

"Ethan, I can't do this." She turned with a heavy heart that felt as though it were cracking in two. She retreated into the kitchen. When she turned around, he was gone.

In that moment, she realized he was a hero in every sense of the word. He couldn't walk away from firefighting any more than she could walk away from baking. So where did that leave them? Nowhere good.

CHAPTER TWENTY-FIVE

Hannah yawned...again.

The sun wasn't even up yet.

It was the following day and Hannah was tired. She'd been at her brother's place until late. She'd finished making the pancakes and then proceeded to add hash browns, eggs, and bacon to the menu. And then her family had quietly gathered around the kitchen table. Each had been lost in their own thoughts as they ate the quiet meal.

When Hannah had gotten home, she'd knocked on Ethan's door but he hadn't answered. It wasn't until later when she was lying in bed, staring into the dark that she heard him come up the steps. He'd lightly tapped on her door and called her name, but she hadn't answered.

She felt as though she'd just fallen asleep when the alarm had gone off. It went off again. This time she pressed the silence button instead of the snooze.

No matter how much she didn't want to get out of bed, the children of Bluestar were counting on her to hide the Easter eggs.

In zombie mode, she moved quickly through her morning routine. She could do this. She yawned. It was going to be an extremely long day.

With her coffee topped off, Hannah tightened the lid on the thermal cup. With four large bags full of eggs hanging off her arms, a flashlight, and three copies of the map of the park. Hannah headed for the door. It was past time to start hiding eggs.

She tiptoed past Ethan's door and headed down the stairs. She knew that he'd volunteered to help her, Josie, and Lily hide the eggs, but that was before the fire—before she realized that his occupation would always stand between them.

The ride to Beachcomber Park in her golf cart was quiet as was the town. She met up with Lily and Josie. They didn't look much more awake than she felt.

Lily glanced around. "Where's Ethan? I thought he was going to help."

"Don't tell us that he gets to sleep in while we're out here in the middle of the night." Josie frowned.

"He's not coming." She didn't want to talk about it. "It doesn't matter. We've got this."

Lily arched a brow. "What did we miss?"

"Nothing." Hannah avoided her friends' inquisitive gazes.

"Here he comes," Josie said. "This should be interesting."

"What?" Hannah spun around. Sure enough Ethan was headed in their direction.

"Maybe we should get started," Lily said.

"Can't we stay and watch?" Josie asked.

"No. Come on." Lily hooked her arm in Josie's.

"Okay. Stop pulling." Josie grabbed a bag of eggs and headed off with Lily.

Hannah's traitorous heart thudded at the sight of Ethan. When he finally stood in front of her, she said, "What are you doing here? We said everything last night."

"You might have had your say but I didn't have mine."

She didn't want to hear what he had to say. It wouldn't change her mind. They couldn't continue this—whatever this was between them.

"First, I have to hide the eggs," she said, hoping to end the conversation before it'd even begun.

"And I'll help."

With a sigh, she handed him a bag of eggs. At least now she'd have a little breathing space—a chance to figure out what to say to him in order for him to take her seriously.

By the time they finished, there was a glow in the horizon as the sun was about to make its grand appearance. She took off to catch up with Ethan and help him hide his remaining eggs.

"How many do you have to go?" she asked.

"Hang on one second." He placed a pink egg in a bush. Then he turned to her. "I'm done."

"Did you remember to mark the map?"

He held up a finger for her to wait and then he made a mark on his map. "All done."

When he handed over his map, she glanced at it, finding the eggs were evenly distributed throughout his section. She folded his map and then placed it in her backpack purse. She could see Josie and Lily off in the distance still hiding eggs.

"Thank you," she said. "But you don't have to stay."

"Yes, I do. We have some talking to do. Or at least I do."

"Ethan, it isn't necessary."

"I disagree. Now the way I see it, we can talk here or we can go sit over on the wall. Which shall it be?"

With an exasperated sigh, she led the way across the street to the stone wall that separated the beach from the parking lot. Hannah picked a spot on the wall and sat down. Ethan sat next to her. They quietly stared off at the horizon as shades of oranges and pink splashed across the sky.

"Hannah—"

"Shh...you're going to miss it."

Ethan was quiet for a minute or two. "Hannah, we need to talk—"

"There it is." The darkened sky grew brighter. "Do you see it? The sun has just crept above the horizon."

"I see it." He didn't sound the least bit interested.

She glanced at him. "Okay say it."

"I think you and I have a good thing going and I don't want it to end—"

"Don't—"

"Don't, what? Say what I feel." He hopped down off the wall and stood in front of her. "Are you trying to say you don't feel anything for me?"

245

She clasped her hands together and stared at them. "It doesn't matter."

"Of course, it matters. It matters very much. I'm falling in love—"

She pressed a finger to his lips. Her heart was breaking. He was saying the exact words she'd longed to hear before last night's fire drove home the reason they didn't belong together.

He wrapped his hand around hers and pulled it from his lips. "Hannah, why are you fighting this? Don't you care about me?"

She yanked her hand from his. "I care. I care too much."

"What does that mean?"

Tears pricked the backs of her eyes. Why was he making this so hard? She blinked repeatedly. "It means I can't go through that again."

"What again?" And then his eyes widened in understanding. "You mean the fire. But everything turned out okay. Everyone is safe."

"This time. My father was safe for years until he wasn't—until his job killed him!"

"Hannah, it doesn't mean that will happen to me."

"The risk is...it's too much." She glanced down at her clasped hands.

"So you'd rather just throw away any chance we have at happiness?" Frustration rang out in his voice.

Her gaze met his. "Are you willing to give up firefighting?"

He raked his fingers through his hair. "I...I don't know."

The anguish reflected in his eyes was all the answer she needed. She swallowed hard, struggling to control her emotions. "We're both kidding ourselves to think you and I could work out." Her chest grew heavy with a deep sadness. "I...I can't expect you to quit your job—a job you love. But I can't stick around and worry every time you go out on a call. I'm sorry."

She got to her feet. Her heart felt as though it'd sunk down to her sneakers. She turned and started walking.

"Hannah, don't do this. Hannah, stop."

As the tears streamed down her face, she kept walking. She told herself that he would be happier this way. He'd find someone who didn't have an issue with his occupation. He deserved someone who could fully support him.

She wished it was her. She wished that when her father had died that something hadn't broken inside of her.

Now she had to figure out how to be happy without Ethan. Was that even possible?

CHAPTER TWENTY-SIX

She was so tired of fake smiling.

Inside her heart was broken.

As Hannah moved through the events of the day, she found herself looking for Ethan but he'd been absent from the Easter egg hunt. The whole time she'd been questioning her decision about ending things with him. Had she done the right thing?

In the end, what other choice did she have? He was always going to be a firefighter. And one loss to that profession was more than enough for her. This knowledge didn't ease the pain she felt.

Buzz. Buzz.

She had no interest in talking to anyone—until she glanced at the caller ID.

Hannah pressed the phone to her ear. "Emma? What's wrong?"

"Nothing. Why would you say that?"

"Because...oh, I don't know. Never mind. What did you need?"

"I heard about the fire. How is everyone doing? Do I need to come home?"

Hannah filled her sister in on the details of the fire. Conveniently, she left out any mention of Ethan. Just the thought of him sent a wave of sadness over her, but she worked hard to hide it from her sister.

"So you see, everything is fine and there's no need for you to drop everything and come home." Hannah hoped her voice didn't betray her. "What's going on with you?"

"We're getting ready to go out on the road next week." Em went on to mention the famous country star she would be opening for, and Hannah was extremely impressed.

"Wow, Em! I'm so happy for you. I knew you could do it."

"Hey, aren't you supposed to be at Spring Fling?"

"How did you know?" Hannah was surprised her sister, who'd been gone for quite a long time, would still be on top of the happenings in and around Bluestar.

"You do realize you can take the girl out of Bluestar, but you can't take Bluestar out of the girl. I still keep track of what's going on with the town on the island's blog."

"Oh. Right." Hannah recalled how Mayor Banks had launched a Bluestar website a year or so ago, but she wasn't aware there was a blog. "This blog, it's just about the public events in Bluestar, right?"

"Actually, there's a lot more like wedding, baby, and birthday announcements. Last week they had an update on your bakery—"

"What?" Why hadn't she heard about it? "What did it say?"

"That the flood had delayed the opening, and they weren't sure if you'd be open for the beginning of tourist season at the beginning of May. And then they mentioned other places in town that people could get their baked goods. None of it was bad."

Her stomach dropped. "That all depends on how you look at it."

"Oh, Han, don't worry." Em was the only one to call her Han. "Once your bakery is open, you know you'll have more business than you can deal with." There was a distinct pause. "Is that what has you so down?"

"I'm not down." Even to her own ears, her voice sounded like she was trying too hard to be convincing.

"So if it's not the bakery, it must be the new guy who has been helping you."

"You mean Ethan?"

"Yes. What's going on with you two?"

"Nothing good." And then it came spilling out.

"Wow. I have missed a lot. If he's as awesome as you say, you need to give him another chance."

"I don't know." All the reasons to hold back flashed in her mind like big warning signs.

"Han, you've always been the cautious one. You stayed close to home. You took forever to get serious with a guy—"

"And look how that turned out."

"But you say Ethan is different. And...and he's a firefighter, just like Dad." The tone of Em's voice said she was connecting the dots. "And you're worried that Ethan might meet the same fate as Dad."

"I couldn't go through that again. Every time he went out on a call, I'd worry about him."

"And you're saying if he did anything else for a living that you wouldn't worry about him?"

"No, but—"

"What happened to Dad was the worst. And I miss him as much as you, but it was an accident, Han. You can't think that it's going to happen again."

Her sister was right. Logically she agreed, but it was her heart that wasn't so certain it was up for taking a risk again with a firefighter. "It doesn't matter anyhow. His job is in New York and mine is here on the island."

"Unless you tell him the truth. Tell him you love him. You do love him, don't you?"

Hannah opened her mouth to deny it, but she couldn't. She wordlessly pressed her lips together as she thought of Ethan. Was her sister right? Had she overreacted? Should she try to fix things?

"Enough about me," Hannah said. "When are you coming home?"

"I...I don't know." Em went on to tell her about the cross-country tour.

"Now I can tell everyone that I knew you before you were famous."

"You could tell them a lot more than that, but don't you dare." In the background, there was knocking and someone calling out Em's name. "Sorry, Han, I have to go. I know

250

you've been hurt before, but if you don't take a chance on Ethan, you'll regret it. Bye."

And with that her sister was gone. Hannah wished her sister was there in Bluestar. She missed Em a lot. They didn't agree on everything. Their mother always said it was because they were opposites. But they did have a lot of fun together.

As for telling Ethan about her feelings, Em had some good points. But since when did she start taking advice from her younger sister—the same sister who'd broken up with her soulmate to chase her singing dreams?

She was home.

At last.

Birdie clasped her hands together as a smile pulled at her lips. She'd missed Spring Fling but from what she'd heard, it had been a huge success. Now she wanted to thank Ethan and Hannah for all they'd done in her absence.

Ethan's parents, who'd taken Peaches to pick her up at Sunny Days, stood with her in Beachcomber Park. Birdie's gaze searched the lingering crowd. Where was her nephew and Hannah? Her reports from Betty had all been positive. Her little bit of meddling had worked.

"Where are they?" Birdie asked.

"Who?" Ethan's mother asked as she held onto Peaches's leash.

"Ethan and Hannah. I thought they'd still be here, helping with the cleanup."

Ethan's parents, Clara and Marshall, glanced at each other. Worry lines creased their faces as the silence dragged on.

A sense of foreboding came over Birdie. "Out with it."

Marshall cleared his throat. "We didn't want to upset you with this being your homecoming."

"It's too late for that." Birdie turned to Clara. "Is it Ethan?"

Clara shook her head. "He's fine. But there was a fire last night."

"Oh no." Birdie released a hand from her walker to press it to her chest. No wonder they'd been hesitant to tell her. "Where?"

"The Bell Farm. And luckily no one was hurt."

Birdie's mind raced with possibilities. "Was it the house?"

Marshall shook his head. "It was a new barn."

Birdie shook her head. "This is unbelievable. Sam has been through so much—too much for someone his age." When they both looked confused, Birdie continued. "Sam lost his young wife, Beth, not long after they had their daughter. And more recently his father unexpectedly died. When they say bad things come in threes, they weren't kidding."

"Everyone feels terrible for him and his daughter," Clara said. "I wish there was something we could do."

Birdie wasn't sure how to help, but there had to be something the town could do. "Let me think about it."

"Anyway, everyone was up late," Clara said. "Maybe Ethan and Hannah decided to skip the festivities today."

It didn't sound right to her. Both Hannah and Ethan were responsible individuals. They'd want to see Spring Fling through until the end.

Betty strolled up to Birdie and hugged her. "Welcome home."

"Thanks." Birdie resumed searching the familiar faces.

"Did you lose something?" Betty asked.

"Yes. Where are Ethan and Hannah?"

Betty shrugged. "I don't know. I saw Hannah a little while ago, but come to think of it, I haven't seen Ethan all day."

"Maybe he's finishing up at the bakery," Ethan's father said. "I'll walk over and see."

"They were so happy yesterday, well, before the fire. You heard about it, didn't you?"

Birdie nodded. "It's just awful."

"Agreed. But before that Ethan and Hannah were having a good time together. Entering them in the jelly bean relay worked out just like you thought."

Ethan's mother agreed. "I've never seen him so happy."

Betty sighed. "I suppose this means I owe you an apology."

Birdie finally tore her gaze away from the crowd of people. She noticed the way her friend's brows knitted together in a frown. "Apologize for what?"

"I told you to stop matchmaking, but it appears you were right about them."

Birdie glanced back at her best friend. "I have a feeling that by this evening, they'll be an official couple. It'll be so great to have Ethan on the island permanently."

Peaches barked her agreement. Birdie bent over to pet her four-footed friend. Oh how she'd missed Peaches. She'd missed this island. She didn't know it was possible to miss a place that much. There was something special about Bluestar. It might not be perfect all of the time—her thoughts turned to the fire—but its residents looked out for each other. It was exactly what her nephew needed after all he'd gone through. And she would love to be a regular part of his life.

Jingle. Jingle.

"Sorry to interrupt," his father said. "I tried your phone but you didn't pick up."

"Oh. Sorry," Ethan said. "I was just finishing up a couple of things. What did you need?"

"I know you're leaving today, and I wondered if you'd mind giving me a ride as your mother is going to stay with your aunt. I need to get back to work too. Anyway, I wanted to leave your mother the car at the parking lot on the mainland so she can get Aunt Birdie back and forth to her physical rehab appointments."

"Ahh...sure. Not a problem. I was planning to leave in an hour or so."

"I'm already packed," his father said. "Shall we meet up at Aunt Birdie's?"

Ethan nodded. "I'll see you there."

His father looked around. "You did a beautiful job. I can't wait to visit it the next time I'm on the island."

"Thank you." His voice didn't sound right, not even to his own ears.

Ethan was holding back a wave of sadness that was threatening to engulf him. Because hearing his father speak made him realize he wouldn't be back on Bluestar Island any time soon.

Even though he'd been through a rough patch, being a firefighter was as much a part of him as breathing—just as baking was an integral part of Hannah. He wished she understood how important it was to him.

After his father had gone, Ethan had to accept that Hannah hadn't changed her mind. She had made her choice. There was nothing left for him at The Elegant Bakery.

With the bakery completed, thanks to his friends at the fire department, there was nothing keeping him there. It was time to go home.

He grabbed a piece of paper and jotted Hannah a note. And then he laid his key to the bakery atop of it.

Spring Fling was over for another year.

Hannah knew she would never forget this event—nor the man who'd help make it possible. Ethan's image came to her mind. It was followed by the memory of him preparing to walk into the burning barn. Her body shuddered at the memory. She banished it to the back of her mind.

She'd noticed how he'd stayed away from the egg hunt. She told herself it would be easier if they avoided each other until he left town, but that was unrealistic as they both lived above the bakery. And she wanted to see him.

She wanted to tell him how well the egg hunt had gone, that she'd spoken to her sister and Birdie was home. There was so much to share. Maybe it would help smooth over this rough patch they'd found themselves in.

Excitement bubbled up in Hannah at the thought of seeing the progress at the bakery. But right on its heels came sadness at the thought of Ethan leaving tomorrow. Even though they'd officially ended things, she wasn't ready to say goodbye. She shoved the thought to the back of her mind.

She'd delayed this moment as long as possible by agreeing to have dinner with her mother at The Lighthouse Café. When her mother suggested they include Ethan, Hannah had brushed off the suggestion. She was so grateful her mother hadn't pursued the subject.

As she rode to the bakery in her golf cart, she focused on the bakery. Hannah's dream had started many years ago in her grandmother's kitchen. And now Ethan had helped her make this dream come true.

She didn't know how to thank him. What was the appropriate way to repay someone who saved your dream from being utterly ruined? She didn't know but she'd think of something.

When she pulled to a stop in front of the bakery, it still looked the same from the front. The paper was still on the windows blocking out any curious onlookers. She hadn't seen the inside in days and she wondered how much work would be left for her to complete.

When she stepped up to the front door, she was surprised to find it locked. Usually, Ethan left the doors unlocked when he was working. He must be upstairs as she just saw his family at the café without him.

She rummaged in her backpack purse to find her keys. She unlocked the door, all the while wondering what she'd find inside. No matter the state of things, she would finish it. She could do it. At least that's what she wanted to believe.

Hannah opened the door, letting the last rays of sunshine in. With the windows covered, she couldn't make out much. Using her hands to make sure she didn't run into anything, she slowly made her way toward the counter.

She skirted around a table in the middle of the room. *Where had that come from?*

After bumping into a couple of things, she made it behind the counter. She ran her hand over the wall and finally located the light switches. The spacious room was flooded with light. Her heart leapt into her throat.

This can't be real. She blinked just to be sure she wasn't imagining things. But the beautiful room still existed. It was like a dream come to life.

In the middle of the room stood a round pedestal table. It was made of light-colored wood with a whitewash. It was shabby chic beach. In other words, it was perfect.

She moved forward and ran her hand over the smooth finish. "I love it."

Above the table hung the chandelier from the estate sale. It looked perfect in the middle of the room. It was definitely a center piece. She couldn't believe Ethan had gotten all of this done in such a short amount of time.

She had to see him. She had to thank him. Though she doubted she would ever be able to find the words to express what this all meant to her, but she had to try.

She rushed to the door that separated the bakery from the private residences. She called upstairs. "Ethan? Ethan, come here!"

While she waited for him, she moved back inside the bakery. There was so much to see—so much to enjoy.

She turned on the lights in the new display cases. She lightly clapped her hands as she grinned while bouncing on the balls of her feet. This was like taking all of her childhood Christmases and bundling them into one day. No. It was better.

On the wall behind the display cases was the giant mirror she'd opted to turn into a chalkboard. On the board in white chalk was scrolled out: *Welcome to The Elegant Bakery*.

This moment felt wrong to experience by herself. Ethan should be here with her. Without him, none of this would have been possible. She ran back to the bottom of the steps and yelled, "Ethan, hurry. Please."

She worried he was purposely avoiding her until he left sometime tomorrow. She placed her foot on the bottom step, but then she hesitated. She'd give him a little more time.

Hannah stepped back into the bakery. She turned in a circle, taking in the navy and white tile floor that fit so perfectly with the classical charm of the bakery. The walls and ceiling were sanded and painted in a soft white. How did he get this all completed so quickly?

Unable to wait another moment, she ran up the stairs, taking them two at a time. She had to thank him. She had to tell him what an amazing job he'd done.

She rapped her knuckles on the door. "Ethan?" She knocked louder. "Ethan, please don't ignore me."

Nothing.

She tried the doorknob. It turned. "Ethan?"

Inside all of the lights were out. She checked the time on her fitness watch. It was too early for him to be asleep. Maybe he was hanging out with Greg.

Hannah expelled a disappointed sigh as she closed his door. She moved to her apartment and let herself inside. Her excitement over the bakery abated a bit without Ethan there to share it.

They'd been partners through the whole process. She'd been the visionary and he'd made it a reality. The bakery was their creation. They'd been an amazing team.

She flipped on the lights and then closed the door. On the floor she found a white envelope. She picked it up and found her name scrawled on the front. Not sure what it was, she opened it.

Hannah, by now you've seen the bakery. I hope it's everything you wanted. I made the table from some scraps of wood. I knew you wanted a special piece for the middle of the room and with your limited budget, I thought you might like this until you find something better.

I can't take credit for getting the bakery done so quickly. I had a lot of help. The guys at the fire department wanted to chip in. They worked in shifts to get it finished.

Hannah's legs grew weak. She leaned her back against the door and slid down to the floor. Guilt assailed her for keeping her distance from the firehouse ever since her father's death. She would have to do something special for them, starting with Firefighter Monday where they received free donuts. Her father would have approved of it. He loved donuts.

Would her father have approved of the bakery? Her heart said *yes*. Maybe the reason he'd steered her away from being a fulltime firefighter was that he knew her heart lay elsewhere. Maybe he just wanted her to follow her own dreams instead of his.

Tears spilled onto her cheeks. It was more than the amazing surprise of her dreams coming true. It was learning just how much the people of this small town cared about her. It was like a healing balm upon her heart.

And then there was Ethan—the man who orchestrated all of this. He'd shown her that she didn't have to do things alone. It was all right to lean on others. It didn't make you weak. It just meant you were human.

I enjoyed working with you. I'm sorry I missed seeing your expression upon finding the bakery completed. But it was time for me to head home.

I hope all of your dreams come true. You are a special person who brings happiness to those around you. I'll miss your blueberry muffins.

Ethan

He was gone. A teardrop splashed onto the page. She never got to thank him.

More than that she never took her chance to tell him how she truly felt—how much she'd come to care for him—how much she loved him.

And now it was all a moot point.

CHAPTER TWENTY-SEVEN

He hadn't wanted to leave.

But it was what Hannah wanted.

Ethan maneuvered his truck southbound along the busy highway. He'd like to say he was anxious to go home, but as he tried to think of something he'd missed about his apartment, he struggled. And then he knew what he missed— his buddies at the fire department. Though he wondered if they'd ever see him as he had been before the accident—the way the crew in Bluestar saw him.

He already missed Bluestar—especially a certain baker.

He knew if he were still on the island—if he were to see Hannah again—his resolve to leave, his determination to retake his life, would dissolve. And he would be left with questions. Could he have been a big city firefighter once more? Could he still do what was asked of him without hesitation? Or could he be happy without being a firefighter?

For most of his life, he'd prided himself on being a firefighter. Firefighting was what defined him. If he walked away from it—and it was a huge if—it had to be on his terms. He wouldn't let an accident drive him away or let someone else choose what made him happy. Even though being with Hannah made him the happiest he'd ever been.

"You're quiet." His father's voice interrupted Ethan's thoughts. "You must be tired after all you did while you were in Bluestar."

Ethan kept his attention on the road. "Actually, I'm not. The work was relaxing and even rejuvenating."

"I'm glad you got a break. You've been through a lot this year. But you must be anxious to get back to the city and the job. I know your mother and I had the time of our lives in Europe, but I can't wait to get back to my life."

Ethan found it interesting how his father viewed his return to New York so different from him. Ethan wasn't anxious to get back to what he'd been doing, but he was anxious to prove to himself that he hadn't lost his nerve. Would the drive needed to do his job day in and day out return? Would he ever be the man he used to be?

Deep inside a resounding *no* resonated within him. He'd changed. And it'd started before he'd stepped foot on Bluestar Island. In fact, it'd started before he'd been caught up in that fiery accident. Maybe it'd started the first time he'd volunteered his time off to build affordable housing.

But he had to admit that taking the leap from a reliable job with benefits to starting his own business was a bit intimidating. It wasn't like he was a kid anymore. In fact since being in Bluestar, he'd been thinking it was time to settle down with a family. How was he supposed to do that without a reliable income?

"Ethan, what is it?" His father's voice cut through Ethan's internal debate.

"What are you talking about?"

His father cleared his throat. "There's something going on with you. You're quieter than normal. There's something weighing on your mind. Is it Hannah?"

"Yes. But no."

His father chuckled. "I should have known it was a woman."

Ethan gave a slight shake of his head as he signaled to pass a slow-moving car in front of them. "This isn't about Hannah."

"So there is something going on." His father grew quiet, as though waiting to hear what was on Ethan's mind.

He didn't want to disappoint his father. He knew some people might find that ridiculous since he was a grown man, fully capable of making his own decisions. But he'd always had a close relationship with his parents, so what they thought was important to him. He didn't think he'd ever reach an age where that wasn't true.

Ethan swallowed hard. "Here's the thing..." It was easier to say in his thoughts than to actually put a voice behind the

261

words. "I'm thinking about stepping away from firefighting full- time."

His father was quiet for a moment. "This is about the accident. It's okay. I understand that you're nervous about going back. Anybody would be after what you've been through. But it'll be okay with time."

"Dad, it's more than that." How did he make his father understand what he was feeling? "Didn't you ever wonder what it'd be like if you'd made another choice? Done something other than be a firefighter?"

"No. It was what was expected. It's what I wanted to do." His father shifted in his seat so as to look at him. "If it's not the accident, it has to be Hannah that has you talking like this."

"No. It's not her either." Though he did miss her. "This is something that's been building for a while now."

"Then how come it's the first I'm hearing about it?"

"Because I knew you wouldn't be happy."

To that his father had nothing to say. Ethan told himself it was better that way. At least heated words weren't spoken—words that couldn't be taken back.

And to honest, his father might be right. When he got back to the firehouse and was around his buddies, everything might fall back in place. He might not long to have sandpaper or a hammer in hand. He might get caught up in his career again and not have time to think about Hannah. He wouldn't know until he gave it all a chance. But he didn't think there was anything that would help him get over her. She was unforgettable.

CHAPTER TWENTY-EIGHT

Days blurred into each other.

Hannah made sure each minute of each day was filled with work. Because when she stopped, she thought of Ethan and how much she missed him.

Not long after Ethan had left town, she'd asked Birdie for his mailing address. She'd thought of calling him, but she decided a thank you card was better. It gave her a chance to write out her feelings without getting all tongue-tied.

She'd apologized for the way things ended. The barn fire had gotten to her more than she'd been willing to admit. And he'd ended up getting the brunt of her emotions.

She let him know how much she loved the bakery and told him that he was extremely talented. And she included a check. It was her first payment for the chandelier all of her patrons complimented.

She wanted to tell him how desperately she missed him. That there were countless times she reached for her phone to tell him something, but each time she resisted the urge.

She entertained the thought of starting a long-distance relationship with him. It wouldn't be ideal, but it would be so much better than this big gaping abyss where he'd once been.

But there was still the issue of him being a firefighter. Could she learn to live with him putting his life on the line every time he went to work?

She didn't have an answer and she was so tired of questioning her actions, so she submerged herself in her work. At last, the bakery was cleaned from top to bottom. And yesterday afternoon she'd passed her inspection the first time—something she heard didn't happen for everyone. Thankfully she was one of the lucky ones.

And now it was time for her to rush over to the Lily Pad to pick up the decals for the front door. The words *The Elegant Bakery...everything to satisfy your sweet tooth* were to be printed in black while encircling the silhouette of a cupcake in the center. It would be the finishing touch.

Hannah rushed out the door and headed down Main Street. She wondered what Ethan was doing now. Was he out on a fire call? The thought sent a wave of worry skittering through her.

She shoved the thought to the back of her mind. Instead she imagined him at his apartment. What would his apartment look like? Would it be messy? She didn't think so. Ethan cleaned up the tools he'd borrowed and kept the toolbox organized. And while he'd lived across the hall from her, his place had always been neat enough.

Was he thinking of her? She had no idea but she hoped so. Maybe she should call him, just to check in. She retrieved her phone from her back pocket. She pulled up his contact info and then her thumb hovered over the call icon.

If he'd have wanted to talk to her, he could have called after receiving her thank you card and yet he hadn't. His silence was his answer. Her heart pinched. He didn't want anything to do with her.

Up ahead her mother stepped out of The Lighthouse Café and she wasn't alone. She was with Chief Campbell. But that wasn't what caught Hannah's attention; it was the way her mother was smiling at the chief. It was the kind of smile that lit up her mother's entire face. She hadn't seen her smile like that since—since her father was alive. This wasn't some casual flirtation. She was in love with Chief Campbell.

Hannah came to a stop on the sidewalk. She knew she should turn and walk away, but she couldn't move. Her mother and Chief Campbell stood outside the café. They were talking and laughing. They seemed to be in their own little world. They...they were in love.

The fact swept the air from her lungs. She knew it shouldn't surprise her that things were serious. The signs had been there all along. Hannah had just been too caught up in her own life to see that her mother's life was moving on.

Hannah thought she'd be angry over her mother finding happiness with someone else, but surprisingly, she wasn't. There was a part of her that was happy for her, but another part that still longed for the way things used to be. Her grandmother used to say that change was never easy. She was so right.

When Chief Campbell set off in the opposite direction, her mother turned toward Hannah. Her mother's eyes widened with surprise. At last Hannah's feet cooperated and she resumed walking.

Her mother approached her. "Good morning."

"Hey, Mom."

"I guess you saw that," her mother said. "We bumped into each other this morning. Walt was just telling me a funny story from when we were in school."

Was her mother blushing? "You went to school together?"

Her mother nodded. "All three of us. Your father, Walt, and myself. Those were some great times. And Friday night football games were the best."

This was new information to her. She knew her father and the chief were old friends, but she didn't know that they were that old of friends. She'd thought they'd become close as firefighters. And then she realized that was what bothered her about her mother and Walt—he was a firefighter just like her father.

"How can you do it?" The words slipped past Hannah's lips before her mind registered what she was saying.

"Do what?"

Since she'd already opened up the subject, she might as well keep going. "How can you get involved with another firefighter?"

Her mother glanced around and smiled at the passersby. Then she lowered her voice. "Hannah, it's not like that."

"Then how is it? Because I want to know. I can barely bring myself to walk into the fire department since Dad died. If it wasn't for that place, he'd still be alive."

Her mother's mouth gaped. It took her a moment to gather herself. "I had no idea that's how you felt. Why didn't you talk to me?"

"I...I knew you had enough to deal with."

"Is this why Ethan left?" Her mother stared at her as though she could automatically tell if Hannah was speaking the truth or not, just like when she was a child.

Hannah glanced away and shrugged.

"Let's have some coffee," her mother said.

Hannah walked with her mother into the café. With it being mid-morning, not many people were inside. They found a booth and ordered two cups of coffee.

"Hannah, you can't blame the fire department for what happened to your father."

"Why not? If he wasn't a firefighter, he'd still be alive." The pain and anger came rushing forth, surprising Hannah.

"No matter the danger, your father would have saved those horses. He took care of others, even if it meant risking his own safety." Her mother reached out, placing her hand over Hannah's. "Your father loved us, but he was driven to help others. It's who he was."

For a few moments, they quietly drank their coffee while Hannah digested this information. Her mother seemed to make peace with the whole situation. Maybe it was time that she did. But she still had another question for her mother.

"Doesn't it worry you to get involved with another firefighter?"

Her mother blushed again. "We aren't involved. We're friends."

"I saw the way you smiled at him. You only ever smiled like that at Dad."

Concern reflected in her mother's eyes. "Are you upset with me for moving on with my life? I need to know."

266

"Surprisingly, no. I want you to be happy...even if it's another firefighter."

Her mother reached out and gave her hand a quick squeeze. "Hannah, you need to let go of the what-ifs. They'll drive you crazy if you let them. I know. I had to accept that it was your father's time to go. As much as I wanted him to stay with us, it wasn't the plan. He loved you and your brother and sister with all of his heart. You couldn't have asked for a better father. I will always love him. But your father wouldn't want this for you."

"Want what?"

"I saw you with Ethan. There was something special between the two of you. If you're pushing him away because he's a firefighter like your father, please don't."

"It's more than that." Hannah drank some more coffee. "His life is in New York. Not here."

"Did you ask him to stay?"

Hannah glanced down at her coffee cup.

"Hannah..."

"No. I didn't."

Her mother finished her coffee. "You should consider calling him. I'm sure he'd be happy to hear from you." She checked the time. "I have to go. We can talk more later if you want."

At the door, her mother went one way on the sidewalk and Hannah went the other way. Hannah replayed her conversation with her mother. Was it possible she'd been upset with the fire department all of this time because it was easier to be angry with them than deal with the pain of her father's absence?

And if she was ready to move past being upset with the fire department and her father, did that mean she'd wrongly put up barriers between herself and Ethan because of his career?

CHAPTER TWENTY-NINE

Cleaning. Check.

Inspection. Check.

Baking. Check.

The Elegant Bakery was officially open for business. And Hannah felt as though she were living a dream—well, almost. It just didn't feel complete without Ethan to share this moment.

And yet everywhere she looked around the bakery, she saw his touch—in the beautiful trim work, with the chandelier that gleamed overhead, and then there was the table he'd created from some scrap lumber. She wanted to call him—to hear his voice—but she resisted the urge. She was certain he was busy settling back into his life. Just as she was settling into a new routine of being up before the sun to fill the display cases with her finest pastries.

As one week became two and two weeks became three, she was certain she wouldn't hear from him again. He must have realized the thing between them—the springtime romance—had been fleeting. The thought made her heart ache.

Sometimes late at night, she let herself imagine what might have happened if she'd have told him about her true feelings. She let herself imagine he felt the same way.

And then the logical side of her reminded her that if he'd have stayed in Bluestar just for her, he would have eventually resented her. She didn't want to be responsible for him giving up everything in his life, from his home to his closeness with his parents. And then there was his career—his family's legacy. They just weren't meant to be. But she was still having a hard time buying that too. Because when they were together, it felt so right.

As she walked through Beachcomber Park, she searched for something to make this feel right—for a way to let go.

Maybe what she needed was closure. She just needed to hear that he was happy back in his old life.

Not giving herself time to change her mind, she reached for her phone. She selected his number and the phone started to ring. Once. Twice. It continued to ring. She should hang up. But she hesitated, hoping he'd take her call. And then the call switched to voicemail. The sound of his voice still made her heart beat faster. Deciding not to leave a message, she disconnected the call.

She continued walking to Birdie's house. She gazed out at the ocean, wishing that she had time to walk along the sand. But that would have to wait. She had more work waiting for her back at the bakery.

Moments later, she stepped onto Birdie's covered porch. She rapped her knuckles on the door. While she waited for Birdie to answer, she couldn't help but wonder why Ethan hadn't answered the phone. Was he working? Or was he avoiding her?

Perhaps he met someone since he'd been back in the city. It was extremely plausible, considering he was drop-dead gorgeous and so easy to talk to. Her heart sank at the thought.

"Hannah?" The sound of Birdie's voice drew Hannah from her thoughts.

"Yes."

Birdie's brows knitted together. "Are you okay?"

Peaches barked her greeting as she sat next to Birdie. Hannah wondered if Peaches missed Ethan too.

"Um, yes. Why?"

"Because you're awfully quiet lately."

"Sorry." And then Hannah remembered the box of blueberry crumble muffins. She remembered how much Ethan had enjoyed them and hoped Birdie would like them too. She held out the box. "I brought you these."

"Thank you, dear." Birdie backed up. These days she was moving about without the aid of a walker. "Come in."

269

Hannah had made a point of checking in on Birdie every couple of days since Ethan's mother had gone back to New York. She stepped inside the little seaside bungalow. "I can't stay long. I have to get back to the bakery."

Birdie made her way over to an easy chair and gestured for Hannah to have a seat on the couch. "How are things going with the grand opening?"

"Better than I ever imagined." She just wished she could share it all with Ethan. "We were able to open in time to be listed in Bluestar's Visitors Guide and with the early spring, business is in full swing. And I wouldn't have been able to do any of it without your nephew's help. I hope he knows how much I appreciate everything he did to help me."

"You don't talk to him?"

Hannah shook her head. "Not since he left the island." Her gaze met the older woman's puzzled look. "How did he sound when you talked to him?"

"I've only talked to him a couple of times. Each time he sounded rushed and tired. We never talk for long. I...I just thought you two were in communication."

"I...I'm sure he's busy getting back to work and everything." Even as she said the words, she didn't believe them. There was a reason Ethan hadn't called. And the thought that they would never speak again pained her heart. Hannah choked down her emotions. "How are you doing?"

Birdie's brow was still creased in frustration. "I'm doing good. A couple more weeks of physical therapy and I should be good as new."

"Is there anything you need?"

Birdie smiled. "That's sweet of you, but I've got everything I need."

Hannah got to her feet. "I'm sorry I can't stay, but if you think of anything, just call me."

"I'll do that." She frowned. "Are you sure you can't stay just a little longer?"

"I'm afraid I can't. But I'll stop back tomorrow."

"For lunch. We insist." Birdie glanced at Peaches. "Don't we, girl?"

Peaches barked her agreement.

Hannah smiled. "How could I resist such a lovely offer? Thank you."

"Good. We'll see you tomorrow at noon."

Hannah said her goodbye to both of them and then made her way out into the cheery sunshine that seemed to mock her gloomy mood. Without Ethan in her life, her heart ached. She wondered if she'd ever see him again. She hoped so. Maybe after the busy tourist season, she'd take a trip to New York. She could do with a shopping spree and perhaps a visit to a certain firehouse. The thought gave her a little comfort.

What had happened?

She'd been so certain about those two.

Birdie frowned as she watched Hannah walk away. She was certain more now than ever that Hannah had feelings for her nephew—deep feelings. So why wasn't he doing anything about it?

She moved to the phone and dialed his number. It was time they had a serious conversation about matters of the heart. She needed to understand what was going on with him.

The phone rang and rang. Then it switched to voicemail. Birdie considered leaving him a message, but this was too important for a message. She would call back later.

In the meantime, she opened the white pastry box with four large muffins in it. Birdie's mouth watered as she looked at them. The doctor did say she should eat a little more. Now appeared to be the perfect moment to follow the doctor's orders.

CHAPTER THIRTY

He'd missed a call.

No. He'd missed two.

Ethan noticed Hannah had just called followed by his aunt. He wondered what was going on. Neither had left a message so it couldn't have been anything urgent.

He would call Hannah back in just a moment. He clutched his phone in his hand as he kept moving. His strides were long and fast as the sunshine warmed his face and invigorated him. This was going to be a good day. No, it was going to be a great day.

In the three weeks since he'd left Bluestar, he'd missed Hannah so much—more than he'd thought possible to miss anyone. He knew he should have called her before now, but he'd forced himself to slow down and think things through. When he made a decision about the future, he wanted to be certain what would truly make him happy in the long term. Now he had to hope that Hannah would understand his reason for the silence.

He was finally ready to call her. He dialed the still familiar number. As the phone rang once, twice, his heart beat faster. What if she was furious with him for not calling sooner? What if she didn't give him a chance to explain?

"Hello." In the background dishes and pans clanged. People called out to each other. However above it all was the sweet lilt of Hannah's voice.

A smile immediately pulled at his lips. "Hi, Hannah. How are you?"

There was a pause as though she wasn't sure how to answer his question. "Good. Busy." She muffled the phone to say something to someone else. "Sorry. And you?"

"Better now."

"Now? Why now?"

Clang. Bang. Ding.

He continued to smile as he imagined the kitchen of the bakery abuzz with activity. "Hannah, step outside."

"I'm sorry if it's hard to hear me, but I can't take a break now. Can we talk later?"

"No. Please. I wouldn't ask you if this wasn't important." She hesitated, considering his request. "Hang on."

She muffled the phone again to talk to someone in the kitchen. Then he heard the sound of the exterior kitchen door opening. The next thing he knew she was standing in front of him, wearing her white work clothes. She'd never looked so beautiful.

"Hello, Hannah."

She blinked as though making sure he was truly standing there in front of her. "Ethan, what are you doing here?"

It wasn't the greeting he'd been hoping for, but at least she was speaking to him. "I'm back." He held out an arrangement of purple, pink, and white tulips he'd bought at Bea's Posie Patch. "These are for you."

She stepped forward and accepted them. "Thank you." She gazed at the floral arrangement for a moment before meeting his gaze again. "I don't understand. Has something happened? I just saw your aunt. She seemed—"

"Can we take a walk?"

"I, uh...wait." She rushed inside and then returned a couple of minutes later without her apron or the flowers. "Let's go."

They started in the direction of the beach. He could see in her eyes that his abrupt departure without a goodbye had hurt her. He never meant to make things worse for her. By his way of thinking, he'd been trying to protect her by not leading her on when he'd been so confused about so much.

He cleared his throat. "When I left Bluestar, I was confused. I was torn between the life that had been laid out for me in New York and the life I'd come to love in Bluestar."

Hannah chanced a glance at him. "You love it here?"

He nodded. "I do. How could I not? There's something so refreshing about waking up to the island breeze, not to mention the friendly residents and the amazing views. And then there's this baker who creates the most amazing muffins." He noticed the color that flooded her cheeks. It looked good on her. "Hey, you wouldn't have any on you, would you?"

She shook her head. "I just gave the last of today's blueberry muffins to your aunt."

"Lucky lady. Maybe I should go visit her now."

When he turned as though to walk toward his aunt's house, Hannah reached out to him. "Stop. That can wait." She stopped and stared deep into his eyes as though she were trying to read his thoughts. "This can't. I don't understand what you're doing here."

Ethan gestured toward the stone wall where they'd watched the sun rise—where things felt as though they'd ended. He hated that such a beautiful spot would be stuck with such a negative memory. Maybe it could be remembered as the place for second chances. "Let's sit over there and talk."

They moved to the wall and took a seat. They weren't the only ones enjoying the beach. There were a number of people walking along the water's edge.

He raked his fingers through his hair. "I'm not sure where to begin."

"At the beginning usually works best."

He nodded as he stared out at the ocean, watching the swells of water. "When I left here, I didn't know if I was still the same man I was before the accident. I know that I dealt with the fire at the farm, but it wasn't quite the same. I needed to know if I'd lost my nerve. I needed to know that I'd finally and fully conquered the ghosts of my past." He turned to her. "I hope you understand."

She gazed at him and nodded. "I have some idea. I had to prove to myself that I could open this bakery. I know it's not the same thing, but I had to prove to myself that I could see my dream through just like my brother and sister had done."

He reached out to squeeze her hand but then hesitated and placed his hand back in his lap. "You did it. You made your dream come true."

"And what about you? How did it go back in New York?"

"I did it. I..." He hesitated. For starters, he'd been able to rescue a child from a horrific car accident, helped clean up a dangerous fuel spill from an overturned tanker, and walked into an apartment fire to make a rescue.

"You what?"

"Never mind."

"No. I want to know."

He turned his head and stared into her eyes. "Do you want to know? Because I know my profession makes you uncomfortable."

She sighed. "Since you've been gone, I've learned that I was holding onto some lingering anger about my father's death. It was easier to be angry than to deal with the pain. And instead of being angry with my father, I aimed all of that pain at the fire department. I shouldn't have done it. It was wrong."

"It wasn't wrong. There's no right way to grieve. You lost someone close to you and it's not something you get over. I know that Aunt Birdie still loves Uncle Gil and misses him every day."

"My...my mother is moving on with Chief Campbell."

"And how does that make you feel?"

She shrugged. "I thought I would be upset. I never imagined my mother with anyone other than my father, but then I saw her with Chief Campbell and she's happy. Truly happy. Why would I want to take that from her? If she's happy then I'm happy." She turned her head so their gazes could meet. "So tell me about New York."

275

He told her about the things he'd experienced and how he'd felt doing them. "But the thing is while I was in New York, it didn't feel like home any longer."

"It didn't?"

He shook his head. "My home is here on the island. It's where I choose to be."

"What about your job?"

"Well, that's the thing...I'm unemployed. At least until I get my own business started."

Her eyes widened with excitement. "You're going to do it? You're going to start your own contracting business?"

He smiled and nodded.

She immediately leaned over and hugged him. "I'm so happy for you." She pulled back. "How did your father take it?"

"I talked to him on the way back to the city. I tried to explain to him how much I enjoyed working with my hands and the sense of accomplishment I got from creating something new. I didn't know for sure what I wanted at that point, and I have to say that he was shocked. He didn't say much to me."

"I'm sorry—"

"It's okay. When my mother got home, she talked to him and in the end, we all had dinner. My father told me that he only wanted me to be happy. If starting my own business was what I wanted to do, he would respect my decision."

"So things are okay with you two?"

"I think so. It might take me getting my business off the ground for my father to truly believe this was a good idea. But he's trying to be supportive and that means a lot to me."

Was this really happening?

Hannah could hardly believe that Ethan was sitting next to her. Her heart pitter-pattered. Now she needed to find out if he wanted the same thing as her.

Because she couldn't put her heart on the line and have it rejected. As soon as the thought came to her, she realized that's what she'd told herself before he'd left the first time. And she didn't want to make the same mistakes. If she'd learned anything since meeting Ethan, it was to take chances because you only get one go around in this life.

"You want to live here permanently?" Her heart thumped louder. She wrung her hands together. "You aren't moving here just because I'm here, are you?"

"Absolutely not." He sent her a teasing grin. "Yes, you played a part in my decision. I needed time to sort out what I truly wanted for the future. And that's the reason I didn't call you while I was gone. I didn't mean to hurt you."

"I could have called you too." She'd picked up the phone many times before putting it down. "I...I thought you'd moved on and forgotten me."

"Not a chance." He took her hand in his and squeezed it. "I needed to know that I was making the right decision about my career."

"And now you're sure? You want to change your life?"

Ethan gazed into her eyes. "I need you to know that I'm a firefighter. I'll always be a firefighter. But I don't want it to be the sole focus of my life."

"What are you saying?"

"That even though I walked away from firefighting full-time in New York, I'm still going to be a volunteer here on the island. It's a part of who I am, just as your baking is a part of you. Is it something you can live with?"

She was quiet for a moment as she gave his question serious consideration. "If you'd have asked me that question a month ago, I'd have said no. But I've learned a lot about myself since then. Yes, I can live with it. I love you."

"I love you too."

He got to his feet and then held his hand out to her. He helped her to her feet. As they stood next to the stone wall, he gazed deep into her eyes while his hands rested on her hips. "Hannah, you showed me that there is more to life than what is expected of me. You helped me find the courage to go after what I truly enjoy—what fulfills me. And I thank you. Hannah, I love you with all my heart."

She blinked repeatedly, holding back her tears of joy. He'd just said exactly what she'd been longing to hear. Her heart beat so loud it echoed in her ears.

Her hands rested on his solid chest. "You helped me see that I was clinging too tightly to the past—to the pain that I needed to let go in order to enjoy the memories. Thank you. You've given me back my past and my present. I love you too. And I hope you'll be a part of my future."

"I couldn't think of anything I'd like more."

Her hands slid up over his broad shoulders. As her fingers wrapped around the back of his neck, drawing him to her, she lifted up on her tiptoes. He met her halfway, pressing his lips to hers. It felt as though she were floating on a cloud.

When they parted, Ethan asked, "Does this mean I get a blueberry muffin every day?"

She grinned at him. "Every day? Don't you think you'll get tired of them?"

"Not a chance. Just like I'll never get tired of this." And then he kissed her.

She agreed.

This was the best.

And it was only just the beginning.

The Elegant Baker's Blueberry Crumble Muffins

(makes 12)

Ingredients:

4 oz cream cheese, softened
½ cup granulated sugar
½ cup light brown sugar
1 ½ tsp baking powder
½ tsp baking soda
¼ tsp salt
3 tsp vanilla
2 eggs
½ cup canola oil
½ cup buttermilk
1 tsp lemon zest
2 tsp fresh lemon juice
2 cups flour
1 cup fresh blueberries + ¼ cup blueberries reserved for topping

Streusel Topping:

¼ cup flour
¼ cup brown sugar
2 Tbsp butter, cold

Preheat oven to 375°F.

Coat the 2 cups of blueberries with 2 Tbsp of the flour. Set aside.

Fill cupcake trays with liners. Set aside.

Mix cream cheese until smooth.

Add granulated and light brown sugars. Mix.

Add baking powder, baking soda, salt, and vanilla. Mix.

Add eggs. Mix.

Add oil and buttermilk. Mix.

Add lemon juice and zest. Mix.

Slowly add remaining flour, a little at a time. Mix just until moistened.

Fold in blueberries.

Fill cupcake liners ¾ full.

Press remaining blueberries into the top of the batter.

Streusel Topping:

In small bowl, mix flour and sugar.

Cut butter into mixture.

Evenly sprinkle mixture over tops of muffins.

Bake 20-22 minutes or until lightly browned.

Enjoy.

Thanks so much for reading Hannah and Ethan's story. I hope their journey made your heart smile. If you did enjoy the book, please consider...

- Help spreading the word about Love Blooms by writing a review.

- Subscribe to my newsletter in order to receive information about my next release as well as find out about giveaways and special sales.

- You can like my author page on Facebook or follow me on Twitter.

I hope you'll come back to Bluestar Island and read the continuing adventures of its residents. In upcoming books, there will be updates on Hannah and Ethan as well as the addition of some new islanders.

Coming next will be Sam's story in HARVEST DANCE! Thanks again for your support! It is **HUGELY** appreciated.

Happy reading,
Jennifer

Other titles available by Jennifer Faye include:

WHISTLE STOP ROMANCE SERIES:
A Moment to Love
A Moment to Dance
A Moment on the Lips
A Moment to Cherish
A Moment at Christmas
WEDDING BELLS IN LAKE COMO:
Bound by a Ring & a Secret
Falling for Her Convenient Groom
ONCE UPON A FAIRYTALE:
Beauty & Her Boss
Miss White & the Seventh Heir
Fairytale Christmas with the Millionaire
THE BARTOLINI LEGACY:
The Prince and the Wedding Planner
The CEO, the Puppy & Me
The Italian's Unexpected Heir
GREEK ISLAND BRIDES:
Carrying the Greek Tycoon's Baby
Claiming the Drakos Heir
Wearing the Greek Millionaire's Ring
Click here to find all of Jennifer's titles and buy links.

About the Author

Award-winning author, Jennifer Faye pens fun, heartwarming contemporary romances with rugged cowboys, sexy billionaires and enchanting royalty. With more than a million books sold, she is internationally published with books translated into more than a dozen languages. She is a two-time winner of the RT Book Reviews Reviewers' Choice Award, the CataRomance Reviewers' Choice Award, named a TOP PICK author, and been nominated for numerous other awards.

Now living her dream, she resides with her very patient husband and two spoiled cats. When she's not plotting out her next romance, you can find her curled up with a mug of tea and a book. You can learn more about Jennifer at www.JenniferFaye.com

Subscribe to Jennifer's newsletter for news about upcoming releases, giveaways and other special offers.

You can also join her on Twitter, Facebook, or Goodreads.

Made in United States
Orlando, FL
25 June 2022

19153084R00157